THE SACRED PATH OF
TEARS

M.B. TOSI

WestBow
PRESS
A DIVISION OF THOMAS NELSON

WestBow Press books may be ordered through booksellers or by contacting:

WestBow Press
A Division of Thomas Nelson
1663 Liberty Drive
Bloomington, IN 47403
www.westbowpress.com
1-(866) 928-1240

Because of the dynamic nature of the Internet, any web addresses or links contained in this book may have changed since publication and may no longer be valid. The views expressed in this work are solely those of the author and do not necessarily reflect the views of the publisher, and the publisher hereby disclaims any responsibility for them.

Certain stock imagery © Thinkstock.
Any people depicted in stock imagery provided by Thinkstock are models, and such images are being used for illustrative purposes only.

Author's photo was taken by Stevie Grand, www.grandlubell.com

The Kansas towns depicted in this book are real places. All characters, however, are fictional. Any similarity to real persons, living or dead, is purely coincidental and not intended by the author. The battles during the Indian Wars were real events and the commanding officers real people. The facts given about those events and officers are documented in the bibliography.

All quotations used are public domain.

ISBN: 978-1-4497-2167-1 (e)
ISBN: 978-1-4497-2168-8 (sc)
ISBN: 978-1-4497-2169-5 (hc)

Library of Congress Control Number: 2011911784

Printed in the United States of America

WestBow Press rev. date: 9/30/2011

Dedication

To my mother, Daisy Beschenbossel, who always told me I could do anything if I put my mind to it. Her Swedish perseverance was an inspiration to me, and I am who I am because of her belief in me and her generosity of spirit.

To my wonderful children, Christa, Julia, and Nick – I believe you can accomplish anything you set out to do. You are all truly amazing, and I am very proud to be your mother!

And to all my friends – Thank you for your support, especially Mary Ann for your time and help, and my mentor, Jim, for your words of encouragement.

Preface

The Sacred Path of Tears is Book One of *The Indian Path Series*. Each book focuses on a different Indian tribe during the Indian Wars in the late 1800s, and the lives of fictional characters are woven into the true events. The theme of *The Indian Path Series* is how to find life's purpose and a path of peace, love, and faith in times of trouble. As American poet Henry Wadsworth Longfellow said, "If we could read the secret history of our enemies, we should find in each man's life sorrow and suffering enough to disarm all hostility."

Man's inhumanity to man makes countless thousands mourn!

Robert Burns

Introduction

My name is Mokee'eso, which means Little Woman in the language of the Cheyenne Indians. I was given my name by my aunt, Anovaoo'o, which means Falcon Woman. I think my parents hoped I would someday have the strength and grace of a falcon, so they gave the honor to my aunt to name me, hoping her attributes would rub off on me.

The problem was I was as scrawny and shriveled as a prairie chicken when I was born, and I barely survived. I've often thought how awful it would have been if my aunt had actually named me Prairie Chicken or even Chicken Legs. I get teased enough for my abbreviated size, so that would have made life even more difficult. It also doesn't help that instead of the beautiful, coppery bronzed skin of my people, I have the light tan skin of a desert lizard. I must have had an ancestor way back that was white, because here I am, not red or white, just kind of a dreary, splotchy sand color.

My other less than desirable attribute is my hair, or lack of it. Although my hair is black like my people, it has the texture of a brittle heap of tumbleweed. I keep cutting it shorter and shorter with my hunting knife, because it sticks out like angry, unruly pokes of buffalo twine in what used to be my braids. Pretty soon, my hair will be so short it will resemble a mound of stiff, black vegetation atop my tiny, tan head, which actually, if the truth is known, looks like the shape of a small prairie turnip.

Needless to say, I'm not a beauty, and I've often wondered what the Great Spirit had in mind when He created me so unlike the others. In a way, it's good to be unusual, a word I definitely prefer to a less complimentary one like mousy or homely. I never have to take the time to try to be pretty like the other maidens, which for me I know is an impossible feat. Instead of trying to make myself marriageable (which seems as distant as the white man's ocean I once heard about), I focus on having a good sense of humor about my obvious physical flaws and living a life filled with sometimes strange, unconventional behavior. After all, it's best to be what I am, and there must be a reason I'm so different, although I haven't been able to figure it out.

So, I've decided I like my name, even though it reminds my Cheyenne people how small I am. I also like myself most of the time. I have many friends as no one is ever intimidated by me. Be serious now. Would you feel threatened by a skinny chicken with a prairie turnip for a head and vegetation growing in a mound on top of it? My friends all call me Mokee for short, no pun intended, and this is my story.

The oral history of my Cheyenne people reveals we have been in the place known as America for thousands of years. We originally lived in what is known as Minnesota around the white man's year of 1500. From there, we migrated west into the Dakota and Montana territories. We were the first Plains tribe in the Black Hills and Powder River Country until the Sioux took over much of our territory. As we were pushed westward by the Sioux, it resulted in us pushing the Kiowa south. I've always found it rather sad how people continually push people out of the way instead of getting along with them. Most recently, we have been allies with both the Sioux and the Arapaho, and the Crow Indians have always been our traditional enemy.

Although the Cheyenne began as an agricultural tribe staying in one location, we abandoned that lifestyle for the nomadic way of life of the Plains Indians. This change was brought about by the acquisition of horses. We began using tepees made of buffalo skins that were easily moved to new locations, and our diet changed from mainly fish to buffalo meat, wild fruits, and vegetables. We came to depend on the buffalo for our survival and over the years, we lived in many hunting places from the upper Missouri River to the Wyoming, Montana, Colorado, and Dakota territories.

Woven into the lifestyle of all Plains Indian tribes is an unbreakable thread of spirituality and belief in the Great Spirit and the sacredness of the earth. A common belief in seeking the supernatural in the ordinary occurrences of daily life has created many similar ritualistic ceremonies among all the Plains tribes. Some of these observances include the Sun Dance, purification in a sweat lodge, vision quests, and smoking a sacred peace pipe. It is not uncommon for one tribe to share these rituals with another tribe.

The thing that makes my tribe unique from the others is our highly developed organizational structure. Whereas the other Indian tribes are divided into autonomous and self-governing bands, which don't always yield to a central authority, the Cheyenne bands are politically unified in a central government system. The Cheyenne have ten bands or tribal units which, when added together, make up the Cheyenne tribe. Each of these ten bands has four elected leaders or chiefs.

An additional four chiefs make up a higher body, and they are principal advisers to the other forty delegates. These four have the power to elect one of their four to be head chief of the entire tribe. The total assembly of forty-four men, which is called the Council of Forty-four, meets regularly to discuss any problems facing the tribe as a whole. It also regulates the Cheyenne military societies, enforces tribal rules, and conducts ceremonies. The meeting of the council usually occurs around the Sun Dance at the summer solstice.

There's also another ceremony of Sacred Arrows, which is very special to my Cheyenne people. A bundle of forty-four, red-painted invitation sticks, which symbolize the Council of Forty-four, is kept with the sacred medicine arrows of the tribe. This set of medicine arrows is sent around the assembly of our leaders when it is convened. The medicine arrows are also carried into battle when a tribal level war is waged. Each arrow has a different color, which is said to have come from the beginning of the world. Because the arrows are so sacred, no woman, white man, or mixed blood of the tribe has ever been permitted to come near them.

In the middle of what the white man calls the 1800s, my people divided into the Northern Cheyenne, with some bands choosing to remain part of the year near the Black Hills in the Dakota territory, and the Southern Cheyenne, who remain year round near the Platte River in the central Colorado territory. Although I am a member of a Northern Cheyenne band, we choose to spend the cold part of the year in the south with our Southern Cheyenne brothers. Our common heritage means we are unified as Cheyenne no matter where we are, and it is not uncommon for a band, if threatened in one area, to rejoin other bands in a different area.

One of the earliest peace treaties with the Cheyenne was signed in the white man's year of 1825, and the United States promised unending friendship, along with its right to regulate trade with the six tribes of the upper Missouri River. As time went on, more and more white emigrants traveled the Oregon, Mormon, and California trails. Many headed to the California gold rush in the time period known as the 1840s.

I was born in what the white man calls the month of December in 1849. The Cheyenne lost almost two thousand members in a cholera epidemic in 1849, so I guess I'm lucky to have survived at all. The disease was believed to have been brought by emigrants heading to the gold rush, and the theory was it spread in mining camps and waterways because of poor sanitation. Nearly a tenth of the emigrants also died of the disease.

Many unfortunate events have happened recently, which are beginning to threaten our way of life. It's sad to say, but I have known nothing but the threat of war since my birth, and my Cheyenne band must move around frequently to avoid hostilities. In the year of 1851, the Treaty of Fort Laramie, which was between the United States and seven Indian nations, including the Cheyenne and Arapaho, was signed.

This treaty was very important to my people. In it, the United States accepted that the Cheyenne and Arapaho held a vast territory of all the lands between the

North Platte and Arkansas Rivers and eastward from the Rocky Mountains to the western Kansas territory. This area included the southeastern Wyoming and southwestern Nebraska territories, most of the eastern Colorado territory, and the westernmost portions of the Kansas territory.

Between the years of 1855 and 1857 in what was considered Indian land, there were several skirmishes between the Cheyenne and the increasing number of emigrants to the western territories. Colonel Edwin Sumner of the United States was ordered to go against the Cheyenne in the year of 1857, and it was the first battle which my people fought against the United States Army.

The real trouble for my people began a year later in 1858. Gold was discovered in the Rocky Mountains in the Colorado territory and in part of the Kansas territory, bringing on what was called the Pike's Peak Gold Rush. There was a flood of European and American emigrants, and the Colorado territorial officials pressured the federal United States government to redefine the extent of Indian lands in the Colorado territory and to negotiate a new treaty. In what was to become a pattern for peace treaties, a previously existing treaty, which had been accepted by my people, was overturned by another more constrictive treaty.

The new treaty was signed in the year of 1861, just ten years after the previous treaty, and it was called the Treaty of Fort Wise with the United States. The treaty was signed by four Arapaho chiefs and six chiefs of the Southern Cheyenne, one of whom was Moketavato (Black Kettle). At the time, he was on the Council of Forty-four as one of the additional four chiefs. These four chiefs had elected him head chief of the Cheyenne tribe.

Many of the other Cheyenne bands, especially the Northern Cheyenne, believed the new treaty was signed without the consent of the remaining chiefs represented on the Council of Forty-four. They protested, saying the signers had not understood the concessions they had made.

Basically, the new treaty ceded most of the lands designated to my people by the earlier Fort Laramie treaty. The new reservation was less than one-thirteenth the size of the previous 1851 reservation, and it was located on a small parcel of land in the eastern Colorado territory between the Arkansas River and Sand Creek. This new, smaller allotment of land was not suitable for growing crops and did not have buffalo to hunt, which threatened to create famine and poor living conditions for my people.

Because it had not been ratified by the entire Council of Forty-four, many of the Cheyenne bands refused to follow what they considered to be a false treaty. To the Cheyenne, the Council of Forty-four is a governing body similar to the Congress of the United States. These bands, including my own, continued to follow the previous Treaty of Fort Laramie and to live and hunt on our traditional lands between the Arkansas and South Platte Rivers and near the Smoky Hill and Republican Rivers.

Angered the United States was trying to take away traditional hunting lands, radical and militaristic bands of Cheyenne and Sioux, called the Dog Soldiers, began making random attacks on the white settlers. These independent, renegade bands had been evolving since the 1830s, and they were growing very powerful, though they did not represent the peaceful intentions of a large majority of Cheyenne. The Colorado territorial government officials, however, said any Indians who refused to abide by the new Treaty of Fort Wise of 1861 were hostile and planning war. Suddenly, even peaceful Cheyenne bands, who were hunting on the lands previously given them, were now considered enemy combatants.

The year of 1861 was made more complex by the beginning of the Civil War, and military forces were organized in the Colorado territory to fight for the Union Army. After the Coloradans defeated the Texas Confederate Army in 1862, they returned home and were mounted as a home guard and militia under the command of Colonel John Chivington.

Chivington and the Colorado territorial governor, John Evans, adopted a hard line against all Indians. Without a formal declaration of war, they began attacking and destroying a number of Cheyenne camps in the spring of 1864. They initiated what was known as the Colorado War, their goal being to kill any Indian in sight. General warfare broke out. In retribution, the Indians began making raids on the trail along the South Platte River, which the city of Denver depended on for supplies.

When the state army later crossed into Kansas, which had become a state by that time, the policy of killing any Indian in sight continued. Two well-known Cheyenne chiefs approached the soldiers to greet them in peace, only to be gunned down. This action set off a war of retaliation by the Cheyenne bands in Kansas.

It is an awful thing to be young and to think constantly of war, though I try to hide my anxious thoughts from the others. I should be thinking of the joys of having few responsibilities yet, and the eager anticipation of girls my age to marry one day and have children of their own. I try very hard to remain cheerful and optimistic, and I try to act as fun-loving as people expect me to act.

When I am alone, however, there are times I contemplate my future death. I often wonder whether I will live to see another sunrise. Every noise I hear in the night makes me flinch and in my fear, I think we are being ambushed and the end is near.

I frequently think of my cousin, Ešeeva'e (Day Woman). While she was hunting with her brother and his friends, their Cheyenne camp, maybe three days from mine, was attacked, and any women and children who did not escape were slaughtered. Ešeeva'e lost her baby sister and mother that day, and now she is struggling to be her father's squaw, although she is only ten years old.

Life in a time of war can be cruel for a Cheyenne child. Whenever I think of my cousin, I inevitably look into my mother's worried eyes and lined face. I wonder what horrors she has seen in her young life, and how many of her friends and family have been killed. I think of a future time when I might be without my mother's love and comfort, or when she might lose me to death at the hands of a soldier. Would either of us be able to endure life without the other, or would we be overwhelmed with grief and living in constant fear? I often wonder whether white women love their children as much as my mother loves me. I think it must be so, because I can't imagine it any other way.

I can't seem to understand why life is so violent, especially when there is such beauty and peacefulness all around us in nature. Can it be innocent women, children, and others who want peace are being killed because their skin is red? Do white people believe the Great Spirit has made it their destiny to remove the Indians from the land they have lived on for thousands of years? I once heard our elders say the white men see themselves as superior to a people they view as primitive and inferior. Is there not enough land for all people to share in peace?

Sometimes, I lay awake on my sleeping mat and pray to the Great Spirit. Although some of my friends make fun of me for my continued trust in the hearing ability of the Great Mystery Power, I've always told them it makes perfect sense. Why wouldn't the Creator of the beautiful stars and infinite skies be able hear the cries of His people? No matter what the others say, I believe my Creator loves me and listens to me, and I continue to pray for peace for my Cheyenne people.

Because there is so little I comprehend about my life and my purpose, I do have many more questions for Him. Why do some people find such pleasure in killing others who are different? Aren't we all your people, Great Spirit, and don't you love us all? Is the only choice we have to kill or be killed? I keep hoping there is a third path, a sacred path yet unseen we can choose, and every day I promise the Great Spirit I will choose that path if He shows me the way.

This, then, is the story of my life's very small and unimportant footprints trying to find the hidden path of peace, hope, and love in a world spinning out of control with violence. I would one day be blessed to read the words of the poet William Wordsworth, who said, "Fill your paper with the breathings of your heart," and so I have breathed my heartbeats upon this paper. My story begins quite ominously on the white man's date of November 28, 1864.

In war, truth is the first casualty.

PART ONE

Chapter One

It had been a long, dusty trip, but my best friend and fellow mischief-maker, Tovôhkeso (Swift Fox), and I had an exciting time, especially racing our horses like a wild buffalo stampede through our camp last night. My mother was not amused by our unbridled exuberance.

Although Tovôhkeso is fifteen years old, he is only a half-year older than I am. I will be his age when the snows come, although I don't look that old. We have been inseparable since I was about eight years old. He is the handsomest young warrior I know, and I like to stare at his beautiful, bronzed face to get my mind off of my worries about war.

The only reason I think he likes to be with me is because I can be a troublemaker, in a nice way of course. I also make him laugh at the predicaments I get myself in, like the other night when I tried to spear a fish, but got my spear wedged between two rocks. I tried to yank it out and wasn't successful. Instead, I broke my spear in half and fell, with a huge splash, into the icy water. Tovee, which is my nickname for Tovôhkeso, quickly wrapped me in a warm blanket and carried me back to the tepee of my father and mother, who were not pleased at my carelessness. I'd fall in the river again if Tovee would carry me in his arms some more.

My older friends, who are all very pretty, are envious of the attention Tovee wastes on me. I'm always expecting him to tell me he is courting one of them, which wouldn't surprise me as many Cheyenne maidens marry when they become fifteen. But, he seems to pay them no notice. Because they'd be even more jealous, I didn't tell my friends Tovee braided me a necklace made of thin strips of elk skin, and I never take the necklace off except to bathe. The necklace probably meant nothing to him, but it is really special to me. I wish I would hurry and grow up before someone else snatches him away from me.

There were several bands of us, including the Arapaho, traveling south for the winter to join up with our Southern Cheyenne brothers near their new reservation land at Sand Creek in the Colorado territory. Cheyenne camps are very portable. Within minutes, the tepees can be dismantled, the central poles crisscrossed over the back of a horse, and the buffalo hide walls stretched between the poles behind the horse, forming a travois. The word for travois is from the French

1

word "travail," and it is a frame for restraining horses. As the poles drag on the ground, the belongings of each tepee, even the most precious belongings of little children, are loaded on top of the hides.

On our buffalo hunts in summers past, I was one of the children balancing atop a travois with Tovee, and he and I used to figure out ways to shove the other one off onto the prairie grass. I was usually the one who ended up with burrs on my behind. On our current journey from the northern Plains to the south, Tovee was old enough to ride with a group of new warriors. Astride his appaloosa stallion, he strutted by so proudly, though it was very cold, and he had his poncho huddled around his shoulders.

It was my mother's wish that I still ride on top of her travois. Her excuse was she couldn't pay attention to me and concentrate on steering her travois over a maze of gopher holes at the same time. Although she didn't realize it, I was freezing sitting in the crosswinds on the hides. So, I decided to make a pest of myself, which is one of my specialties, and I deliberately dumped one of my family's parfleches, which is a storage place for clothes, on the well-traveled ground. There were buckskin garments everywhere, and my mother, Paveena'e (Good Feathers Woman), yanked her mare to an angry stop.

"Mokee'eso," she started shouting above the din of neighing horses and poles scraping the ground. "Pick up those clothes before they get dirty, and get back on the travois." I knew she was annoyed because she used my full name, which is a mouthful.

I hid my smile. Everything went according to plan, and we began to fall behind the procession. Dawdling on purpose, I leisurely picked up each individual item and folded it ever so carefully, causing my mother to look nervously ahead at the trail dust and the backs of her friends getting smaller.

"Please, Mother, I'm so bored and cold," I complained as only a fourteen-year-old can do and grate on a mother's ears. "I just know I'll have another accident again. Please let me ride with Tovee. I'll be warmer, and I promise it will keep me out of trouble." I gave her my most coaxing smile, which is probably my best attribute. My mother gazed at me with frustrated affection, and I knew she'd give in. She is usually very kind.

My mother always felt badly for me, because I wasn't maturing or as shapely as the other girls my age. Instead, I was skinny, plain as a little wren, and flat as a tree stump. I knew it wasn't fair to give her my poor Mokee look, which I had perfected. But I also knew she'd do anything to erase that look, even send me out on the overcrowded trail on my pony. I think she harbored a secret wish I would marry Tovee, even though I was young, so she and my father wouldn't need to worry about me anymore. *Maybe next year*, I thought, my lifelong dream the same as my mother's.

Moments later, I was off catching the brisk wind on my wiry mustang pony with its thick winter coat of honey-colored fur. I galloped as fast as I could toward the front of the caravan, leaving a cloud of trail dust swirling behind me. The wind went right through the seams of my buffalo skin clothing, and I pulled my poncho tighter. Like all Cheyenne, I was a skilled rider since practically my birth, and I wove expertly in and out of the crowd of animated warriors until I spotted Tovee and his friends, Haeohe'hame (Fast Horse), and Ma'enetse (Red Eagle). I waved excitedly, almost needing to catch my breath at how Tovee's coppery skin shimmered in the sunlight and his black, braided hair glistened.

"Mokee," all three shouted gaily. They waved at my approach. Eagerly, I trotted into the center of their circle of mammoth horses, and I felt a bunch of hands robustly clap me on the back like I was one of the warriors, which was fine with me. I had given up trying to look like a girl long ago. The only hand I really noticed was Tovee's, which seemed to burn a hole through the shoulder of my outer garment as it rested there momentarily. I hoped he didn't see me grow flustered, as I didn't want him to think I had a crush on him, which, of course, I did.

"It looks like it might snow tonight," said Fast Horse, pulling his collar of buckskin even higher and pointing to a distant, darkening sky with rolling black clouds. "Maybe not, though. Those clouds are moving way too fast. It seems too early for snow anyway."

"Do any of you get to go on the buffalo hunt later today and tomorrow?" I asked with interest, wondering if I'd have to figure out ways to occupy my time after we set up camp. The older warriors sometimes selected a few of the younger ones to tag along on the first winter hunt. Fast Horse and Red Eagle chimed in they were going for sure, and I realized it was probably because they were closer to being sixteen than Tovee, who had just turned fifteen five full moons ago.

Tovee immediately changed the subject to something he found more appealing. "I thought I'd pick you up before dawn, Mokee, and we could go exploring for treasure in the hills," he said spiritedly, apparently not bothered by being excluded from the hunting expedition. "I thought we'd even try panning for gold, like the white man." His masculine face shone with anticipation. "I know a perfect spot just south of where we're going to be camped. How about it? Do you want to come?"

My heart leaped with joy and nearly burst out of my chest. It would be another adventure with my future husband, though, of course, he didn't know that yet, and I would have been absolutely mortified if he could have seen my thoughts. I nodded self-consciously, giving him my best smile of cooperation and hoping he couldn't read my constantly wandering mind. It was foolish of me to keep thinking about him, as I'm not pretty enough to end up with someone as good-looking as Tovee. Worse yet, who knew how much time we all had left? We had been hearing rumors the white man was determined to kill us all.

While our slow procession of travois made its way south nearing its destination in the eastern Colorado and Kansas prairielands, one of our scouts came back and said Black Kettle, who was the chief, not only of a Southern Cheyenne band, but of the entire Cheyenne tribe, had reported to Fort Lyon in the Colorado territory. He wanted to confirm his intentions for peace before moving his band to its new reservation land at Sand Creek.

The reservation was near a northern branch of the Arkansas River, which was located south of the westernmost headwaters of the Smoky Hill River. Many other Cheyenne bands, mine included, were unsure about the newest treaty, and we still set up our regular encampments on the land previously allotted us.

The rivers all flowed eastward from the High Plains region of the northeastern Colorado territory. Both the main course and the north fork of the Smoky Hill River, which according to the white man's measurement was more than five hundred miles long, flowed through the Smoky Hill region of north central Kansas. The region got its name from the hazy smoke, which often surrounded the isolated buttes and foothills in the area. Two main tributaries, the Saline and Solomon Rivers, joined up with the main part of the Smoky Hill River near a settlement called Salina, just before it merged with the Republican River.

The Republican River was further north and flowed along the southern border of the Nebraska territory and eventually curved southward, meeting up with the Smoky Hill River to form the Kansas River. The settlement where the two rivers joined would eventually be called Junction City. Because of the plentiful buffalo, the entire area was the traditional hunting grounds for many Indian tribes. Winter encampments were scattered all along the entire basin as far south as the Arkansas River, which also flowed eastward from the Colorado territory through the middle of Kansas until it turned southward into the state of Arkansas.

Much later, I found out Black Kettle, who was one of the main advocates of the peace process and one of ten chiefs who signed the new treaty at Fort Wise, was confident the promises of peace he had received from the soldiers at Fort Lyon would keep his band safe from any attack. When he returned to his new encampment at the Sand Creek reservation, which was less than forty miles north of the fort, he flew both an American flag as well as a white flag over his tepee. It was his way of showing he was a friend of the white man. He then accompanied most of his warriors to hunt, leaving the older men, women, children, and the infirm in the village.

I also found out the date of our arrival, according to the white man's calendar, was November 28, 1864. It was a beautiful sunny, but frigid day as my band of Cheyenne set up our encampment about twenty miles north of Sand Creek. Of course, I wasn't aware of the date or the distance until recently. I only knew it was late fall and bitterly cold. The weather was typical for our annual fall trek to spend the winter with our southern brothers. The colorful leaves, which had painted the isolated forests with dazzling colors along our journey, had begun to wither and turn brown as winter approached.

Although I didn't realize it at the time, the beautiful prairieland where we set up camp had been almost entirely claimed by the white man. Mixed in among the tall prairie grasses were patches of deciduous forests, buttes, and canyons. The plains state of Kansas and the Nebraska territory, which both bordered the Colorado territory, were also claimed by the white man, and vast prairies overlapped any boundary lines to the east and northeast.

After we arrived, it was an afternoon of strenuous work. Indian women were responsible for setting up the new temporary encampment, while the men secured the area. It was cold enough to freeze the twine fasteners on what was left of my chopped braids. Many of the warriors, including my father, Vohpeaenohe (White Hawk), had already left to scout the area. Others went on a quick buffalo hunt, as our food supplies needed to be replenished after the long trip. Because I was getting older, I helped my mother situate our tepee and fasten the buffalo hide walls in place. After several hours of tedious work, my mother and I collapsed on our leanbacks, which were comfortable folding chairs sitting on the ground, and we rubbed our hands together for warmth by our central fire, which we had just gotten started.

Both of us were starving and wondering what we should make for dinner. We really didn't have many supplies left. Suddenly, Tovee came strolling through the tepee flap with two skinned rabbits in hand, and we were both effusive with our thanks, as we were so tired. Tovee's sudden appearance was no surprise. He was a frequent visitor to our tepee, and I knew my parents liked him. My mother eagerly took the rabbits from his hands, and she began to prepare a rabbit stew, browning the meat and chopping a few prairie turnips we had carried along on the trip.

"Mokee, I just wanted to remind you of our search for gold in the morning." Tovee wiggled his eyebrows comically, and I saw my mother smile. "Dress warmly, and I'll bring the horses and food for the day. Don't forget, I'll be here before dawn." With a pleasant wave and nod at my mother, he left.

Had I known what was in store for the next morning, I might have jumped on my horse that night and ridden away.

Chapter Two

"Hey, short stuff," Tovee whispered so as not to rouse my parents. They were sound asleep under thick buffalo hides. My father had returned home in the middle of the night, assuring us the area was safe. I was already up and dressed for warmth, eagerly anticipating my new adventure hunting for gold. Although I knew what gold looked like and that it was thought to be valuable, I had no idea why people killed for it.

All of the Cheyenne knew the gold rush had caused major problems for our tribe, resulting in broken treaties by the white man's government. Many times, I prayed to the Great Spirit to protect my people from the greed of those who valued rocks over human lives. It saddened me to see the Indian people being cast aside in an insatiable quest for gold-laden land. Putting my pensive thoughts away, I skipped out of the tepee with an energetic smile on my face, deciding to have a good day, which was how most of my days were with Tovee. It was not to be the case that day, however.

We quickly rode away from camp and into the timberline, following a narrow branch of the Smoky Hill River, which meandered from the southwest. Although dawn had not quite broken, we were conscious of the dangers of being spotted and tried to remain inconspicuous in the dark shadows of the underbrush. The land began to roll gently with more wooded hills, and the river was narrower as the hills became higher.

"Let's head out into the prairieland for a while until we spot an offshoot of the Arkansas River," Tovee said. "It will make our ride easier."

At a fast clip, we rode for what seemed a long distance until we spotted another river branch. Once again, we headed into the protection of the thick forest for safety. Tovee seemed to have a specific spot he remembered from past years for our adventure. As the sun was beginning to rise into the early morning sky, we saw the perfect place to begin panning for gold. We were on a promontory of land high above a twisting river, and a small, rocky stream of icy cold water gurgled its way down a steep hill to join the flowing water below. A herd of does, which was bedded down by the stream, startled at our arrival and scampered into the undergrowth.

Before we dismounted, Tovee unfastened his parfleche, which was tied to the back of his saddle, and he took out the strangest-looking tin pan I'd ever seen. Part of it was a flat piece shaped like a screen with little holes in it. "What do you think?" he asked proudly, showing me the unusual object.

"I have no idea what that is," I said skeptically. "Where did you get that piece of junk anyway?"

"Patience, sweet Mokee," he said proudly, leaping from his towering appaloosa horse and tying him to a bush. I also jumped down with ease, in spite of the fact I was a lot shorter than Tovee, and the ground was a lot further for me. "My friends and I found the pan near a river at our camp last year in the Wyoming territory. Look, here's how it works. I dip the entire pan in the swiftly moving water, and any sediment, or gold, remains on the filter to examine. If we don't find the prize, we'll dump it all out and try again."

"Pretty clever," I mused, not sure whether dipping our hands in icy water sounded like much fun, especially if we did it all day long. "It also sounds like it's a pretty lengthy process," I added, trying hard not to grumble in spite of being cold.

"Well, that's why we have a warm blanket for the ground and another to wrap around us. We'll pretend it's a hot summer day, and we'll have a breakfast picnic," he said, having taken care of all the details. "My mother made your favorite muffins last night," he added coaxingly. "But I think we owe it to ourselves to find our fortune first. Then we can run off together and see the world." We both laughed at the silliness of his comment. Neither of us had any concept of the extent of the world.

Tovee dumped the first pan of water, which was a mixture of worthless sludge and pebbles. He was just about ready to dip it in the icy water for a second try. All at once, we heard the rhythmic, piercing sounds of bullets ringing out against the silence of a peaceful morning. Somewhere in the nearby area, there was a volley of relentless gunfire and the roaring blasts of cannons.

Momentarily frozen by fear, Tovee suddenly spun into action, and he grabbed me bodily by my waist and tossed me like a weightless sack onto my horse. He quickly shoved the pan into his parfleche, untied our horses, and mounted all in one swift motion. His stallion began stepping in an impatient circle. "We've got to figure out what that was, Mokee," Tovee hollered anxiously. "I think it came from another encampment. Follow me."

With the skills of a new warrior, Tovee tore through the underbrush, ducking under tree branches, while his horse leaped over fallen logs. He and his horse became a blur, and they charged expertly through the forest and its tangled undergrowth. My shorter mare was not as agile and definitely not a jumper. That was probably better, as I hoped my slowness might cause Tovee to go a safer speed. It definitely would not be a good idea to plunge recklessly around a curve in the hill and into the crossfire of a gun battle.

When we reached another bend in the river below and its corresponding timberline, the echoing sound of gunfire suddenly got louder. We were on top of a steep incline looking down on the river, and we cautiously slowed to a trot and then dismounted, taking cover behind the brittle brown leaves of a hedge of low bushes. A protective wall of barren trees stood guard in front of the bushes, and we felt safe enough to try to peer around the dead foliage to see what was happening.

Telling this part of my story is difficult. Tears fill my eyes and sometimes leave a trail of smudges on my paper. Across a vast space of barren land on the opposite bank of the river, there was a large encampment of tepees. We determined it was the Sand Creek reservation, where Black Kettle's band had set up camp the previous evening.

Everywhere Tovee and I looked, white soldiers were charging defenseless Indians, killing and then mutilating them. It was an ongoing slaughter. Screaming women and children were scattering in the melee and trying to escape, but they were being gunned down in their backs as they ran. Other victims were on their knees, weaponless and begging for mercy, and the soldiers, ignoring their pleas, butted them in their heads with rifles and then executed them in cold blood. I had never seen so much blood.

As if their acts of violence weren't savage enough, the bloodthirsty soldiers took their knives and began scalping and ripping apart the bodies, treating the victims like useless animal carcasses, not people. Some of the victims remained alive only briefly, and a few shrieked with pain just before the soldiers began to pull out their hearts and other organs and then display their prizes to one other. The soldiers went so far as to mount some of the freshly bleeding body parts on fallen branches, like trophies. But in the worst display of man's inhumanity to man my mind could not even grasp, a young pregnant squaw was thrown to the ground and executed, and her baby carved out of her body and then murdered.

I started shaking uncontrollably, never imagining human beings could treat other helpless human beings in such a maniacal, frenzied way. They acted like sadistic predators descending on a killing field of worthless animals. Sobbing and choking with tears streaming down my cheeks, I began heaving violently in the bushes, toppling forward into the underbrush. The rough branches of the bushes cut my face as I helplessly fell toward the ground.

With an overpowering revulsion, I nearly blacked out. My poor Cheyenne sisters and their children and unborn babies lay lifeless on the blood washed ground, their bodies indiscriminately attacked even in death. I had just witnessed the brutal killing and carnage of more than a hundred Cheyenne in what would one day be known as the Sand Creek Massacre.

Tovee rescued my limp head out of the bushes, where I had collapsed and wasn't able to find the will to go on. "Are you okay?" he asked tensely, his eyes searching my pale face. He tried wiping some of the dirt off. Gathering my strength in honor of my fallen sisters, I nodded, swiping my face angrily with the back of my hand. "Let's go then," Tovee ordered urgently, lifting my limp body to my feet and then onto my horse. Feeling completely weak, I didn't know if I could ride or even hold on, but I had to. It was not the time to be a coward. I prayed deep inside me to the Great Spirit for strength.

"We have to alert the other camps," Tovee said with a steely readiness, spinning into action. I could see he was enraged and barely in control of his emotions. Knowing the remaining Cheyenne encampments were spread out at a great distance, mainly along the Smoky Hill River to the northeast, Tovee and I began to ride as swiftly as we could to warn them of impending danger. An eerie calmness slid over my body. With a sense of urgency, we galloped through the forest to warn the closest camp, which was our own.

Much later, I would find out Colonel John Chivington set out from Fort Lyon shortly after Black Kettle's friendly visit, ignoring any assurances of peace given to the chief by the soldiers at the fort. The officer was accompanied by nearly eight hundred troops of the First Colorado Cavalry, the Third Colorado Cavalry, and a company of First New Mexico Volunteers. At dawn on November 29, 1864, Chivington ordered his troops to attack, disregarding both the American and white flags on Black Kettle's tepee. His troops massacred as many of the unarmed villagers as possible, mutilating and scalping the bodies, according to the Congressional testimony of many witnesses.

Any survivors set out toward the Cheyenne camps further north and east along the Smoky Hill and Republican Rivers, and individual survivors met up with other groups, who had escaped with part of the horse herd. There were devastating losses. Eight members of the Council of Forty-four were killed, in addition to mainly women and children. In a striking irony, the chiefs who were killed had advocated peace with the United States government.

The massacre not only weakened the authority of the Council of Forty-four, but it strengthened the emergence of the militaristic Cheyenne Dog Soldiers, who would begin to seek retaliation on white settlers throughout the Platte valley in the Colorado territory. Remember the Sand Creek Massacre became a battle cry of vengeance, and the inhumane massacre was one of the major turning points away from a path of peace to a brutal path of war.

It is difficult to put the obscene acts committed that day into words, but it is well-documented Chivington and his men publicly displayed battle trophies, including body parts of human fetuses and male and female genitalia, in Denver's Apollo Theater and saloons.

Chivington, giving his views on attacking Indians, said, "Damn any man who sympathizes with Indians! . . . I have come to kill Indians, and believe it is right and honorable to use any means under God's heaven to kill Indians."

Kit Carson, a well-known frontiersman who lived in the Colorado territory, said of the massacre, "Jis to think of that dog Chivington and his dirty hounds, up thar at Sand Creek. His men shot down squaws, and blew the brains out of little innocent children. You call sich soldiers Christians, do ye? And Indians savages? What der yer 'spose our Heavenly Father, who made both them and us, thinks of these things? I tell you what, I don't like a hostile redskin any more than you do. And when they are hostile, I've fought 'em, hard as any man. But I never yet drew a bead on a squaw or papoose, and I despise the man who would."

Despite the recommendations of the Congressional Joint Committee on the Conduct of the Wars and the damning testimony of many witnesses, I was stunned to find out later no charges were ever brought against those found guilty of the brutal and cowardly acts in the Sand Creek Massacre, and none of them were ever removed from office or punished.

My heart grieved as Tovee and I rode to warn our people. Why, Great Spirit? Why? My only question became one with the wind. My nightmare of war was here.

The stars are scattered all over the sky
like shimmering tears,
there must be great pain in the eye
from which they trickled.

Georg Buchner

Chapter Three

With our hearts in our throats, Tovee and I took off for our encampment at a mad gallop. Deciding to stay as close together as possible for safety, we raced through the thickest part of the timberline on the incline above the river, not knowing whether any of the ruthless soldiers had spotted us and were already in pursuit. From our vantage point, we could see random groups of Indians fleeing the battle by following the curve of the river. We knew the soldiers wouldn't be far behind with their lust for blood.

After the gory massacre at Sand Creek and the soldiers' indiscriminate desecration of the dead bodies, Tovee and I were positive our camp and the remaining Cheyenne camps further east would be next. Only one thought prevailed. We had to save as many lives as possible, even if it took us several days to reach all the camps. Leaving the carnage and protection of the forest behind, we made our way diagonally across the prairieland until we spotted the timberland leading to our camp.

By the time we got to the encampment, it was early afternoon. Our camp was teeming with activity, and we rode at a fast clip among the tepees. We shouted our warnings to everyone within hearing distance, telling them to flee the area immediately as there had been an attack at Sand Creek. Everyone began running for their loved ones and making plans for escape. Some were already beginning to dismantle their tepees.

We continued on to our parents' tepees to make sure they knew the devastating news firsthand about our Cheyenne brothers and sisters. Tovee shouted to my parents he would take care of me, and he motioned with an urgent look in his eyes we should continue our journey to warn the other encampments. I saw my parents exchange a look of relief I would be safe with Tovee, and my mother, with great sadness in her eyes, reached up to my horse to kiss me one last time. With longing, I would remember her kiss for a lifetime.

My parents hurried inside their tepee to prepare to leave. I watched them go with a lump in my throat and a look of yearning and love on my face. Although I was almost fifteen, it was painful to think I might never see my parents again.

As Tovee and I galloped out of camp and continued downstream in an easterly direction, my mind mulled over why the soldiers had ignored Black Kettle's overtures toward peace. He had not only flown the American flag, but he had accepted the tiny reservation land at Sand Creek. What had he done to make the white soldiers act so violently?

Years ago when I accidentally eavesdropped on a meeting of our elders, I got to see a few white men up close. They were negotiators, and they had ridden with their interpreters to different Cheyenne bands, explaining the peace process and the government's offer of reservation land. I actually picked up a few English words and phrases by listening to them, not knowing if the words would be useful someday.

Other than the negotiators, I really had never seen any other white people. Could it be they were liars, saying one thing and meaning something else? Were they cruel and merciless like the soldiers, their goal being to commit an act of genocide on the entire Cheyenne population? Or, were there some who were peacemakers like Black Kettle? Were there any who could be trusted? I wished I knew what to believe. It was shocking to think an entire race of people could be wicked, but I had no evidence to the contrary to make me draw a different conclusion.

Tovee and I seemed to be the only ones who had witnessed the attack and escaped to safety. The other survivors from Black Kettle's camp were still struggling to get away, and their chances didn't look very good. It became our responsibility to reach the furthest encampments of our brothers, and we rode at breakneck speeds, eventually forgetting about the cover of the forest and heading straight across the flat prairieland, rather than following the slower curve of the river.

Toward evening, we reached the next camp, and our surprise arrival and words of terror brought forth a frenzy of preparation and gathering of loved ones. Most of the warriors were off hunting buffalo, and the women who remained invited us to spend the night. They decided they were temporarily safe enough not to dismantle the camp until early the next morning. Because the sky was black and the air bitterly cold, we decided to stay. Our bodies were bone tired, and we desperately needed to rest. The camp was disassembled at dawn and after a welcome breakfast, we set off for a different encampment.

After another five hours of hard riding, we came upon a camp of Arapaho. They had traveled with us from the Nebraska territory. After retelling our story of the massacre at Sand Creek and sharing a meal with them, we were back on the trail heading further downstream. Once again, we went across the prairieland to make the best time. The Arapaho told us of two more camps they knew of to the east, and we kept up our fast pace, reaching the next village just before dark.

Similar to the first night, we gave our warning and spent the night, leaving at daybreak as the camp began to disband. The final encampment was further away than all of the others, and we didn't reach it until late afternoon. After issuing our final warning, Tovee and I left for the solace of the riverbank, each of us absorbed in our own thoughts.

Our mission was done, and we were exhausted from riding for nearly three days straight. As we watered our horses in the river, we contemplated where we should go next. We no longer had a camp to return to or any possessions. The two of us were alone now without the help of our parents, and we needed to rely completely on each other.

As we gazed at the serenity of the icy water flowing swiftly over a jumble of rock formations, I wondered about the contradiction of it all. The sacred earth, which was the Great Spirit's creation, was peaceful and overflowing with unending beauty, and yet the human beings He also created were continuously filled with discord and evil intent. I wondered how good and evil could exist at the same time in such a beautiful place.

"What do we do now?" Tovee suddenly asked, breaking my contemplation of life's mystery and injustice. I could tell the realization we were alone in the world had also struck Tovee. We knew our decision would have to be made in haste. The soldiers, so hell-bent on killing, would be close behind and enraged the Cheyenne camps had disbanded.

"Let's head further east into Kansas," I suggested quickly, not even knowing where the idea came from in my mind. I wasn't even sure exactly where we were now, except on the bank of the Smoky Hill River. Indians didn't recognize the borders of territories like the white man did. "If we temporarily separate from the general location of all the Cheyenne bands, we can find shelter until the atrocities have ended," I said logically, surprising even myself. "It may take a few sunrises before the soldiers quit their pursuit, and it's safest if we hide out away from our people until the situation has settled. When it's calmed down, we can return and try to find our parents."

I could tell Tovee was hesitant to leave the general area of the battle, preferring to turn around and join the fight for revenge with the other warriors. It was the first time I saw a side of Tovee I had never noticed before. His black eyes flashed angrily for retribution. If he returned before he thought things through, I knew he might impulsively join up with one of the militaristic groups of Cheyenne warriors, who were constantly escalating the war with raids on the white man.

Without waiting for him to answer, I said, "C'mon, Tovee." My voice was more forceful in tone than usual, and he looked startled at my self-determination. "If we die, we will be of no use to our people. Let's go somewhere to be sheltered until the fighting stops." I pushed myself up from the hard ground, which was nearly frozen, and brushed the twigs off of my buckskin pants. The time for sitting had passed, and we had to find cover before nightfall. I extended my hand to help Tovee stand up, not knowing if he would consent to my plan.

Surprising myself with my deep resolve, I had already made up my mind to ride a little further into Kansas myself, even separating from Tovee if he stubbornly insisted on returning to the slaughter. If he tried to continue the fighting before being prepared, it would probably result in his being killed. I was overwhelmed at the perseverance rising up within me. If anyone had asked me to relate the defining moment I became a woman of purpose and left my childhood behind, it was that moment.

With reluctance, Tovee nodded a grudging assent to my plan. Once again, we remounted our horses and took off to the east, trying to stay camouflaged in the cover of any scattered forests along the way. This time, we rode more slowly as we were well ahead of the soldiers. We also knew the soldiers would be distracted by the evidence the other Cheyenne camps had vanished. Just like my dreams, war had caught up with me in the end.

It was an exhausting afternoon with little food. We were able to eat a few provisions the last camp had given us for our journey, but both of our stomachs were growling with hunger as evening approached. As it was bitterly cold, we knew it was time to make a decision where to settle in for the night, especially when we saw the sun set beyond the distant tree line to the west. We knew we had to find cover, or we might not survive the harsh drop in temperature.

Much to our surprise, we came upon a small settlement of houses, which I would later find out was called Salina. In the white man's measurement, it was about eight miles west of where the Smoky Hill River was joined by the much smaller Saline River, which was named for the salt marshes in the area. One day, I would learn the settlement, which was founded in 1857, became the county seat in 1860. It also became an important supply station on the stagecoach line for emigrants heading to Pike's Peak and continued to grow in importance after the Civil War.

Wanting to avoid the settlement, which wouldn't look kindly on two roaming Indians, we headed southeast away from both the river and the town. After a while, we found ourselves in rich farmland, which looked as though it had been partially plowed. Although the sky was blackening, the moon's brightness silhouetted an unpretentious barn in the distance. Tovee obviously had the same thought I did, and we both slowed our horses to a cautious trot. We slowly approached what we hoped might be a safe haven for the cold night.

As we surveyed what appeared to be the only large farm we had seen on our journey from Sand Creek, we noticed a well-built, but modest two story house, a small corral for animals with a feeding trough, some farm equipment to plow the fields, and several fields, which had been recently harvested for the winter.

The house was unusual. The others we passed were tiny log cabins or made of sod, whereas this one was made of wood. It must have been very late, and there was no movement in the house. Hopefully, its inhabitants were asleep.

With the utmost of caution, we both dismounted and gingerly led our horses to the double door on the front of the weathered barn. As quietly as he could, Tovee slid a large bolt of wood to the side. Along with our horses, we sneaked into the small enclosure, shutting the door carefully behind us and simultaneously breathing a sigh of relief we weren't discovered.

The barn was only slightly warmer than the outside air, and it was about the size of three tepees. The floor was sprinkled with sweet-smelling, fresh hay, and there were three tiny stalls, one with two immense pink hogs bedded down for the night against each other and another with two work horses, which neighed restlessly at our sudden appearance. The third stall was empty, and we ushered our tired horses into it, removed their saddles to use for our heads, put some hay in a feeding trough for them to eat, and shut the gate. *At least they had food,* I grumbled enviously to myself, rubbing my empty stomach.

I'd always pictured what Tovee's and my first night together would be like, and this definitely wasn't it. We were ready to collapse from exhaustion after our grueling, three day ride. On top of that, we were famished. Every time I closed my eyes, I saw nothing but the blood-spattered ground of Sand Creek.

After a second, more thorough search of his parfleche, which was still tied to his saddle, Tovee found some old buffalo jerky stashed in the bottom, and he shared his meager provisions with me. At least it would tide us over until morning, when we would leave and hopefully hunt or fish.

Tovee motioned us to a protected corner, which was cushioned with loose hay, and then he pointed to some coarse horse blankets draped over a slanted railing. Motioning for me to be quiet with a finger over his lips, Tovee grabbed a ratty blanket and headed for the mound of hay. I followed and sank down next to him. The hay was surprisingly soft under our tired bodies.

"Thank you for taking me with you, Tovee," I murmured self-consciously as I sat on the hay next to my best friend. My wandering thoughts strayed back a few days to the devastating morning at Sand Creek. "I hope our parents made it to safety. They are better off without us to worry about." As I chattered, I realized I was an unwanted responsibility forced on Tovee by circumstances, and that realization made me feel awkward.

"Come here, Mokee," he whispered softly, his wiry, but muscular body already sprawled out on the hay and his arms open in welcome. Somewhat reticently, I nestled against his chest, which was wrapped in a thick buffalo skin poncho. I immediately felt warmth and comfort as he covered me with a blanket.

With a shiver not from the cold, I felt Tovee's breath against my forehead. To my surprise, he gently kissed my thatch of unruly black hair.

"I never once thought I wouldn't take you with me. We're meant to be together, short stuff. You know that, don't you?" His warm, black eyes looked at mine, as if wondering how I could be so stupid not to know he wanted to be with me.

I shut my eyes with a sigh of relief and nodded my flustered agreement with his words. The truth was, though, I had never thought someone as handsome as Tovee could have feelings for someone as homely as me. I always thought the reason he was with me was because I was funny and made him laugh.

Although war was raging in the Colorado territory and maybe even here in Kansas, my heart felt peaceful in this brief moment of safety. I silently breathed a prayer of thankfulness to the Great Spirit for Tovee's arms of comfort. I only wished his arms could erase the indelible pictures of horror, which would forever be etched in my mind.

Some minds seem almost to create themselves,
springing up under every disadvantage
and working their solitary but irresistible way
through a thousand obstacles.

Washington Irving

Chapter Four

I heard a harsh, clanking sound before I saw its source. With panic, my frightened eyes flung open in alarm. Because we had been exhausted, Tovee and I foolishly overslept. Where slats of wood didn't quite match up with other slats, streams of bright sunlight forced their way through tiny cracks. Suddenly, the barn door flung wide open. It ushered in a burst of frosty air and let in even more light, which outlined three astonished white people. There was a rather pretty older woman in a plain fabric dress and cloth coat, a teenaged boy about Tovee's age, who was much rounder and shorter than Tovee, and a tallish, rather confident man of maybe twenty years. He was standing with his feet resolutely planted apart and holding a shotgun, which was cocked and ready to blow us to pieces.

Under the blanket, I could feel Tovee's hand tense on his knife. For whatever reason, I was not afraid and thought the gentleness in the woman's lined face made me form that conclusion. When I was younger and knew I wasn't pretty, I developed other qualities to make up for it. I knew I had a skill for reading other people's emotions, and this ability would be important for our survival. I whispered to Tovee to let me handle the tense situation and not to draw his weapon.

With a broad smile on my face, I faked a peaceful yawn and rubbed out a few kinks. Slowly, I sat up so as not to be threatening. Then shocking the three strangers, I spoke in the best English I knew after listening closely to the interpreters, who had once visited our camp. "Hull – oh," I said pleasantly, keeping a smile planted on my face.

The woman's face softened under her curly top of speckled gray hair, and she scolded the taller man. "Oh, Jebediah, she's but a sweet young girl. Put that gun down before you frighten her." I couldn't understand her words, but I did realize the threatening man's name was Jebediah.

It was the younger man who answered the woman, and his face had an unpleasant sneer. I took an immediate dislike to him. "Ma, they're just Indians. Why don't we just kill them and be done with it? Or, at least let me take them over to Fort Riley near Junction City. It's not that far of a ride." His tone was demanding and harsh, and I realized the woman's face had an expression of uncertainty. I also noticed Jebediah's rifle was still pointed at me. He must have thought I was still a threat. I decided I would have to put on my best act.

Giving a casual stretch of my arms like nothing in the world was bothering me, I slowly stood up to my full height, which might have been the size of a small pony at best and definitely non-threatening. With a big grin, I pointed at myself and said, "Mokee." Then I pointed at the woman and with a questioning look, used another English word I had learned by eavesdropping. "You?"

The kindly woman gave a little gasp of delight. "Why, Benjamin, she just told me her name. What a smart little girl. And she asked me what my name is." The gentle woman returned my smile and spoke very slowly. "My name is Catherine." She pointed at herself.

Now I knew the younger, angry-looking one was named Benjamin, and the woman's name was Catherine. *Their names are as long and difficult as Cheyenne names*, I thought to myself. Continuing to try to charm her, I held my arms irrepressibly outward, as if I wanted a hug. "Mama, Cat," I said, shortening her name and using another English word I had picked up.

The woman's pleasure was real, and it warmed me inside. I genuinely liked her, not caring she was white and I was an Indian. "Oh my goodness. What an amazing little girl. She just shortened my name to Cat and called me Mama, and she wants to hug me. Jebediah, put that fool gun down right now! I'm warning you. I will not have killing at my house."

The woman's tone of voice became demanding with the older one, and I realized he was her son and the brother to the shorter one. Before I could say anything further, the one called Jebediah spoke fiercely. "It's a trick, Mother, can't you see? She's trying to get you closer so the Indian under the blanket can attack you. It's probably how they plan to escape."

Next, Benjamin chimed in with his opinion. "C'mon, Ma, let's at least kill the guy. You can amuse yourself with the girl if you want." Although I couldn't understand what they were saying, I could tell the situation was deteriorating. The woman had an indecisive look on her face. I had never been one to be shy, and I plunged forward with conviction, knowing I had to win the kindly woman to my side.

I pointed to the younger boy, who seemed to be a little older than Tovee and said, "Ben." Next, I pointed to the older one and said, "Jeb." Then I pointed at both and said another English word I knew, "Bruthers." All three of them looked surprised I had understood their names, but I always had the knack of picking up on words.

I pointed at me again and said, "Mokee." Then I pointed at Tovee, who had a blank, confused look on his face. "Tovee." Finally, I said deceitfully, "Tovee, bruther." Quickly speaking in Cheyenne to Tovee, I explained I had told the people he was my brother, and I warned him to be peaceful and cooperate with whatever I did. I also told him he had to promise he would not attack these people. He nodded.

I began rubbing my stomach in circles, then said, "Mokee, Tovee," and finally made gestures like I was using an eating utensil and eating. My eyes turned to the woman's face and with a look of yearning, I said softly, "Mama Cat, please."

Just as my own mother couldn't resist my pleading eyes and smile, neither could the white woman, Catherine. Jebediah was on to me, however, as his tongue was in his cheek, whether in amusement or disgust I couldn't tell. His unyielding eyes scrutinized my appearance and assessed my pluckiness at the same time. All at once, he lowered his gun in defeat, and I knew I had won the brief skirmish, but not the battle.

Benjamin was definitely mad at the turn of events, and I sensed he was disappointed no blood was going to be shed that morning. Catherine, the sweetest, kindest woman I had ever met, came forward slowly with her arms out, and she hugged me to her ample breasts in a non-threatening way. I hugged her back with sincerity, even though I could tell Jebediah and Benjamin thought I was pretending.

I whispered for her ears only, "Mama Cat, thanks," and I knew my vocabulary of English words was almost depleted. A tear glistened in her eye as she looked at the brave little ragamuffin in her arms, which was me, and I knew for the time being I was safe. Releasing me from her arms, she gently took my hand and motioned for Tovee to take her other hand.

I told Tovee in Cheyenne to take the kind woman's hand, and we were going in her house for breakfast. I also told him he was to be on his best behavior, and if he did anything bad, I would kill him myself. He looked askance at my threat, but gave a forced smile, deciding to show he could be amiable too. He looked dumbfounded I had maneuvered our way into their house. Neither of us knew what to expect. We'd never been in a house before or for that matter, held hands with a white person or even seen a white woman up close. *It was a rather exciting adventure, more so than panning for gold*, I thought excitedly.

When Tovee stood up, the woman's sons glared at him with distrust. Thankfully, he ignored them and took the woman's hand, keeping a faint smile of cooperation on his face. Our motley group crossed the frost-covered ground to the warm, inviting house, and the men of the family uncomfortably brought up the rear.

We entered what I would later find out was called a kitchen, and a welcoming fire was burning brightly in a wide brick fireplace. Jebediah had picked up a few extra logs on our brief walk to the house, and he added them to the fire, stoking them with a heavy black stick. Catherine pulled out two substantial, wooden chairs from under a large planked table and motioned to Tovee and I to sit on them.

It was a fascinating experience to sit on something so high up off the floor, and my delight was obvious. I kept squirming my bottom in different directions to figure out which way was best to sit, and I crossed and uncrossed my legs several times. The furniture was made of sturdy oak and very rustic. Benjamin was disgusted at his mother's decision to invite two savages into their house, and he slammed out the kitchen door.

Jebediah, meanwhile, sat down at the table across from us, having set his shotgun in the corner of the kitchen. He watched me spin around like a child on the chair. I couldn't tell if he found it offensive to sit at the same table with two Indians, or whether it didn't matter to him. White people were a complete mystery to me, but I had a sudden interest to learn about them. Jebediah was obviously protecting his mother from two strangers, which I decided was a good attribute and how it should be. Perhaps he was the man of the house and had no father.

Catherine busied herself with cooking the most wonderful mixture of ingredients on top of a strange piece of equipment, which I would find out was called a stove. As she stoked the fire underneath, the cast iron skillet on top sizzled with a blend of fresh eggs, a white vegetable similar to a prairie turnip called a potato, and a salty meat called ham. When we were in the barn, Tovee and I must have missed seeing the chickens, which laid the eggs.

The aromas were mouthwatering. The woman put some pretty white dishes on the table, and I was astonished they weren't made of wood like most Cheyenne bowls. Because they were shining, I held mine upright to see my reflection, which I wasn't usually used to seeing, except on the surface of a still pond. I made my smile broader and then scrunched my lips shut and finally, I started examining my teeth. They appeared to be pretty straight. Both Tovee and Jebediah stared incredulously at my strange behavior, but Catherine merely smiled, delighted I was so interested in my surroundings.

When she dished up a generous portion of the yellow concoction for all of us, I noticed she served some for herself and Jebediah. She also set an extra portion on a side counter for the missing Benjamin. I'm very observant, and I knew Benjamin's absence was not a good sign. But I also knew it was a good thing the woman and her older son were eating with us. That meant they didn't consider us too filthy or savage to share a meal with them. They regarded us as people. Making a quick judgment, I decided they were decent white people, which was a welcome revelation after seeing all of the bloodthirsty white soldiers at Sand Creek.

After I figured out how to use the pokey thing called a fork, I showed Tovee, of course, and then I wolfed down every bite of eggs. It was delicious. Jebediah seemed to watch each morsel fly into my mouth. He appeared to be wondering where I was putting it all in my small body. I couldn't remember the last time I had eaten anything so delicious. When my plate was empty and my stomach feeling incredibly full, I patted Catherine's arm and smiled. "Thanks." She smiled back and patted my hand, which was on her arm. "You're welcome." I listened very closely, wanting to impress her with my ability to remember new words and phrases.

"So, what's next, Mother?" Jebediah asked impatiently, drinking a steaming black, smelly substance looking like oil. "What are you going to do with them?" Although I couldn't understand his words, I could tell he was respectful to his mother. Wondering if I guessed his age correctly, I decided I'd been right, and he appeared to be about twenty years old. His face was very serious-minded for being so young. He was also very nice-looking for a white man, but very pale and not as handsome as Tovee, with his bronzed skin and healthy glow.

Catherine rolled her pale blue eyes and shook her head in answer to her son's question. She also sipped the black oil as she contemplated an answer. Tovee and I had glasses of a white substance called cow's milk. I drank it to be polite, but I thought it was rather sour. "We can't just make them leave. You know what you heard over in town yesterday. There are rumors about a brutal massacre at Sand Creek in the Colorado territory, and Chivington and his militia are still looking to kill any remaining Cheyenne who escaped." When I heard the words, Sand Creek, and the English word for our tribe, Cheyenne, which I had heard before, I surmised they were talking about the massacre.

"What if the army comes to the door on a house to house search? Are you going to turn them over?" Jebediah had an impassive look on his face.

"We can't do that, Jebediah. It wouldn't be Christian to turn them over to be killed. What have they done? They're just children, and their only sin is being born Indians and not white. I can't believe their skin color means they should be killed. I think we need to let them stay here for a few days, at least until the danger has passed. If the army comes, we could always hide them in the root cellar.

"Besides, there's something very special about Mokee. I knew it the moment I set eyes on her. She's very bright and so eager to please. While she's here, I'd like to try to teach her a few things, maybe even some more English words. She's already picked up words on her own, which means she wants to learn. She doesn't really look like an Indian, do you think, Jebediah? I've never seen such pale skin on an Indian."

Jebediah eyed me with wariness. I knew the two were talking about what to do with us and by the woman's expression, she had expressed she liked me. "I think Mokee is the strangest-looking Indian girl I've ever seen," he admitted with a half-smile. "Her hair is chopped in every direction, and her skin is splotchy tan, like she has the mange. If she got cleaned up, I guess she could almost pass for being white. Worse yet, she looks like she has malnutrition as she's so small and skinny. But I don't trust the other one, Mother, and I doubt he's really her brother. That Mokee is clever as a whip. Look at her watching me and assessing what she's going to do next."

"I know he's not her brother," Catherine said quickly, not wanting her son to think she was naïve. "She did that to protect him as she knew we liked her. I find that very admirable and quick-thinking. So, how old do you think she is? I don't think he's her boyfriend. She seems too young to have a boyfriend."

Jebediah gave a grunt. "She looks about nine, but I bet she's at least a teenager. They say Indians get married young."

"I'm not sensing any romantic involvement from them, but I could be wrong. It's more like they were thrown together to survive. I'm thinking he won't leave her side, though, as he seems a little older and feels responsible for her. My inclination is to give her a bath and wash that God-awful hair, give her some fresh clothes, and let her sleep in a real bed in the spare bedroom.

"I saw they had horses in the barn and sleeping bags on their saddles. They didn't even need the sleeping bags with all the hay in the barn. I guess we can let them sleep in the same room, but he can use his sleeping bag on the floor. It's just temporary, you know, until they're safe." Catherine looked deep in thought, contemplating the dilemma of what to do with the Indian runaways.

"And, just what will he do while you're playing mother hen to the little orphan?" Jebediah asked with a smile, not really being critical. He knew his mother didn't just talk about being a Christian, but she was the type of person to spring into action.

"Well, I thought you could handle that part," Catherine said hopefully. "There are all kinds of chores around here we never have time for, and he can earn their keep, that is if he'll leave her side, which I doubt. Before she goes back to her people, I'd really like to teach Mokee as much English as I can. It might come in handy for her someday and help her survive."

"So, how do we tell them our plan, Mother? Have you forgotten neither one can understand English yet?" Jebediah looked at his mother with disbelief at the major flaw with her idea.

"I think Mokee will be a big help," she explained, pushing her chair back dismissively from the table and standing up. "You're going to have to keep an

eye on Benjamin when he gets back. I don't trust him around either one of them."
Jebediah nodded in agreement.

I went to stand up too, gathering their conversation was finished. Catherine gently pushed me back down in the chair and told me with a smile, "Stay." Another word I would have to remember. I hoped she meant we were staying for a while.

Chapter Five

On the first floor of Catherine's house, there was a small room called a bath closet. The tiny room, which barely fit two people, was near the kitchen, where water could be warmed for baths. A hot bath was apparently a favorite activity of white people. Jeb, which I'm sometimes calling him now in my thoughts as Jebediah is way too long for my tongue, brought a huge metal tub into the room. He began filling it with pot after pot of steaming water, which he heated on the stove.

I followed him like a puppy dog, back and forth, watching him curiously as he poured the water. Then he went back outside to a small well, and he sent a pail down a hole and got more water. I never knew water could come up from a hole in the ground, so that intrigued me. Jeb wearily rolled his warm blue eyes at my persistence in following him, but his reaction just made me work harder at winning him over with my cheerful disposition. I smiled at him until he finally smiled back. There was no point alienating our white saviors.

Mama Cat, which I like to call her sometimes though I think Catherine is a pretty name, was upstairs assembling items I would need for my first indoor bath. Tovee was not particularly happy about the entire process, worrying Catherine would attack me when I was at my most defenseless. Resolutely, he had decided to guard the bathroom door, weaponless, of course, as we were asked to turn over our knives to Jeb, who was storing them in the kitchen until our departure. Tovee, looking sullen-faced and uncooperative, sat cross-legged on the floor in the hall outside the bath closet, refusing to budge.

Jeb's brother, Benjamin, after returning from his walk or whatever it was he did, seemed calmer but still angry. In my mind, I continued to call him by his full name, Benjamin, because I didn't like him. He slammed out the kitchen door again, saying he was off to see his friends in the settlement Tovee and I passed, which I heard him call Salina. I gathered Benjamin didn't want to stay in the house with Indians, so he decided to spend the night with friends in town. Mama Cat, who had walked back into the room before he left, warned him not to say anything about Tovee and me, or she would punish him. I wondered if he would listen to whatever it was his mother asked. He seemed unusually belligerent and not as kind to his mother as Jeb.

It was finally time for my bath, and Mama Cat's strong arms were overflowing with necessary items like a towel and washcloth, a nightgown, special shampoos and soaps, a scissors, and a comb and brush. As it wasn't very appealing to bathe in a cold stream in the fall and winter, I was eager for the new experience.

Catherine very carefully tested the water with her elbow, making sure it wouldn't scald me. She had decided the best way to communicate with me was through acting out what she wanted me to do. All at once, she pretended to undress. "Undress, Mokee," she said with simplicity. I smiled and obeyed, saying the new word, undress, over and over out loud, trying to memorize it.

When I was done, I very neatly folded my soft deerskin undergarments and thicker buffalo skin outer garments for winter, which included a long sleeve shirt, pants with fringe, and a poncho. I added my well-worn moccasins and leggings to the pile, and the very last thing I removed was the braided elk skin necklace from Tovee.

Catherine helped me step over the high rim of the metal tub, holding my hands while I carefully sat down. The hot water felt heavenly and so different from my usual frigid baths. I smiled appreciatively. In a matter-of-fact way, as though seeing naked bodies was something she did every day, Mama Cat soaped her hands and began lathering my entire body. She patiently said the English word, which I repeated, for everything about the bath like soap, water, rinse, hot, and cloth.

Next, she took her fingertips and massaged the scalp of her head, saying the word, "shampoo." She poured something pink and smelling like berries in the palm of her hand, sniffed it and let me smell it, and then began rubbing it into my scalp. It became very bubbly. It was wonderful, and I was so relaxed I trustingly shut my eyes. Catherine leaned her head way back and said, "tilt," then told me to do the same. Before long, all of the sweet-smelling shampoo was rinsed off into the sudsy water.

My bath done, she lifted my dripping wet body gently from the tub and stood me on a loopy mat made of woven cloth, wrapped me in an amazingly soft, nubby towel for warmth, and gave me a sweet, quick kiss on my cheek. As I gazed into her warm, loving blue eyes, I had a crystal clear moment of understanding. The Great Spirit had heard my prayers for help and had temporarily taken me away from war and put me under this kind woman's protection. Experiencing my first moment of insight, I suddenly knew the Great Spirit loved Indians as well as white people.

Next, Catherine showed me a comb and brush set with shimmering pearl handles, and she ran the teeth of the comb and then the bristles of the brush through her curly hair, saying their names while showing me how they worked. After doing the same thing to my wet hair, she cut a tiny piece of her hair with the scissors and then motioned she was going to do the same to mine. I was very glad she was going to even out my hair. Cutting it with my hunting knife had left it jagged and uneven.

Very patiently, I let her do her magic, and I was completely startled when she said, "Mokee, mirror," and showed me the lovely reflection of a clean young woman, who was almost pretty under her neat cap of black hair. *Was it possible I was becoming pretty?* "Thanks," I said with simplicity, carefully handing Mama Cat her mirror so I wouldn't break it.

With very tiny scissors, Catherine trimmed one of her nails and then motioned she was going to do the same to my long, uneven ones. I watched her very carefully, and I bravely splayed my hands, thinking it was going to hurt. It didn't hurt at all. After completing both hands, she tackled my toenails, and I giggled as my feet seemed ticklish. I was sure Tovee wondered what was going on in the bath closet.

When my grooming was done, she removed my towel and helped me into a soft camisole and underpants. She watched me carefully tie my elk skin necklace on my neck, and then she lifted a cotton nightgown with long sleeves over my head. I had never seen anything so pretty, with its pale blue satin ribbons flowing down over a front panel of lace. I felt like a princess. "Thanks," I said shyly, overwhelmed by the kind white woman's generosity.

"Mokee, Tovee bath?" Mama Cat asked curiously. "Water hot. Ask Tovee." I nodded I would, and we opened the door to find Tovee still sitting in the hall, his ramrod straight back leaning like a prison guard against the wall. His eyes gazed over my appearance with approval, and he gave me a faint smile, glad I was safe.

"Tovee, Mama Cat says you can have a bath if you want and use my water while it's still warm," I said excitedly in Cheyenne. "You can be in there alone, and she'll bring you a towel. You can put your own clothes back on, but it feels wonderful to have warm water for once. You should try it," I coaxed animatedly. I could tell by his expression he didn't like my acceptance of the things white people liked to do.

Very carefully, Tovee gave his measured reply. "Mokee, I'm glad to see you happy, and you look beautiful after your bath. I even like your hair for a change." I blushed at his compliments. "It's good you feel safe from the white soldiers. I know how hard it was for you to watch the massacre. Please try to understand. I am in training to be a Cheyenne warrior, and it is difficult for me to be staying with the enemy."

"Enemy?" I said aghast, not understanding his thinking at all. "Catherine and Jeb could not be nicer or more decent. If not for them, we could be dead." I was silent about Benjamin. I didn't trust him either.

"I guess it's okay to stay here for a few days, but soon I am returning to our people to fight in the war against the white man. You can choose to stay here for a while, where you feel safe. You are not a warrior, Mokee, and the white soldiers go after killing the women and children first. If you return with me, you will have no one to watch after you as I will be gone with the warriors.

"Perhaps you should think about it and consider staying here, and I will come back for you. After the war, we will be together someday." He suddenly stood up, tired of having to explain his thoughts any longer. "I'm going for a walk. And no, I don't want a bath in the enemy's house, today or ever." With a stubborn finality, Tovee turned away and marched outside to get some fresh air.

Apologetically, I turned to Mama Cat, who had been standing there curiously listening to the lively barrage of Cheyenne dialect. I hoped she didn't think I shared Tovee's obvious animosity. "Tovee, no bath," I said with a sad smile, motioning with my eyes at the slammed door.

Catherine, not knowing what to do next, leaned her head on her hands like she was sleeping. "Sleep? Bed, Mokee?"

"Tovee," I said, shaking my head no. I knew she realized I wanted to wait for him to return. Suddenly, my face brightened. "Jeb?"

The kindly woman smiled and took my hand. We padded into another room, which I found out was called a living room. Her long-legged, rather serious-minded son was seated on a wide tan leather sofa. An oil lamp was positioned on a wooden end table, and the pensive man was relaxing and reading a thick book. His reading glasses were perched comically on the bridge of his nose.

I stared at him sitting there and felt a warmness in my heart. This kind man had accepted me into his home, in spite of his reluctance. I had never seen anyone read a book before, and I was fascinated how the pages flipped and then flipped again. I was eager to see what Jeb was looking at so intently, but I remained quiet. I didn't want to be too forward.

"Doesn't Mokee look lovely, Jeb?" Catherine asked, breaking his concentration. Jeb carefully put down his book on its belly and took off his reading glasses. For fun, I pirouetted in front of him to show off the new me. Both he and Mama Cat laughed, and I smiled appreciatively. I always liked making people laugh.

"What a remarkable change," he assessed thoughtfully, almost in disbelief. "She was actually beautiful under all that grime. You did a great job with her, Mother, especially her hair. If I didn't know it, I couldn't even tell she's an Indian. She must have white blood in her to have skin that light."

"I only bathed her, Jeb, and let her natural beauty shine through," Catherine said modestly. "By the way, she's the sweetest young girl I've ever met, very polite and cooperative. And, she's trying so hard to learn our language. I bet I taught her fifty words in the course of her bath."

As if on cue, I looked into Jeb's face and said, "Thanks, Jeb. Bath good. Good water." I smiled my gratitude, knowing he had gotten the water from the well, and Jeb chuckled at my attempt at humor and smiled back. *He's got a very nice smile for a white man*, I thought. Then I unintentionally shivered, berating myself for my straying thoughts, especially with Tovee, my future husband, brooding outside in the darkness over my affinity for Catherine and Jeb.

"I wish Benjamin was coming back," Catherine said nervously. I could tell the atmosphere in the room got immediately tense at Mama Cat's mention of her younger son. I was already sensing Benjamin was trouble.

"He's probably just staying with his friend, Dillon," Jeb answered quietly, trying to ease his mother's mind by mentioning one of his brother's friends. If he were being honest, Jeb had no idea where Benjamin had gone. He knew his mother was as concerned as he was about his brother's drinking and carousing.

"Don't worry," he continued. "I warned him again not to say anything about our visitors. Just in case he gets drunk and spills the beans, we better be prepared to hide them tomorrow. In fact, I'll go out to the barn tonight and hide any of their belongings and their saddles. If we have to implement a plan quickly, you'll have to explain it to Mokee in the morning."

"I'll do it first thing," Catherine said, lines of worry creasing her face.

Just then, the kitchen door squeaked open and in walked Tovee, still in his soiled clothes from the long ride. Hearing our voices, he continued on to the living room. I smiled at him, glad he had returned.

"Let's take you to bed, Mokee," Mama Cat said, extending her hand to lead me upstairs. "Did you fix the sleeping mat on the floor, Jeb?" He nodded, looking suspiciously at Tovee. One day, he would tell me he had been worried putting Tovee in the same room with me, but he knew there'd be trouble otherwise. He also thought it was strange how, even from the beginning, he didn't think of me as an Indian, though he knew I was.

Excitedly, I followed Catherine up the stairs. As I had never climbed up steps before, I walked very slowly. I wished there had been time to try jumping from step to step. It looked like it would be fun. "C'mon, Tovee," I said impatiently in Cheyenne. "They're giving us a room." Reluctantly, he followed us up the stairs, almost acting like he was selling his soul to the white man by entering further into the bowels of the house.

When the door opened to what was to be our bedroom, I gasped in awe. I had never seen anything so beautiful or feminine. The room was quite small with a narrow, twin-sized bed and a matching dresser with a big mirror. Because this was the second mirror I'd seen, I decided white people liked to look at themselves. A white, ruffled bedspread trimmed with lace was pulled back to reveal a puffy pillow and sheets edged with little holes, looking like eyes.

On the soft bed, there were several thick wool blankets, and I noticed the only source of heat in the room was a small hearth in a corner. There were also frilly white curtains on the room's two windows. Wooden shutters were closed over the windows to keep out drafts.

"Thanks, Mama Cat," I said. I gave her a quick, but affectionate hug, which I could tell Tovee didn't like. The older woman discreetly left the room and shut the door.

At the end of the bed on the hardwood floor, I noticed Tovee's sleeping bag from the barn, and I knew Mama Cat was suggesting we sleep apart. After thinking about it, I realized it might hurt Tovee's feelings if I didn't share the soft bed with him. After all, he only thought of me like a younger sister, or so I'd always thought.

As if he agreed with my silent assessment of the sleeping arrangements, he crawled into the soft bed without invitation and held his arms open for me to join him. I smiled self-consciously and sank into his arms, just as I had done in the barn the night before.

"This is some place, isn't it?" he asked uncomfortably, fidgeting in the foreign bed of the enemy. As he pulled me closer, I felt his lips touch my newly cut nest of soft hair in a brief kiss.

"It's like a dream," I whispered with disbelief and awe. "Can you believe white people sleep on beds this comfortable?"

"Go to sleep, Mokee," Tovee responded irritably, making it obvious he didn't approve of how I liked Catherine and Jeb. "It's really been a long couple of days, and we need our rest. I'm really worried the soldiers will find out we're here. So, enjoy the bed tonight. Tomorrow night, we might be back in the woods."

I knew what he said was true, but I had even more troubling thoughts than my own problems. Whose room had this been? It surely wasn't decorated for Jeb or his brother. *Had Mama Cat had a daughter?*

Chapter Six

It was early dawn, and the rising sun was just starting to peek through the top cracks of the shutters. For a moment, I startled, not knowing where I was, the soft sensations of a bed unfamiliar to my senses. I glanced over at Tovee, who was still in a deep sleep and making little snoring sounds. Then I realized what had awakened me. There was frantic pounding on the wooden entrance door to the bedroom.

All at once, Jeb and Catherine flung the door open. It was obvious they couldn't wait any longer for one of us to get up and open it. It struck the wall with a crash. They marched into the room, their faces etched with fear. Without noticing or caring that Tovee and I were sharing the bed, they exchanged anxious glances about how to tell us some important news. By this time, I was sitting up straight, and Tovee had awakened and sat up as well. We also exchanged nervous glances.

Catherine was the first to speak, and it was with urgency. "Mokee, soldiers." She paused, wondering what to say next. All of a sudden, she said, "Sand Creek." I instantly knew soldiers were coming to search the house, and we needed to hide. I conveyed the information to Tovee in a burst of Cheyenne language. We both bounded out of bed, ready to do whatever they told us to do.

"Mother, why don't you put Mokee in regular clothes. If anyone sees her, at least she'll look like one of us. I'll take Tovee to the root cellar to hide, and you bring Mokee when she's dressed." Catherine nodded, hurrying to a dresser drawer, and Jeb grabbed Tovee by the hand and rushed him away. I shouted after Tovee to cooperate, knowing how he hated touching Jeb's hand as they ran through the hall and down the stairs.

Catherine dressed me in a long-sleeved, dark green dress of soft material called velvet. It had a narrow white collar and cuffs. Next, she whipped some thick, white leggings on my legs followed by the most uncomfortable, black shiny things called shoes on my feet. They pinched my toes like crazy.

Like a whirlwind, the older woman grabbed my buckskin clothes, moccasins, and also Tovee's sleeping bag, and she hid them deep in a drawer of frilly clothes. Then she yanked up the bedspread and made the bed look like no one had ever spent the night there. Mama Cat did a quick onceover of the room to make sure everything was in place. Rather than have me fall on the stairs in the slippery-bottomed shoes, she easily scooped me up in her arms and sprinted from the room. Hurriedly, she rushed down the stairs. Any thoughts I had the previous night of jumping and playing on the steps had vanished from my mind.

The main floor of the house was deserted and silent, and Catherine quickly looked out the front window of the living room. Comfortable the soldiers hadn't made their approach yet, Mama Cat charged out the kitchen door in the back. The root cellar was a little ways from the back door, and it had a wooden door on the ground level slanted against the house and a huge sliding wooden bolt as a lock.

Catherine yanked the door open with a burst of strength and then, with me still in her arms, hurried down some rickety wooden steps. There was an oil lamp flickering on a wobbly wooden table, and the eerie light exposed a huge cavity with a dirt floor. Built against the cool earthen walls, there were shelves and closets with wooden doors. There were even bins for additional storage.

Another room around the corner, which was also carved out of the earth, had more storage space with enclosed closets and shelves. Sacks of supplies and edible things like onions, turnips, carrots, and potatoes filled the shelves, and household equipment, extra coats, blankets, and tarps overflowed in the closets.

Jeb had found what he thought was the perfect place for our concealment. It was a bin in the room around the corner and deceptively, it didn't look large enough for even one body. There were more ideal places for hiding right next to it, and the bin looked too small to contain human bodies compared with the larger hiding places.

Tovee climbed in first and adjusted his body to the small space. Then, Jeb picked me up and dropped me gently into Tovee's arms. Surprisingly, there was room to spare for both of us once we readjusted our limbs. Catherine brought over a cloth tarp and threw it over us. On top of that, Jeb started randomly scattering light gardening things like gloves, scarves, empty sacks of seeds, and rags. Tovee readjusted the tarp in the back so we could breathe, and Jeb shut the lid imperfectly with a few of the seed bags caught in the hinge, allowing us to continue to get fresh air.

Quickly, Jeb and Catherine did a run through on both rooms of the cellar, leaving closets ajar and other bins slightly propped open to suggest the rooms were supposed to look untidy. Extinguishing the lamp and taking it with them, Catherine and her son exited the dark, cold root cellar, securely bolting the door. They raced into the kitchen, stored the lamp above a cabinet, and slowed their pace as they finally reached the living room.

Jeb casually sat down on the sofa, and his hands shook uneasily. As a distraction, he resumed reading his book from the night before. Catherine carefully peered around a lacy curtain. "They're coming, Jebediah," she whispered, going to her favorite chair and casually picking up her knitting. "It looks like about five or six of them."

Jeb shook his head sadly. "I just can't believe Benjamin did this, but we haven't seen him since last night. What else can I think? He was the only person who knew."

Catherine also didn't want to believe her younger son had betrayed them all. She had always blamed Benjamin's erratic behavior on the deaths of his sister and then his father. But, this went beyond the pale. Hadn't he realized if Mokee and Tovee were discovered on their property, his mother and brother would be in danger of being arrested or even executed as traitors? Not only would Benjamin be responsible for the deaths of two innocent Indians, but his family as well.

No, I can't think that about my son, Catherine said to herself in denial, her heart distraught. She began silently praying to the Lord who had sustained her throughout her life, even when her young daughter and husband had died. Please help us, she said in spirit, and keep Mokee and Tovee invisible.

There was a stern rap on the front door. Jeb calmly walked over and opened it, using the book as a prop to steady his hands. He gazed over the rims of his reading glasses at the small group of soldiers. "Can I help you gentlemen?" he asked with an authoritative voice as the man of the house, although he was barely a man.

"Who is it, Jebediah?" Catherine asked from her chair, pretending she hadn't known the visitors were coming. Jeb had only heard about the soldiers that morning. His closest neighbor had stopped by at the first light of dawn to share the gossip, and the neighbor had heard the rumors in town at the general store the previous night.

"May we come in?" an unyielding voice asked. The militia officer definitely meant business.

"Certainly." Jeb stepped aside and ushered five soldiers into the living room, which was near the front door. The large uniformed bodies filled the small space. Catherine stood up, and she casually took off her glasses and put down her knitting. She approached the men.

"Well, hello gentlemen," she said pleasantly, offering her hand politely to the leader of the group. "You're out bright and early this morning."

"Ma'am." The spokesman doffed his cap after shaking her hand, and Jeb noticed he was the only officer, a captain in the Kansas militia. The others were enlistees. "I'll make this quick. There was a rumor circulating in Saline County about Indians fleeing from Colorado. Several were said to have been spotted in this general area. To satisfy ourselves the rumor's false, we've decided to do a sweep of any outlying farms. We hope to reassure the settlements of Salina and even Abilene they're in no danger. If you don't mind, we'd like to search your house and barn."

"I guess that's all right," Jeb replied with a disinterested shrug. "Be my guest.

My mother and I have been sitting here talking this morning, and we haven't seen or heard anything unusual. I assume you're from Fort Riley. Where exactly did you hear the rumor?" Jeb asked curiously with a puzzled look on his face. He was almost afraid to hear the answer.

"One of our soldiers reported it. He was on a leave of absence and said he heard it in Salina. If you don't mind, we'd like to get started. There are a few other farms we have to get to this morning," the captain said. Jeb nodded, and the officer began directing a few soldiers around the house and the rest out to the barn.

Catherine almost gave a sigh of relief. If they were searching other farms, it meant Benjamin hadn't specifically ratted on his own family. Jeb silently drew a different conclusion. Benjamin was obviously the only one who had known the truth. Jeb was convinced he had gotten drunk with his friends and blurted part of the story in a general sort of way. His brother's rebellious nature and temper were only part of the problem. Jeb feared he was an alcoholic, and he knew his mother refused to believe the truth. Having Indians in the house had brought the problem to a head.

The two of them settled back down in the living room, pretending to be unworried about the search. They could hear the soldiers' boots clattering on the wooden staircase, as well as in the kitchen. The footsteps were moving along quickly, and doors were creaking open and slamming shut almost simultaneously from different locations. Before long, the soldiers were done, and they clambered out the back door to join the others in the barn. Before leaving, the captain stuck his head in the living room to thank them for their cooperation.

Jeb went in the kitchen to watch the remainder of the search and noticed the captain pointed a couple of the men to the root cellar. *The perfect time for a prayer was now,* Jeb thought, as he silently prayed God would protect Mokee and her friend. It gave him pause to think he was so worried over the safety of the impish Indian girl.

Pretending to be busy in the kitchen cooking breakfast, Jeb tried to keep tabs on the soldiers, and his stomach was tied in knots. The soldiers in the root cellar hadn't returned yet. In what seemed an eternity, the two finally came up the steps empty-handed and returned a lantern they had used to the barn. Jeb wanted to shout for joy. Instead, he began actively assembling food for what would be their belated breakfast. He figured everyone would be starving after all the tension. Just to be sure the soldiers were all together, he counted them one more time, and then he watched them hurriedly ride away on their horses.

Slowly, Jeb walked into the living room. "They're gone," he said quietly with a smile.

Catherine jumped to her feet and threw herself into her son's arms. "Oh,

Jebediah, I'm so relieved. I was so worried about poor little Mokee." Tears of relief were streaming down her pale face. It was just like his mother to worry about the small Indian girl and not herself.

"I think we should give it at least another twenty minutes until I get them out of their cubbyhole. Why don't you finish cooking breakfast? I already got it started. I'm going to make a quick run through the house and barn to make sure the soldiers didn't forget anything, like gloves or whatever. If they did, they'll be back." Jeb gave her a happy smile and patted his mother's back. "Try to calm down, Mother. We did it!" Catherine smiled through her happy tears and set off for the kitchen.

"Okay, Mokee, you're safe," Jeb said cheerfully. He carefully flung back the lid to the storage bin and tediously removed the clutter of items from the top of the tarp, hoping we would understand things were okay now. When he finally removed the tarp, he gave me and Tovee a big smile and held his hands out to help me from the bin. After blinking at the sudden light, dim as it was, we both smiled back, although Tovee's smile was tentative. It was good to see Tovee not as stern-faced and unfriendly as usual.

Tovee lifted me into Jeb's muscular arms, and Jeb carefully guided me to my feet. I was overwhelmed with emotion we were still alive and safe. With a sudden move, I threw myself into a gigantic hug, flinging my arms around Jeb's high shoulders. I gave my savior a broad smile and said, "Thanks, Jeb."

Jeb looked dumbfounded at my genuine show of affection, especially in front of someone he thought might be my boyfriend. I knew he had no idea how old I was, or whether I was even old enough to have a boyfriend. He obviously didn't want to take any chances Tovee would be jealous, and Jeb quickly broke off the hug and helped Tovee out of the bin. Tovee nodded his thanks grudgingly, and I could have kicked him for his continued anger at our benefactors.

Jeb must have realized his mother's way of communicating with me was the most effective, and he pantomimed eating with a utensil and chewing. Then he motioned for us to follow him. Once we were all seated at the kitchen table, Catherine put a strange circular object on our plates. After calling it a pancake, she proceeded to cut mine into bite-sized pieces, saying knife and fork, then butter as she slathered a mound of yellow on the steaming pancake. The yellow melted and made my mouth water. Then she poured a tiny bit of brown goo, which she called syrup, speared a square with my fork, and put it in my mouth, like a mother bird feeding her baby. It was amazingly delicious, and I happily continued feeding myself after saying thanks.

Tovee, of course, defiantly refused her assistance and rolled the circle, held it in his hand, and took a crumbly bite. I'm sure it was dry and not very tasty. The butter and syrup made it so much better. Tovee was proving to be very stubborn, however. When we were in the bin, he told me he was leaving soon. Explaining his reasoning, he said he couldn't stand being with white people any longer, and he was ready to fight the enemy.

I really was having difficulty understanding his attitude. Jeb and Catherine had been so kind to us, even risking their lives to keep us safe. I really thought kindness was more important than the color of a person's skin, but I didn't dare express that thought to Tovee. He rigidly viewed all white people as the enemy. To be honest, I was constantly worried he was going to attack Jeb or Catherine, and I was actually glad Jeb took away our weapons.

Before we had become silent in the bin, Tovee hinted at a plan he'd put together. Although he said he didn't want to force me to stay against my will, he explained he thought it was safer for me if I stayed on with Catherine and Jeb a little longer. He told me my skin color made it possible for me to temporarily fit in, and he would return someday to get me when the atrocities lessened. I didn't like what I was hearing, but Tovee never gave me the chance to speak. If he went to war against the white soldiers, I knew in my heart Tovee would probably be killed.

Telling me my parents had given him the responsibility for my welfare, he tried to reassure me about his decision. He said if I stayed here and needed to leave before he returned, all I would have to do was head west along the Smoky Hill River to the general area of the former encampments. Although the camps had relocated, the new camps would still be nearby, but further north toward the Republican River.

It was then Tovee startled me. He whispered he loved me, and he always had. He also told me I was beautiful. Even though we were in the dark under the tarp, he tilted my face upward and kissed me very romantically. Although I'm almost fifteen, it was my first real kiss, and I liked it a lot. I have to admit I was surprised. I had always thought Tovee had just put up with me and even thought me homely, but apparently I was wrong. I will have to think more on that new revelation. *Was it possible I was as pretty as the reflection in Mama Cat's mirror?*

My thoughts of our tender moments in the bin totally vanished as the back door to the kitchen slammed open, hitting the wall. All of us jumped. We thought the soldiers had returned. Instead, it was Jeb's hot-tempered brother, Benjamin. He was disheveled-looking, and his unshaven face had the beginnings of a beard.

"Well, isn't this a cozy little family portrait with everyone sitting around the kitchen table having pancakes?" he asked with scorn, tugging his winter coat off and tossing it carelessly on a crowded kitchen counter. "I see the redskins are still part of the family." With hostility, he yanked back a chair, scratching it unpleasantly across the floor.

Whipping it around backwards, he straddled it and sank down next to Tovee, who immediately sensed danger and was ready to fight if necessary. I cautioned him with my eyes to let it go. Suddenly, Benjamin surveyed me up and down with disapproval. "What do you think, Mother? That this scuzzy little redskin is Margaret again?"

I couldn't understand a word Jeb's brother said, but the atmosphere in the room nearly exploded. Jeb threw his chair across the room with a crash, and he grabbed his younger brother by the neck of his shirt, jerking him to his feet and nearly choking him. I threw a restraining arm in front of Tovee, whispering in Cheyenne to stay in his chair and be quiet, that this was an argument between Jeb and his brother.

It would clearly be a mismatch if a fight broke out. Jeb was tall and muscular, though on the thin side, and Benjamin was short and paunchy-looking and definitely out of shape. I hoped there wouldn't be a brawl. I didn't want Jeb to get hurt, even though I knew he would win easily. What surprised me was my growing concern for this family.

"You apologize to our mother after making that crack about our dead sister, Margaret," Jeb seethed, twisting Benjamin's neck to face Catherine. Mama Cat was softly crying, and I wanted to comfort her, but thought it might make matters worse. Benjamin suddenly looked sheepish and mumbled some faint words of apology. All I could figure out was the argument was about someone named Margaret.

Jeb still hadn't released Benjamin, and his younger brother started squirming to get loose, nearly knocking the dishes off the table. Jeb began speaking to him tersely once more. "For your information, Mokee and her companion are guests here, and you will be polite to them until they choose to leave. We did not appreciate it when soldiers showed up at the front door, all because you hinted to your friends about Indians being spotted at a farmhouse in the area." Benjamin turned beet red, guilty of whatever Jeb had said.

Jeb continued his verbal assault. "Just because you're a drunk, brother, that's no excuse for your behavior. You endangered our mother's life as well as my own. If the soldiers who came to the house had found our guests, we would have been arrested. And, I promise you one thing. If you do anything else whatsoever to harm anyone here, I'm going to throw you out. Then, you can live on a corner somewhere like the drunk you are. Do you understand, Benjamin?"

"You're not my father, Jebediah, and you don't have the right to kick me out of this house," Benjamin said staunchly with a whine in his voice, standing up to his older brother. There was a moment of deadly silence.

All at once, Catherine, who had gotten control of her emotions, pushed her chair back and stood up straight, towering over Benjamin. Her voice was stern and unrelenting, unlike the quiet woman who had been so kind to me. "Jebediah might not have that authority, but I do, Benjamin, because this is my house and my farm. And, you will do exactly as your brother has said. From now on, you will be polite to our guests. If you say anything about our guests to anyone outside of this house again, you are out!

"Now, it has been a very stressful morning thanks to you, and I am taking our guest, Mokee, into the living room. I'm going to teach her some new English words." She suddenly held out her hand to me, which I took immediately. I didn't want her to be mad at me too. "Mokee, come," she said. After a moment's hesitation, she said, "Tovee, come. Mokee tell Tovee." I understood she wanted Tovee to come with us, so I explained that to him in Cheyenne, stressing it was better to be away from the arguing brothers. He nodded in agreement.

The three of us went into the living room. Mama Cat and I settled on the sofa, and she started methodically showing me books with pictures and telling me the English words for each picture. I was curious how different things could be printed on paper pages, and I kept rubbing the pages, as if the pictures would come off. There were even exotic birds, like parrots, sitting on the pages and looking ready to take flight. Happily, I kept repeating the words, and soon the altercation was forgotten in the kitchen. Tovee, meanwhile, sat cross-legged on the floor, leaning against the wall under one of the windows. He shut his eyes, either deep in thought or thoroughly bored, or maybe both.

I could hear Jeb's low, masculine voice in the kitchen. It was calmer now, and there actually seemed to be a normal conversation going on. I was relieved. I knew Jeb had defended my presence to his brother, and I also knew I was partially at the heart of the difficulties along with someone named Margaret. *Maybe it would be more peaceful for Jeb if I left with Tovee*, I thought.

There were no further problems for the rest of the day. Jeb and Benjamin vanished together to do some work on the farm. I later found out they were mending a fence to keep the pigs from getting out. The farm seemed to have a lot of land connected to it, and there was probably a lot of maintenance. The whole concept of owning land was foreign to me. Indians believed the Great Spirit owned the land, and it was a sacred trust to take care of it and leave as small a footprint as possible.

I had a wonderful day with Catherine. Tovee eventually spent the day outside, and I hoped he would stay out of trouble and especially not confront Benjamin. Mama Cat and I worked on English lessons all day long, going through things in the house and labeling them, learning names of different foods, and making black marks called letters with what she called a fountain pen. I could tell she was really pleased with my progress, and we were having small English conversations by dinnertime.

Catherine had me help her cook dinner, and she explained everything about the kitchen to me in English, of course. We made a beef stew similar to the buffalo stew of the Cheyenne. My favorite part about the meal was the biscuits and especially the butter melting on the hot biscuits. While I cooked, I couldn't resist nibbling a few crumbs ahead of time.

Thankfully, I talked Mama Cat out of continuing to wear the velvet dress and horrible shoes, which imprisoned my toes. She found some old pants and flannel shirts her sons had worn when they were growing up. Finally, I was comfortable and wore my moccasins on my feet.

Dinnertime was actually very peaceful. After working with Jeb all day, Benjamin went into town to be with his friends. I wondered again if he viewed us as savages and couldn't stand being under the same roof with us. I helped serve dinner, saying to a surprised Jeb, "Want stew, Jeb? I cook." He gave me an astonished smile and nodded, and I proceeded to dish up some stew on his plate.

"Did Mokee learn to speak some English already?" he asked his mother.

"Ask her," Catherine answered proudly. Her blue eyes sparkled.

"Well, Mokee. Do you speak English?" Jeb's eyes reflected his disbelief.

"I speak English okay," I said demurely. "Want biscuit, Jeb?" Without waiting for his reply, I put a fat one on his plate. He chuckled. At the same time I was trying to impress Jeb with my learning, I dished up stew on Tovee's plate and also gave him a biscuit, telling him in Cheyenne he would really like the stew as I made it. He gave me a slight smile, but I wondered what he was thinking. Since returning from the woods, he had been very sullen.

"Mama Cat, more butter please," I chirped, happy with my new ability to communicate. "Butter good," I added. *What a wonderful day,* I thought to myself. We were safe from the soldiers, and I was learning English. Jeb said something to his mother about me being a little magpie, but I had no idea what that meant or whether it was good or bad.

Nighttime came, and Tovee and I went to our room. I didn't know it at the time, but Catherine and Jeb had a lengthy discussion about our sleeping arrangements. Eventually, they concluded to leave the situation alone. They needn't have worried, however. As soon as Tovee and I shut the bedroom door, he sat me down on the bed and sank down next to me with a solemn look on his face.

As Tovee held my upper arms, I knew what was coming before he spoke. "I'm leaving tonight, Mokee," he whispered. "I already retrieved my weapons from the drawer, and I secured my horse in the woods." I looked down and saw his sleeping bag was gone.

"So, that's what you were doing today?" I asked sadly. "Why didn't you tell me? I would have gotten ready also."

"No, Mokee, I already explained I've made the decision for you, and I want you to listen to me. You're not coming, at least not yet. You fit in well here. You're safe. They like you and won't mistreat you, and your skin is light. You're enjoying learning new things, something you'd never have the opportunity to do. You'll be safer here than with me on the frontline of war. When the threat of war lessens, I will come back for you when I have the opportunity." He was adamant about his plan.

Tears fell from my eyes. I knew in my heart the war would never be over as long as men's hatred ran so deep. If I stayed, I might never see Tovee again. "Please take me with you," I whispered, feeling a hollow ache inside. I felt as though my life had just fallen apart. I had always planned on being with Tovee and never thought of an alternative.

"No, Mokee, you're staying." He studied my face for a long time. "Please." Tovee held out his arms for me, and we lay back gently on the bed. There were no more kisses, however, as Tovee appeared anxious to be on his way, and he didn't want to make our parting any more difficult. "I will hold you for a while until the others are asleep, but then I'm going. It's better to travel at nighttime. Tell them thanks, and I never hated them personally." Sadly, I understood.

The soul would have no rainbow had the eyes no tears.

John Vance Cheney

Chapter Seven

When I awakened the next morning, it was gloomy outside, and I was as low-spirited inside. There was no sunshine, just gray, overcast skies, and there was a chill in the air, almost like it was going to snow. My heart felt heavy and sad, as if it could fall from my chest with its weight and shatter into tiny pieces on the floor. As I rubbed my eyes before crawling out of the empty bed, I could tell they were swollen and sore from my night of tears. Tovee was gone, and I was alone in the world.

Forlornly, I threw on my pants, flannel shirt, and moccasins, and I went down the stairs to the kitchen, where I heard pots and pans clattering. Catherine heard me coming and turned around to give me a cheerful greeting. It was then she noticed my puffy red eyes and splotchy face, and even my disheveled appearance. With motherly concern, she hurried over and put a calming hand on my shoulder.

"Mokee, what's wrong?" she asked in English, not knowing if I even understood her question. Her eyes searched my face with worry.

Although I didn't know the exact meaning of her words, I knew what her gentle eyes asked. "Tovee gone," I said desolately, breaking into unstoppable tears. Suddenly, there were two consoling arms enveloping me, holding me close to a heart beating in unison with mine. Mama Cat patted my head and rubbed my back while I cried. Eventually, Jeb came into the kitchen for his breakfast, but Catherine hastily motioned him away. "It's okay, child. Everything will be okay," she soothed.

"Did Tovee hurt her?" Jeb whispered angrily. I could tell he was berating himself for not keeping better tabs on Tovee. He was probably thinking he never should have let us sleep together in the same room.

I realized I needed to get control over my emotions. Jeb's tone of voice showed me he was jumping to the wrong conclusions. After sighing deeply into Catherine's chest, my tears finally stopped. There was something important I needed to do. With a silent prayer to the Great Spirit, I searched for the courage. All at once, I looked up into the older woman's kindly face, and then I turned toward Jeb and reached out my hand for him. "Jeb, come," I said softly.

"I'm right here, Mokee," Jeb's low voice said from the door jamb, where he had been awkwardly standing and watching my tearful outburst. He walked slowly to join us and rested his broad hand on my back to calm me down. "What

40

is it, Mokee?" he asked gently with genuine concern. I stared at his blue eyes for the longest time, drinking in their kindness and encouragement.

With suddenness, I took an enormous breath. "Jeb, Mama Cat, Tovee gone. Tovee say thanks." It was then I stood in silence. All at once, I whispered the question I could barely put into words. "You want Mokee gone?" Tears welled up in my eyes once again. I feared their answer. I had brought nothing but trouble to this entire household, and I had put their lives in danger. Jeb and his brother were even fighting because of me.

Jeb and his mother exchanged stunned glances. They realized I was asking whether I could stay more than just a few days, and I heard their deep, worried sighs. Both knew the difficulties my staying would bring, and yet neither wanted to say I had to leave. They both understood I would be thrown back into a violent war in its beginning, and I probably would be killed.

"Mother?" Jeb asked softly, yet carefully. "It's up to you. We'll do whatever you decide." Jeb's eyes met Catherine's with sincerity and indecision.

It seemed as though the older woman was silently praying, as she closed her eyes for a few moments. The silence was almost deafening while I waited for her answer. All at once, Catherine opened her eyes and smiled at me with certainty. Her eyes glowed with conviction and a sense of purpose. "Mokee stay," she said firmly with a broad smile of welcome. "Mokee live here." She gestured to the house with her arms held wide. "Mokee learn English, okay?" Her carefully worded sentences exhausted the English words she thought I would understand.

My heart leaped with joy, and I pulled Jeb into the circle of hugs in my new temporary family. I could almost feel a glow of love and purpose bonding us together and transcending our differences. Although I didn't know why, I was meant to be here. I wasn't replacing my parents nor had I forgotten them, but they had enough worries of their own struggling to survive without worrying about me too. Tovee would tell them I was safe and would return someday.

Catherine and I began crying again, this time with happiness, and even Jeb's eyes were moist. *There is something so honest about a strong man's tears,* I thought, and I implicitly trusted Jeb from that day forward and forged a bond with him. I looked at their faces and pledged silently to never disappoint them. My time with them, however brief, was the Great Spirit's gift of peace to me. I would learn all I could while I was here and one day, I would speak and write English with precision. After that, my goal would be to use my knowledge of the white man's world to help my people find a path of peace.

"Okay," I said with heartfelt conviction. "Mokee stay. Mama Cat, Jeb, Mokee loves." I looked first from one face and then to the other. "Thanks."

I have dreamed in my life,
dreams that have stayed with me ever after,
and changed my ideas;
they have gone through and through me,
like wine through water,
and altered the color of my mind.

Emily Bronte

PART TWO

Chapter Eight

Winter, spring, and summer passed, and I discovered the meaning of joy. I had already known friendship and love in my brief life. I had known the love of my parents, Tovee, Catherine, and Jeb, and the laughter and camaraderie of my Cheyenne friends. But I had never known joy, only a constant, paralyzing fear of violence, hatred, war, and death. As the English poet William Blake said, "He who binds to himself a joy, Does the winged life destroy; But he who kisses the joy as it flies, Lives in eternity's sun rise."

I was determined to kiss the joy as it swiftly flew by. By late summer of the next year, I had not only mastered speaking the English language with its confusing grammar rules, but reading and writing the language as well. Catherine was an excellent teacher. She gave me not just lifeless words on a page, but thoughts that were alive and expressed in beautiful words. My thirsty mind soared. Every day, I studied diligently until my eyes drooped into a peaceful sleep. We studied classics and Shakespeare, poets like Emily Dickinson and William Blake, philosophy, the Bible, and even the dictionary.

"Find ecstasy in life; the mere sense of living is joy enough," said the American poet Emily Dickinson, and I realized the joy of being alive gave me a sense of unlimited possibility and purpose, an ecstasy to every breath.

"The tree which moves some to tears of joy is in the eyes of others only a green thing that stands in the way. Some see nature all ridicule and deformity. . . and some scarce see nature at all. But to the eyes of the man of imagination, nature is imagination itself," said William Blake. I began to see my joy was not only observing beauty, which was all around me, but in using the eyes of my imagination to see future beauty that could exist in my war-torn world.

John Keats, another English poet, told me, "A thing of beauty is a joy forever: its loveliness increases; it will never pass into nothingness," and I knew every experience, from my Cheyenne childhood to my precious time with Jeb and Catherine, would continue to be a joy forever if seen through the eyes of beauty.

Giving me a sense of the harsher realities of life, John Calvin, one of the leaders of the Protestant Reformation, reminded me, "You must submit to supreme suffering in order to discover the completion of joy." I began to realize the violence of war, from which there was no escape, would somehow become the catalyst to complete my joy.

I learned knowledge was the key to unlocking the possibilities of hope and the beauty and blessing of both the present and the future, no matter how difficult my path might become. If I were able to unlock joy and peace in the hearts and minds of those who embraced hatred, I knew I would fulfill my life's purpose.

To help others find joy and peace would be impossible, however, unless I could figure out how to permanently be infused with joy, peace, and love in my own life. And that was the mystery I needed to solve for myself.

It was a beautiful Saturday morning in late August, and it was ten o'clock. Just to state those facts excited me. I now knew the days of the week and the months, and even how to tell time. What a miracle the world was to have so much complexity. Knowing so many facts actually made me appreciate my Cheyenne heritage. Although my people lived in simplicity, I began to see they also understood complexity in their own way. For example, they had great knowledge about moon cycles, seasons, sunrises, constellations, and weather. *Were people innately different, or were they similar in wanting to understand and appreciate the world around them and to give praise to the Creator of all things?*

Summertime meant Jeb was working in the fields from dawn to dusk. He had several crops including wheat, potatoes, and corn, and he was always plowing, irrigating, or threshing. I came to appreciate how hard a farmer's life really was.

Of course, Benjamin's refusal to work with Jeb any longer because of me didn't help, and the farm was too large for only one person to be doing all the hard labor. I knew Benjamin blamed his brother and mother for letting me stay, and Benjamin adopted an either/or attitude, meaning either they kicked me out, or he wasn't helping around the farm. Consequently, Jeb's brother, in a show of anger, left for good and moved either to Salina or Abilene, we weren't sure which. I felt very badly at how Jeb was overworking and wished I could make amends for his brother leaving.

On this fine, sunny morning, Catherine was bent over her knitting, completing a row and switching from knitting to purling. She was making me a woolen scarf for the fall, and it was wheat colored like the harvest. Knitting was something I didn't master, I guess because I was all thumbs and not interested. It didn't bring me the joy books did. With books, I was able to escape into magical corners of the world and faraway dreams, places with no violence.

While Mama Cat knitted, I was gazing into a geography book with pictures of areas I never dreamed existed. There were beautiful beaches and oceans as far as the eye could see. All I had ever known in my short life was the adversity of nature as it affected the daily life of my nomadic tribe. We lived from day to day under harsh conditions, hunting our food and constantly moving our camp when the food ran out, and even battling the elements, such as droughts, blizzards, and windstorms. Now we were warring with the white man, and we were afraid the land, which had sustained us for thousands of years, would be taken away. Yet, I was discovering there was so much more to life.

Looking up momentarily at Catherine who was toiling on her knitting, I reflected on the past nine months I had spent with Mama Cat and Jeb. Shortly after the decision was made for me to stay, I celebrated my first Christmas with my new family. I learned from Catherine about the joyous birth of God's son, and she and I began to read every day from the new Bible she gave me for Christmas.

Jeb gave me the book of geography I was holding on my lap. Because God gave the gift of His son, Jeb said people began to exchange gifts to celebrate God's gift. Not knowing what I could ever give Mama Cat and Jeb to equal their generosity of spirit, I cooked them a Christmas feast with Cheyenne recipes I knew by heart. They seemed to appreciate my efforts.

Being the start of winter, which Jeb and Catherine called the month of December, I realized it was my fifteenth birthday. Every year after my Cheyenne band reached its winter hunting grounds, my real mother celebrated my turning another year older. I shared this information with Catherine, who I think had always been baffled how old I was. She made me a treat called a cake and covered it with a brown, smooth mixture called chocolate. I think I have never tasted anything as good as chocolate, and I hoped I would have more in the future. I even got to blow out a candle on the cake, and Jeb and Mama Cat sang. It was a memorable birthday and a celebration I will never forget.

A few months later, I also reached something Catherine called puberty, and I began to look much older. Mama Cat decided I should let my hair grow longer. By summer's end, it was to the middle of my back and very shiny from so many berries in my shampoo. Now that almost nine months had passed since I arrived, I was also a little taller and shapelier, just like my Cheyenne friends I used to envy. Catherine described me as becoming statuesque. I had to look the word up in my dictionary. I was hoping I had more movement than a stone statue. She assured me it was a compliment, and it referred to my poise.

Among all of her amazing qualities, Catherine was also a wonderful seamstress, and she made me a beautiful wardrobe befitting my new maturity. It was fascinating to watch her push her feet up and down on pedals, pulling cloth under a needle and hearing the steady hum of what was called a sewing machine. It was almost like magic. First, a sleeve appeared and then a bodice, and before long an entire blouse. She sewed me several lovely skirts and blouses, and even a white summery cotton dress. Around the farm, though, I usually wore old, hand-me-down pants, flannel shirts, or short sleeved cotton shirts, and much of my time was spent helping Jeb in the barn as much as I could.

In the white man's world, Catherine and Jeb were considered to be well off. How I figured this out was when she had shoes made for me in a city called Boston. Mama Cat traced my feet on a piece of paper, and then she sent the paper by a process called mail to a store she used to like when she was younger. About a month later, a pair of black leather everyday shoes and a pair of brown leather boots were sent back to me in my size. They were almost as comfortable as my moccasins, which I still wore in secret in my bedroom, though they were almost too small.

Catherine said it was very important I always wear clothes and shoes like white people did. She didn't want anyone to ever question the story about her niece coming to live with her from Boston. Laughingly, she even named me Hannah Smith in case anyone ever asked, and we had fun making up an entire story about my history. She also said not to worry about my new fictitious name. I would always be known as Mokee to her and Jeb.

I didn't know how it was possible I could look like a white person rather than an Indian, but apparently it was so. Even Jeb said my skin color was light, looking like I had a slight tan from being in the sun every day. Although I doubted Mama Cat and Jeb's truthfulness on the subject, I tried to believe them. I didn't want to cause them anymore trouble.

My debut and first appearance in public came in early August. Catherine announced she and Jeb were taking me by horseback for an overnight stay in Junction City, which was about forty miles east near Fort Riley. It was a growing town with more than three hundred people, and she said she had some banking business to do there. Jeb came along for protection as we had to travel near Abilene, which Mama Cat called a rough-and-tumble cattle town with many undesirable elements. Junction City, I learned, was where the Smoky Hill River merged with the Republican River, and it was where they became known as the Kansas River from that point on.

I was very jittery about the trip, becoming a prairie chicken once more like when I was younger. Once Catherine made up her mind to do something, however, she became an unstoppable dynamo, which was a word describing a powerful machine I learned in one of my books. Mama Cat decided the only way we would have any peace was if I could pass for being white. She said it was important not to feel conspicuous in public. So, after reviewing my false biography as Hannah Smith and getting me up to snuff on Boston, according to her expression, we made our way to Junction City.

My English was impeccable by this time, and I guess the main thing I was apprehensive about was my appearance and whether I really looked white. I should have trusted Catherine's judgment, however. Everyone we met seemed to accept our story, especially once I spoke. I accompanied her and Jeb to the bank and waited in the lobby alone, conversing pleasantly with a clerk.

Next, we went to a general store where Catherine and Jeb needed to purchase some supplies. The owner, Mr. Hancock, gave me a licorice stick, which I have to admit was foul-tasting. Unable to help myself, I spit it out in a very unladylike manner on the dirt street. Jeb thought my reaction was hilarious, and he playfully tousled my hair. While we waited for Catherine, we had a good laugh together.

The three of us spent the night at a boarding house owned by a buxom woman named Mrs. Pritchard. Before going up to our adjoining rooms, we ate dinner there in a homey dining room. I read my first menu at dinner and thought it was mind-boggling a person could choose a meal from all the different possibilities listed. I had roasted duck and thought it was delicious. I was more fascinated, however, when Mama Cat extracted some paper, which she called money, from her purse and paid for our meals from a stranger.

Every time I believed I had learned all that was possible to learn, I would discover something I knew nothing about. Such was the case with money, and I made up my mind to have Catherine teach me about it very soon. It seemed to be very important to the white people and their way of life.

I shared a bed with Catherine that night and found boarding houses were very cramped and had just the bare necessities. Although Catherine was an elegant and beautiful woman, it was both endearing and comical to hear her snore. It was one more piece of evidence about the similarities in human nature between Indians and white people. As far as the accommodations were concerned, Catherine's house was much nicer, I decided, and much more comfortable.

Catherine seemed to enjoy the outing as much as Jeb, and it was relaxing for all of us to get away from the routine and hard work of the farm. It was wonderful not to worry any longer whether I could pass for being white. In the morning, we publicly ate a huge breakfast of pancakes at the boarding house, and then we made the long ride back to the farmhouse. I felt a new sense of freedom and confidence after the trip and realized Catherine was right about not hiding me any longer.

"Mokee, come and hold your finger here," Catherine said out loud, breaking my reverie of memories. With a smile on my face, I immediately went to the older woman's chair. Before helping her tie off a section of her knitting with a knot, I gave her a kiss on her soft cheek.

"I love you, Mama Cat," I said, looking straight into her pale eyes. I meant every word.

Chapter Nine

September and October passed by quickly as it was time for the harvest. That meant everyone's help was needed, even mine digging up potato tubers. Farming, I discovered, was as difficult as hunting for buffalo and then tanning the buffalo hides, or even disassembling tepees and transporting them by travois.

Jeb hired several temporary workers to help cut down the wheat and hay and transport it by wagon east to Junction City and Fort Riley, where it was in demand. Although tracks were being steadily laid for a new rail system, they hadn't been completed yet. A railroad would be a boon for this part of Kansas. By growing more wheat and selling it further away, Jeb's profits would greatly increase. We had heard the railroad was going to be extended through Junction City and Abilene, and possibly even as far as Salina in the next two years. The good news was Jeb and Catherine's farm was perfectly situated to make use of the rails in the future.

In addition to his main crop of wheat, Jeb's corn and potatoes had to be gathered from the fields, transported, marketed, and some stored for the coming winter in the root cellar. The fields had to be prepared for spring, removing this year's dead plants and tilling the soil. Additional hay had to be baled and stored for the coming winter in the barn, and these were just the farming chores.

Catherine and Jeb's house, as beautiful as it was, developed a leak in the roof, and it became necessary to repair it before another winter. Firewood needed to be gathered for all of the fireplaces before the cold weather. That meant cutting down trees and chopping the wood into manageable pieces and then stacking firewood and kindling near the house.

Jeb was constantly busy and overworked, and I knew he missed Benjamin's help, though he never complained. I could see the farm was really too big for just one person to manage, and it was good Jeb hired seasonal workers for the harvest. I overheard Catherine and Jeb discussing whether to hire a permanent farmhand, or whether it was possible Benjamin would return someday.

But Jeb's brother determinedly stayed away. It was as if my presence contaminated the house. Once in a while, Benjamin would appease his mother by coming to Sunday dinner, but that was it. No one knew who he was staying with, or in what town, or whether he was working or even robbing banks to get money. I could tell Catherine was worried, but every time I suggested I leave in order to restore peace, she wouldn't hear of it.

Because I could read and write so well, I began to keep up on current events. Although we received it a week late, Catherine bought a subscription to the weekly newspaper in Junction City. I began to read about improvements being made in Salina, from a stagecoach going through the town and heading for New Mexico to a hotel being built with lumber hauled up from Kansas City. There was a combination grist and sawmill under construction and a new ranch store. More people had settled in the area after the end of what was called the Civil War, and the town was becoming well-known as a trading post for westbound emigrants on the Smoky Hill Trail.

I also learned a little of the history of the area and read an eyewitness account of an Indian raid. It happened three years before in 1862, and the raid had intended to kill every settler in the Smoky Hill valley. Although a number of ranchers were killed to the west, the settlers, including the witness, had barricaded themselves in a stockade, and the Indians left without attacking them. That same year, a band of bushwhackers, which were white outlaws marauding the countryside after the Civil War, destroyed everything they couldn't steal from the businesses and residences in the area.

The newspaper, of course, contained the most news about Junction City, which was incorporated in 1859. The city was growing fast, and many of the new buildings were made of brick, rather than lumber. A new school district had recently been organized, which meant there were many residents with children. The newspaper also listed the marriages, births, and obituaries of its citizens. There was very little news about Abilene, which was the town between Salina and Junction City. The only article about Abilene mentioned its origins as a stagecoach town, and there was speculation a future railroad would benefit cattle ranchers in the area.

I was most interested in finding out what happened to the Cheyenne after the Sand Creek Massacre. Nearly every day, I worried about my parents and Tovee. Over the nine month period since the massacre and my arrival at Catherine and Jeb's, the newspaper frequently mentioned the growing threat of Indian raids. One article said the survivors of the massacre rejoined the other camps of the Cheyenne, which had moved north toward the Republican River, and a war pipe was smoked and passed from camp to camp among the Sioux, Cheyenne, and Arapaho. I knew smoking a war pipe was significant news. It meant war had been declared by more tribes than just the Cheyenne.

Another article had a timeline for Indian attacks earlier in 1865. It began with an attack on the Butterfield Overland Stagecoach station and fort at Julesburg in the Colorado territory, which was carried out last January. The successful attack was followed by more raids along the South Platte River both east and west of Julesburg, and the second raid on Julesburg took place in February. Twelve ranches were destroyed along with more than a hundred tons of hay, an important commodity during the winter months.

In the next attack, a wagon train with more than twenty wagons of supplies bound for the growing city of Denver was captured. The Indian war chiefs also ordered the destruction of all the buildings in Julesburg, and the raiding parties destroyed about seventy-five miles of telegraph line to the west, isolating the community of Denver. No stagecoach meant no mail could be delivered, and no telegraph meant there could be no contact with Forts Kearny, Sedgwick, Laramie, and Lyon.

The article went on to say the burning of the Julesburg station was the greatest financial loss the Butterfield Overland Stage Company had experienced. The most recent Julesburg raid also left eighteen dead, and the survivors fled to Fort Sedgwick a mile north of town. After the raid, the remaining Indians moved north into Nebraska on their way to the Black Hills.

Raids continued during the past spring along the North Platte River in Nebraska, and Cheyenne Dog Soldiers were spotted roving in bands in the Colorado and Nebraska territories, and also in Kansas. The raids even extended as far as the Wyoming territory, and troops stationed at the bridge across the North Platte River were attacked.

As I read the most recent news stories, I realized Tovee might still be nearby along the Smoky Hill River. It wouldn't surprise me if he showed up one day to take me with him, and I wasn't sure what I thought of that.

Christmas is a season for kindling the fire
for hospitality in the hall,
the genial flame of charity in the heart.

Washington Irving

Chapter Ten

Another celebration of Christmas came, and I realized it was one of my favorite times of the year with Jeb and Catherine. This year, we were more settled as a family, and there had been no more threats or suspicions about my Cheyenne heritage. Getting into the spirit of the season, we even decorated a little, unlike the past Christmas when my arrival had caused such worry.

I accompanied Jeb to the woods, where he cut down a small evergreen tree and dragged it through the freshly fallen snow back to the house. Then he managed, with some difficulty, to set it up in a corner of the living room. Its fresh pine fragrance filled every room. I had to chuckle to myself about it being in the house. I couldn't imagine my real parents ever bringing a tree inside our tepee, especially when there were so many outside of it.

After searching the attic, Mama Cat found several small boxes of decorations she'd had in Boston as a child. It was wonderful hearing her reminisce about how her family was from a country called Germany far across the Atlantic Ocean. It was a land of tall, snow-covered mountains called the Alps, which were similar to the steep mountains made of rock in the Colorado territory.

With a faraway look in her eyes, Catherine told how her family came over on a clipper ship when she was seven, and they entered the United States in the New York City area. Soon afterward, they made their way north to Boston, where her father's two older brothers had good paying jobs in textile manufacturing. Her own father also got a job there and eventually moved into management. His promotion was a result of his new fluency in the English language, and he had a natural ability with numbers.

"Never underestimate the power of good communication," Catherine interjected, as if she were teaching me the moral of the story. "My father only knew the German language when we arrived in this country, but he conscientiously studied English every night, not just learning enough to get by, but excelling at it and mastering his new language. If anything contributed to his success, it was his willingness to work hard to overcome any difficult circumstances in his life."

Mama Cat then gave me a stern look over the tops of her wire-rimmed glasses, and she said, "Never give up, Mokee. Work hard and become even more fluent in English. Don't just do enough to get by, but excel. Overcome the basic facts that you were born a Cheyenne in a war-ravaged nation. Rise above any discrimination you will face because of your heritage, and set goals and work diligently. If you are conscientious, you'll become a success at whatever you seek to do in life."

Then she added quietly, as if she were revealing the inner workings of her heart, "Never forget God in the equation. If you only remember one thing out of the Bible, remember you can do all things through Christ who strengthens you. If you let Him be the center of your life, you will overcome all adversity, no matter how difficult." My heart was moved by her eloquent admission of faith, and I silently vowed to be a Christian as my mentor, Catherine, was. The only problem with my decision was I didn't know how a person became a Christian.

As Catherine began removing the carefully wrapped decorations, some of them all the way from Germany, she retold how her father brought a handsome young worker home to dinner. His name was Joseph Harlan Preston, and she knew after one look he was the man she would marry. I noticed while Catherine was speaking, Jeb sat down quietly on the sofa to listen, and I realized his mother didn't speak very often about their heritage. I could see her words were very special to him.

"He was a son of a gun, but I loved him," Catherine admitted. "There was nothing in the world I wouldn't do for Joe. So, when he said he'd always wanted to be a farmer, I was all in. I was younger then and full of adventure. For several years, we saved up our money from his job at the textile mill. Together at night, we studied all the different places we could go. The United States was bursting at the seams with possibilities. Because the climate seemed unusually good for farming, we decided on the north central part of the Kansas territory. Off we went, two young dreamers going halfway across this new nation in search of our dream.

"By then, Jebediah had come along and then three years later, Benjamin, and three years after that, precious Margaret. Life was joyous with the laughter of children, and life was tough as we struggled to survive. I guess you can't have one circumstance without the other. Some years, the crops were plentiful, the weather was pleasantly warm, and the rains were adequate, and I would praise God for His blessings. Other years, the droughts came, the land became parched and useless with its sun-baked, crackled ground, and there were no crops to see us through another winter. I learned to praise God in those times as well. He is the God of all times, not just good times.

"Life went on. There were problems with the Indians. They justifiably felt the settlers were taking their land. Some of the settlers in the area were killed, and others left because of the danger. There were also problems with outlaws, whites who felt other people's things were theirs for the taking. During Civil War times, Kansas became known as 'Bleeding Kansas,' and those in favor of slavery fought those opposed to it.

"You see, Mokee. It doesn't matter what color a person's skin is. There are those who want peace, and those who want killing and war. There are some who don't want to work for an honest dollar, and others who want to oppress people. I would venture to say God's blessing is always on those who seek a path of peace and love in a violent world.

"Joe and I faced it all. We had our children, and we had each other. There was the night we had to hold off outlaws, bushwhackers they used to call them, by firing guns out of every window. We made them think there were more of us in here than there were. Another time, we hid in the root cellar when an enormous windstorm came in from the west. A huge funnel cloud, called a tornado, passed five miles south of our farm, and we were fortunate not only to survive, but to sustain very little damage. Our neighbors, the Suttons, lost everything they had, and they moved away. I knew I could endure anything as long as Joe was with me.

"Then bad things started happening. When Margaret was nine, she caught a nasty cold, at least that's what we thought it was. It got worse and worse, and it turned out to be whooping cough, and she died. A year later, when Jebediah was only sixteen, his father was working alone in the woods, and he was severely injured by the blade of a saw. Joe made a tourniquet on his leg, and he struggled to get back home. But he lost so much blood. . ."

Catherine's voice dropped off as she relived the gruesome memory, and her eyes became moist with tears. I glanced hesitantly at Jeb, who was spellbound on the sofa. I wondered if he had ever heard his mother speak so openly before and with so much emotion. My heart went out to him.

Regaining her composure, Catherine continued. "I managed to get Joe into the house and sent Jebediah by horse to get Doc Hutchinson over in Salina. He did everything he could for Joe, just as he had tried to save our poor little Margaret. But, Joe had lost too much blood, and he died.

"It's a heartbreaking thing to lose a daughter and a tragedy to lose a young husband, but imagine how difficult it was for two young boys to lose both within a year. Not only did they lose two people they loved, but they lost their innocence and their childhood."

All of a sudden, Catherine turned to Jeb, startling him and me both. I hadn't known she'd even seen him across the room, where he was listening intently to her words. "Your father's death, Jebediah, made you become a man at sixteen, and I'm so sorry you had your youth taken away and all of the responsibilities of the farm thrown onto your shoulders. I've tried to help you out, but life hasn't been fair to you." Jeb quickly got up and strode across the room to where his mother was seated in her favorite armchair. I was sitting cross-legged on the floor by her feet. He squatted down in front of her, taking her hands in his calloused, working man's hands.

"Mother, you did the best you could. None of us knew Margaret would die or that Father would also die so young. It is what it is," Jeb said softly with acceptance.

"I never should have come west. Life would have been so much better for you and your brother in Boston. It's been nothing but a struggle to survive here in Kansas," she cried. "And, now that Benjamin has gone. . ."

"Stop," Jeb suddenly said with firmness, interrupting her. "You've never wanted to face certain facts about Benjamin. He had troubles long before Margaret and Father died. Remember the time he killed the cat for fun, and the other time he whipped Tommy Carollton so badly the poor boy was in traction for a month. Benjamin has a mean streak a mile wide, and it's time you accepted it, Mother. I won't have you beating yourself up over something that's totally out of your control."

"You've had your life taken away from you, and that is my fault," she insisted. "You've had to become a farmer whether you wanted to or not. I've taken away your dreams and replaced them with your father's dreams. What are your dreams, Jebediah? You've never told me. It isn't right you should have to live out your father's plan for his life. And, you're so busy all the time. You've never even had time to find a life partner like I was to your father, supporting him and sharing a dream together."

I sensed Catherine's outburst was something she had been bottling up for a long time. It seemed to totally take Jeb by surprise. "Mother, I like farming. I wouldn't do it if I didn't want to. Please get it out of your mind you're forcing me to do it. And, I'm only twenty-one. You always tell me the Lord will bring the right person to me when the time is right. Either you believe it or you don't. So, I'm not worried about that either," he said confidently. All of a sudden, he looked at me with a penetrating stare.

I got a little flustered as his blue eyes gazed into mine so intently. *They were a beautiful shade of blue like sparkling mountain water*, I thought. For a moment, they drew me into their depths. It was as though Jeb was letting me dip my feet in the waters to see if I might be the right person for him. After all, I had unknowingly been dropped into his household in what appeared to be a coincidence, although Catherine had always told me there were no coincidences, only acts of God.

I didn't know what I thought of the question Jeb's eyes appeared to be asking. I was very fond of Jeb and knew I loved him in some ways. *I was meant to be with Tovee, though, wasn't I? This was only a detour with Jeb and Catherine, wasn't it?* I felt totally confused.

As if letting me off the hook for now, Jeb abruptly turned to Catherine and said, "You know, Mother, we have a very lonely-looking Christmas tree. Don't you think it's about time we decorated it?" As if all of us were grateful for an interruption in our private thoughts, we began to eagerly sort through the boxes of decorations.

There were a few intricate, hand blown glass balls on the top of the first box, and we carefully tied them onto the tree. Next, there was a lovely, hand painted nativity scene. It was carved out of the wood of an olive tree. Jeb carefully set up the scene on a side table in the living room, all the while telling me in his own words the story of Christ's birth, which Christians celebrate every year in December.

After that, there were some funny little figurines of someone named Father Christmas or St. Nicholas. Catherine explained American children thought of the jolly, bearded fellow as Santa Claus, a mythical figure who rode on a sleigh led by reindeer, and he magically brought gifts down people's chimneys. She said his story was based on an actual saint who lived in the country of Turkey across the ocean, and the real Saint Nicholas, who was known for his generosity, lived more than a thousand years ago. When someone talks about having the Christmas spirit, she added, it means we are generous with each other as God was generous to us by giving us His son.

The next box had some garlands of dried berries strung together on a thick string. Because Jeb was so tall, he got the honor of draping the tree with the garlands. Catherine went out of the room for a minute and returned with a bowl full of apples. She said a tradition in Germany was to hang apples on a Christmas tree to remind us of the Garden of Eden and how, because we sinned, God sent his only Son to save us from our sins.

After hanging the apples with special metal hooks, the finishing touch was to fasten metal candle holders with some narrow tallow candles on a few of the sturdier branches. Jeb used what was called a match to light the candles, and then we all stepped back to enjoy our handiwork. It was indeed beautiful and festive, and I realized I had perhaps changed my mind about the foolishness of having a tree in the house.

Catherine suggested we join hands and sing in front of the tree, and she began singing a carol she had known as a child. It was called *Stille Nacht*, or *Silent Night*. The melody was haunting and lovely as its words told about the nativity, and Mama Cat's hand as well as Jeb's felt warm in mine. Her soft soprano voice blended with Jeb's smooth tenor voice in perfect harmony. *Harmony*, I thought, briefly shutting my eyes and breathing in the love in the room. *God's gift to all humanity was the perfect harmony of His creation loving one another and finding the path of forgiveness through His son.*

On the next day which was Christmas, we had a wonderful feast of a wild turkey Jeb had shot in the woods, squash, dressing, mashed potatoes, gravy, roasted chestnuts, rolls, and pumpkin pie. Because of all the preparations, we didn't eat until late afternoon. In the early evening, we all settled in the living room by the fireplace to share our presents. Catherine seemed a little sad Benjamin hadn't made any effort to see his family at Christmas, and I once again felt guilty. Their estrangement seemed to be my fault. But that was all forgotten as we opened our gifts.

This year, I was prepared for giving gifts, unlike the previous year. I had asked Catherine weeks ahead if I might be able to do some extra chores to earn paper money to buy presents. Happily, she let me do some cleaning she didn't like doing herself. The following week, she took me to the new general store in town and told me to select any items I wanted for her and Jeb. She also was shopping that day and said she would pay for my items at the end along with hers.

It was very brave of her to give me what I now know is called a blank check. I really had no concept of money at the time or what things cost. I only knew what looked pretty to me. After much indecision, I found an exquisite broach with amber gemstones, which I thought would look lovely on the neckline of Catherine's blouses. For Jeb, a marble dish for shaving cream, a brush, and razor caught my eye. I asked the owner of the store if he could wrap the gifts in something, and he put them in festive cloth sacks. I was a little nervous whether I had spent too much money on the gifts and even whether they would like them, but Mama Cat merely smiled and said it was fine.

Finally, we opened our gifts. Catherine had made me a stunning dress of royal blue wool, telling me she thought the contrast would be lovely with my black hair. Jeb must have been in cahoots with her, because he got me a sparkling gold necklace with inch-long pendants, looking like miniature feathers. The necklace was perfect on the bodice of the dress, almost like it belonged there. I was in awe at both of the gifts, never seeing anything so beautiful, and I threw myself into Jeb and Catherine's arms and kissed them both on their cheeks.

Suddenly, the gifts I had gotten them didn't seem very special or large enough, but Catherine and Jeb both seemed genuinely happy and excited I had made the effort to shop by myself. They had given each other books, Catherine receiving a cookbook she had asked for about using different grains in baking, and Jeb getting a book on crop rotation.

All at once, Mama Cat stood up and gave a huge yawn. "It's been a wonderful Christmas, you two, but I'm really tired tonight after cooking all day. I'm going to bed early. And no, I haven't forgotten it's your birthday, Mokee. You're sixteen now, aren't you?" I nodded with a smile. "That's quite a young lady. I haven't finished your present yet, but don't you worry. You'll get it in a few days." With a kiss on each of our cheeks, she quietly left the room.

Jeb and I rarely sat alone on the sofa in the living room, although we frequently worked together in the fields or in the barn by ourselves. For a brief moment, I was tongue-tied, especially remembering his enigmatic look the previous day. Maybe I had misinterpreted his expression, I decided, or maybe I had even imagined it. Jeb seemed completely comfortable and relaxed, asking me what I liked best about the day and what I thought of the feast. Before long, we were laughing and enjoying ourselves as always. I couldn't remember a time I didn't like being with Jeb. He was very easygoing and genuine.

"Even though my mother doesn't have your birthday gift ready, I do. I really want to give you my present tonight," Jeb said happily, extracting a rectangular present from behind one of the gold silk pillows on the sofa. The package had a festive red bow on it and bright wrapping paper.

"Jeb, you and Catherine are so generous to me. I can never repay your kindness," I protested feebly with a sigh.

"Now, let's not hear any more of that. You repay us every day by smiling and just being you," he said with a sweet smile. He nudged the gift toward me. "Go ahead, open it and quit complaining."

That was all the coaxing I needed. I really did love presents, and eagerly I tore the wrapping paper off. The gift itself confused me. It was a book with beautiful flowers on the cloth cover but inside, it was filled with blank pages. I gave Jeb a puzzled look as if there had been a mistake at the publishing company.

"And, here's the rest of your gift." Jeb handed me a smaller box to unwrap.

The new box contained an inkwell, a bottle of black ink, and a fountain pen. I still wasn't quite sure what to make of the gift, and I gave Jeb an inquisitive look.

Jeb could tell my confusion, and he began to explain. "You are an amazing person, Mokee. You've meticulously learned the English language, your grammar is better than most people, and your handwriting is exquisite. I can't imagine a better person than you to keep a journal of your life's experiences. Here you are, in the middle of one of the most violent times our country has faced. You have one foot in the Cheyenne camp and the other foot in the white man's town. One day, I would think your reflections and observations would be both interesting and informative for those of us who can't imagine how your life is torn between two worlds. I would think it might be more than just a story though. In a small way, maybe you'll be able to bridge the gap of understanding between the two cultures and help promote the cause of peace. What do you think? Will you write your thoughts about your life in your journal?"

I was overwhelmed by Jeb's praise of my abilities and gave a huge sigh, feeling the weight of responsibility on my shoulders. Humbled he thought I was up to such a monumental task, I nodded my acceptance of his challenge. As I reached up to give Jeb a kiss of thank you on the cheek, I got tangled in the mess I made of the wrapping paper. All at once, my kiss accidentally slid downward to his mouth. Suddenly, Jeb's lips turned an inch sideways and unexpectedly settled on mine, kissing me warmly, but hesitantly. He seemed unsure whether I welcomed his affection or not.

I felt it was a moment of decision, and Jeb seemed to be leaving it entirely up to me. Briefly, I remembered Tovee's kiss when we were hiding in the bin, but then my mind pushed that unwanted thought aside. This was Jeb, sweet Jeb, and my hand had a will of its own. All of a sudden, it reached up behind Jeb's neck into his soft, brown hair and tugged him closer. His lips suddenly seized mine in passion and caring, unlike anything I ever thought a kiss could be. Jeb's kisses reflected Jeb the man, honest, genuine, sincere, and vulnerable.

As I welcomed his kisses and eagerly kissed him back, I realized I had fallen in love with this kind and caring man over the past year. He had been so compassionate to let a frightened young Indian girl share his home. In a moment of pure awareness, I knew I wanted to continue to be with Jeb, maybe even for a lifetime if he wanted that too.

A nagging question, however, appeared in the recesses of my mind. It was almost like a dangerous undercurrent in a swiftly flowing stream. *How did my love for Jeb affect my future with my Cheyenne tribe, my true parents, and the life I always thought I would have with Tovee?* In confusion and chagrin, I carefully pulled back from Jeb's sweet kisses. I didn't want him to notice my tentativeness.

As he gently stroked my back, Jeb nestled me to his chest with contentment. I breathed in deeply, inhaling the feelings of love, which were overwhelming me. He spoke softly into my ear. "I know you're young and only sixteen, Mokee, and I don't mean to frighten you with my sudden affection or rush you into anything you're not ready for. You totally surprised me tonight as much as I think I surprised you.

"I only want you to think about us, Mokee. There's plenty of time for you to grow up a little more before you decide. Do you think there's a way we could be together, and do you think you could be happy being with me? Or, is your goal to return to your people? I've never really known what it is you want to do, and I guess I've been afraid to ask you. I've always worried you'd interpret a question about your future to mean I wanted you to go.

"The truth is I never want you to go. I want you to stay more than anything. I don't need you to tell me your feelings tonight, but someday when you're ready, let me know if you think you could love me like I already know I love you." Jeb's voice became silent as he wasn't used to baring his heart.

I didn't know what to do or say. Instead, I hugged Jeb as tightly as I could. Although I was confused, I determinedly remained in the circle of his arms. I knew he needed to be given hope for the future, but I wasn't able to do it until I had time to sort through the answers to my questions. With certainty in my heart, I knew I loved Jeb, but if I permanently lived as a white woman, did that mean I couldn't love my Cheyenne people? And where did Tovee fit into my life, if anywhere? Would he come back for me? Until I dealt with these issues, I would have to remain silent about my intentions. Maybe a journal would be good. I could write about my muddled feelings and my quest to find a path of peace and love in my world of violence.

If instead of a gem, or even a flower,
we should cast the gift of a loving thought
into the heart of a friend,
that would be giving as the angels give.

George MacDonald

Chapter Eleven

There was no time to think of my uncertainty over Jeb's affection. Unexpectedly, Catherine got sick in the middle of the January snows. Doc Hutchinson's diagnosis was the grippe, but after her flu-like symptoms subsided, Mama Cat was wracked with a deep, hacking cough. Some days, she was doubled over on her bed in pain.

I kept a vigil in her bedroom, trying to make her comfortable with extra pillows, making her tea filled with honey, which I found in the root cellar, spoon feeding her broth from my homemade soups, and reading to her from the Bible, the only book she wanted to hear. Most of the time, Catherine slept through my reading, but I kept going and covered most of the New Testament, and then I began again. Although I had frequently read portions of the Bible on my own, I began to see more fully how it was relevant to my life. As I read to Catherine, I found I was reading to myself as well.

Jeb frequently visited his mother, oftentimes taking an entire shift with her so I could rest. While he talked to her, he usually kept his hand possessively on my shoulder, and I found I was growing more at ease with his spontaneous affection. It made me feel special when he touched me like that in front of his mother, and Catherine seemed pleased he had taken her broad hint to look at me as a possible life partner. Sometimes as I was relaxing on my bed, I could hear the loud drone of their voices bickering back and forth through the wall of my bedroom. It seemed Jeb and his mother discussed matters of importance more frequently.

At least three weeks passed with the same routine. All at once, Catherine's condition began to worsen, and she was coughing more, sometimes even coughing up blood. In spite of her illness, I discovered she had something important on her mind. After living with Mama Cat and Jeb for a year, I learned she was the most determined woman I'd ever met. If she had a plan, she would do everything in her power to put it into action. As I was reading to her one day, she suddenly confronted me.

"So, Mokee, what do you think about what you're reading?" she suddenly asked in her unequivocal way. Her words interrupted my recitation of the Beatitudes.

"I think it's beautiful," I said with a smile, hoping my response pleased her. It didn't.

"Beautiful isn't enough, Mokee. When are you going to quit sitting on the fence?" Mama Cat asked in an irascible voice. If I had been coughing for nearly a month, I would have been irritable too.

"Sitting on the fence?" I asked in confusion, not knowing what she meant. In my heart, I loved the Great Spirit, God, and now I loved His son Jesus too.

"You remember the story of the brides being dressed in readiness with their lanterns lit. Remember those who thought they had a lot of time. I'm dying, Mokee," she suddenly announced, and my heart plummeted to my stomach. My life had already seen so much death. *Why Catherine?* My intuition had told me she was dying, but I had refused to listen to my thoughts. "But, I'm not afraid to die. I know my savior, Jesus Christ. As soon as I shut my eyes here, I'll be with Him in Heaven. My lantern's lit, Mokee, and I'm dressed and ready."

She stared straight into my eyes with burning conviction. "What about you, Mokee? Your chances of dying are as good as mine, especially if you return to the Cheyenne and become involved in the war again. Are you ready to light your lantern and commit what's left of your life to God's son? All you have to do to make that happen is to confess your faith, right now, on your knees beside my bed, and Jesus will make his home in your heart with the Holy Spirit.

"It's as simple as that. He'll wash away your sins as white as the snow outside my window. One day, when your time is up on this earth, you will be with Jesus in Heaven too." She paused emotionally. "I-I really need to know you will be with me someday in Heaven, Mokee," Catherine said with tears in her eyes. "I love you, and I want to go to my death knowing I'll see you again."

As I gazed into the loving face of the beautiful woman I loved like a mother, I knew I would do anything to ease her passing. I remembered all she had taught me, from English and reading and writing to literature and art and faith. Then I remembered a quote she had shared with me by Leonardo da Vinci, who painted the *Mona Lisa* as well as the *Last Supper*. He said, "I have been impressed with the urgency of doing. Knowing is not enough; we must apply. Being willing is not enough; we must do."

For months now, I had been wondering how one became a Christian. I believed in Jesus and his death for my sins, but I never knew if there was a formal step I needed to take to confirm my faith. There were very few churches in our rural area, or I probably would have been baptized and confirmed as Catherine was as a child. Apparently, confessing my faith to Catherine would also accomplish what I wished for in my heart. I realized I wanted to take this step, not just for Catherine, but for me.

With hope and joy in my heart, I slid to my knees. In spite of her devastating illness, Catherine smiled like a glowing angel, and I confessed my faith, holding her frail, shaking hands. I had never seen her so happy nor had I ever felt as joyous. Whatever uncertainty remained in my life, I was positive I would see Catherine again in God's kingdom.

Because it was another time in my life for shedding tears, I would always remember the cold and dreary month of February in 1866. In a great day of sadness, Catherine died. Jeb and I were on either side of her, holding her hands. In life, she was beautiful, intelligent, elegant, and determined. In death, she was serene and confident.

As I journeyed on my confusing path of life, I never expected to meet another woman of Catherine's depth of spirit. I held Jeb while he wept, and I was moved by the deep love he had for his mother. We both knew, however, that Catherine would not have wanted us to grieve for long. Instead, she would have liked us to celebrate her arrival in Heaven. With certainty, we knew she was with the Lord, whom she had loved all of her life.

The January snows had melted, so we buried Catherine under a lofty oak tree in a distant field. Somehow, Jeb secured the services of a Lutheran pastor, who was temporarily the chaplain at Fort Riley near Junction City. Because the Lutheran faith was the faith of Catherine's birth, the pastor performed the graveside services. The biggest surprise of the day was the appearance of Benjamin at the funeral. He hadn't seen his mother in four months and never visited her when she was sick, yet he wept like a baby for her death.

A few members of the farming community, the general store owner and his wife, Doc Hutchinson, the chaplain, and Benjamin came back to the house for what was called a wake. Jeb and I had prepared food the day before, and I acted as the hostess for the reception, a first for me. As if I were intruding on his life again, Benjamin glared at me the entire time. Jeb, however, proudly kept me by his side and introduced me to the visitors as his mother's niece, who had been living with them for the past year. Once again, he curved his arm protectively around my shoulders, and I was glad for his support in front of the strangers.

When I noticed the chaplain wasn't involved in conversation, I excused myself from Jeb and approached the minister. I told him how I had become a Christian recently. He was genuinely happy for me and said he would like to give me a special blessing. We privately went to the kitchen, and he blessed some water. Then with a cupped hand, he sprinkled it over my forehead and baptized me over the sink. From within his garment, he withdrew a small bottle of chrism oil, and he made the sign of the cross with it on my forehead. From another pocket, he extracted a wooden box, and he took out an unleavened wafer and gave me communion for the first time. I was very moved and knew Catherine was smiling down from Heaven knowing my lantern was fully lit.

Another unforeseen thing happened in February. After so long an absence, Jeb's brother kept showing up at the house. When Benjamin continued walking in day after day as if he still lived at the farmhouse, Jeb was furious. He and Benjamin vanished behind closed doors and went at it. I never heard such yelling.

Because I knew Benjamin's sudden return did not bode well for my staying, I tried to eavesdrop. The most I could hear was a dispute over a document called a will. It seemed Benjamin claimed half-ownership of the farm, and he was using his partial ownership as justification for coming in and going out when he pleased. It also sounded as though Benjamin wanted to sell his half of the farm immediately as he was short of cash. *What's Jeb going to do?*

A week after Benjamin's reappearance, a very stately man in a black suit and tie arrived at the farmhouse, and a meeting was called in the living room. Jeb explained to me the man was an attorney, or lawyer, and there would be a reading of his mother's will to the recipients of her belongings. The recipients were called beneficiaries. To my surprise, I was included in the meeting along with Jeb and Benjamin, and the attorney read my unexpected inheritance first.

Along with her personal Bible and jewelry, Catherine had bequeathed many of her literature and philosophy books to me. Her engagement and wedding rings, however, went to Jeb for his future wife. There was also a savings account of $10,000 in a Junction City bank, which I was told I could use at my discretion. I had no idea what that amount of money meant.

The attorney started to hand me the deposit book for the account and the papers verifying the transfer of the account to my name. Jeb came forward, however, and said if it was okay with me, he would keep the important papers and deposit book in his files. I nodded, and the attorney handed them over to Jeb for safekeeping. Benjamin, of course, voiced his displeasure at my receiving anything at all. I was sure he was going to blurt out I was an Indian, which in Benjamin's eyes, proved I was unworthy of any inheritance.

Benjamin settled down quickly, though, as he thought he would be mentioned next. He looked genuinely excited at his prospects of future wealth, and my mind compared him to a stray dog licking its chops for a bone. The attorney, however, began listing Jeb's assets. He said Jeb inherited the entire farm, the house and barn and their contents, and the full one thousand acres of land, most of which had not yet been farmed except for the fields surrounding the house. Jeb also received $300,000 in a savings account in the Junction City bank, as well as 25,000 shares of common stock of the New York, Providence and Boston Railroad and 15,000 shares of common stock of the Union Pacific Railroad. From the few things I had learned in books about money and stock, I knew Jeb was a very wealthy man compared to most white men, and Catherine must have had great wealth growing up in Boston.

Benjamin went wild with anger at being excluded and jumped to his feet. In an impressive display of expletives, he said he was suing his brother, and he angrily marched to the front door.

"Young man, don't you want to hear what you've inherited?" the lawyer said with dignity. "For your information, your mother changed her will two months ago, and I wrote it myself and got the necessary witnesses. I guarantee it is 100 percent valid, and you would lose in a court of law."

His air supply suddenly deflated, and Benjamin self-consciously strode back into the room. "So, spill the beans, *sir*," he said sarcastically, slouching down in his mother's armchair. "What did I get from dear old mom?"

"You, young man, have received a $20,000 trust fund. . ."

"Now you're talking," Benjamin interrupted, pleased to get something. I could tell he was not pleased my inheritance was almost as large. "And?" he asked, expecting more.

". . . to be administered by your brother, Jebediah, until you reach the age of twenty-five," the lawyer continued. "The conditions of receiving your trust fund are that you are sober and have not been in jail or ever convicted of a felony."

"Twenty-five years old?" Benjamin protested furiously, turning an odd shade of purple. "I'm only eighteen, and I want my money now."

"You also are allowed to stay rent-free here at the farm. The conditions are that you do half of the work, and you behave in a manner Jebediah deems appropriate. If you violate the conditions, Jebediah may throw you out at any time."

As he stomped to the door, Benjamin was seething with hatred. He kept his thoughts to himself as he slammed out, and I hoped it was the last we would see of him for a long time. That was not to be our good fortune, however.

Heaven knows we need never be ashamed of our tears,
for they are rain upon the blinding dust of earth,
overlying our hard hearts.

Charles Dickens

Chapter Twelve

It was the first week in March, and there was a heavy knock on the front door around lunchtime. Before going back out to one of the fields for some fence repairs, Jeb was reading in the living room. I was preparing a quick lunch for the two of us, and then I was planning on surprising Jeb by accompanying him to the field and helping with the fence.

"I'll get it," he said quickly, knowing I was probably elbow deep in mess. I wasn't the neatest of cooks in a kitchen.

"Well, this is a surprise," Jeb's low, masculine voice protested. I walked to the hall and curiously peeked out of the kitchen. To my chagrin, it was Benjamin, and he had a stuffed suitcase in hand. *He's staying,* I thought with shock.

"Well, isn't this a cozy housekeeping arrangement?" he said mockingly, winking at me and making my skin crawl. I felt the hair stand up on my arms, and my intuition grabbed my attention. *Benjamin was plotting something malevolent,* it warned. "I've decided to take Mother up on her offer of a room. My current accommodations, shall we say, fell through."

"Before you bring that suitcase through the door, I trust you remember the stipulations. You're to do half the work on the farm, and you are to be courteous to both myself and Mokee," Jeb said firmly.

It sounded as though Jeb was acquiescing with Benjamin's demands and inviting him to live with us. *For the first time ever, I felt angry at Jeb.* I wondered why he didn't ask for my opinion or talk it over with me. I had plenty to say on the subject of his nasty brother moving in.

"I'm going to be nice to you and the little redskin," he said in a smart-alecky way. His superficial smile didn't reach his cold eyes. "Heck, she's the smartest little redskin I ever heard of, working her way into a white family and even getting an inheritance."

"That's enough," Jeb growled angrily. "You're never to call Mokee a redskin again, or the deal's off. Mother convinced everyone Mokee was her niece from Boston, and you will not make her out to be a liar in her death."

"Hey, bro'," Benjamin said in a silken voice. "I have plans to be very, very nice to. . . Mokee." It was the first time he had ever called me by name, and he made it sound as if it were dirty. Barging into the foyer past Jeb, Benjamin flashed me a lascivious smile. It stretched the entire length of the hall to the kitchen, and I knew trouble was brewing. I quickly looked to Jeb's face for reassurance he thought the same thing, but it was blank of emotion. I was stunned Jeb had accepted his brother's unsettling return.

It was then I remembered reading a proverb with Catherine about blood being thicker than water. Although Jeb thought he loved me, I realized his allegiance would always be to his brother in an unbreakable bond of blood.

March became a tormenting and exceedingly drawn-out month for me. For the first time since I had moved in with Jeb and Catherine, I was unhappy and uncomfortable. Not only was I still grieving the loss of Catherine, but there was no time to explore the new feelings I had for Jeb. His brother was persistently underfoot, never letting us alone for even a second. The strained atmosphere of the house could have been sliced with a knife. Benjamin encroached on every pocket of quiet and peace with his ribald humor and vile language. Worse yet, no matter where I was, he seemed determined to catch me alone.

Whether it was chopping vegetables at the kitchen counter or carrying fresh laundry up to the bedrooms, Benjamin made it a point to corner me and to be as physically close as possible. When he stumbled toward me or rubbed up against me in sensual ways, he acted nonchalant about it and pretended it was an accident. It became obvious to me, however, he was either a clumsy oaf or a vengeful, disinherited younger brother. He was hell-bent on making Jeb pay by torturing the object of Jeb's affections, me. Without Jeb even being aware of his brother's diabolical plan, Benjamin was making my life hell.

How I wished Catherine had been there to confide in. She wouldn't have put up with Benjamin's suggestive behavior for a minute. But she wasn't there. She had given me one thing, though, and that was the armor of God to protect me and help me find my way. I constantly prayed for help, not knowing which way to turn or how to solve the problem myself. I didn't want to alienate Jeb, because, of course, he wanted to think the best of his wayward brother's intentions.

Jeb, I thought sadly. Ever since Benjamin had come home to roost, Jeb had retreated into a shell. He offered up the excuse he was busy consolidating the affairs of his mother's estate, but he was distant as if on purpose. It seemed like Jeb was trying to convince his brother there wasn't anything romantic between him and me. He didn't hold my hand anymore or casually rest an affectionate arm around my shoulders. I had even gotten used to a kiss now and then while I was cooking, but our kisses had also vanished.

Because I was an Indian, educated maybe, but still an Indian, I felt for the first time Jeb didn't think I was good enough to be with him. Unintentionally and perhaps irrationally, my feelings were deeply hurt. At Christmas, Jeb had made it clear he had wanted me to be a part of his future, even sealing it with romantic kisses. Yet his brother's presence seemed to be making him have second thoughts.

Perhaps I was misinterpreting Jeb's actions. I hoped I was. Admittedly, I was insecure about my new life. I really didn't fit in with either the Cheyenne or the white people. Perhaps Jeb was still grieving for Catherine in private and unintentionally turning his back on me. No matter how I tried to justify his behavior, a nagging feeling persisted inside. *I was no longer wanted in this household.*

In the middle of April, I was uncomfortably alone in the house with Benjamin. Jeb had gone to a county office on business, and I was expecting him back anytime for lunch. I busied myself in the kitchen, making his favorite soup out of a ham hock, split peas, and carrots.

All of a sudden, I felt two strong, masculine hands grab my waist and spin me around. Thinking it was Jeb, I turned around willingly only to have Benjamin's nasty, unyielding lips smother mine with defiant, heated kisses. I could smell the stench of liquor on his breath, and I tried to shove him away with all my might. I was still pretty small, however, and couldn't budge his beefy body. When he began to grope me, I panicked. In a burst of strength, I struck him with my knee as hard as I could, aiming for the place it would hurt the most. He yelped in pain and jumped back momentarily, giving me a scurrilous look of contempt and regrouping to attack me.

Before I could reach around and grab the knife off the counter for protection, Benjamin charged forward and harshly seized me, yanking my arm into an iron vise and attacking me with even more debased kisses. All at once, the kitchen door creaked open. Benjamin used the warning to his advantage, gentling his kisses to give the impression I was a happy participant. I knew it would appear I wasn't fighting him off at all, but enjoying our stolen moment of passion.

"What the hell's going on?" Jeb's low voice bellowed loudly. I heard the door slam behind him.

"Jeb, it's not. . ." I started to say it's not how it looks, but Benjamin twisted my arm so painfully I couldn't speak.

"Whoa, Jebediah," Benjamin purred in a syrupy sweet voice. "I'm sorry you had to find out this way, but Mokee and I have had this thing going on for about a month now. We just can't get enough of each other."

"You liar," I hissed at Benjamin, struggling to break away from his punishing grip. "Let me go."

"Is it true, Mokee?" Jeb had the audacity to ask in a spiteful, unforgiving way. His words hung like a black cloud over the kitchen. When I heard the accusation in his voice, I looked at him in shock and disbelief. *Jeb had believed the lying words of his scoundrel of a brother over my kind actions,* I thought. Here I had lived above reproach with him and his mother for a year and a half. I had eaten at their table, learned English, celebrated Christmas and given them gifts, become a Christian, kissed him, and even stupidly fallen in love with him. In spite of all that, Jeb had the nerve to think I was cheating on him with his nasty, wicked, and inebriated brother. The fact I was an Indian and not to be believed over someone with white skin, especially his brother, was the only explanation I could think of for Jeb turning on me.

My eyes blackened with resentment. With a forceful shove, I escaped Benjamin's arms. "I'm going to my room now," I said with as much dignity as I possessed, marching out into the hall and up the steps. I was not only angry with Benjamin for assaulting me, but at Jeb for believing I was a deceitful person, someone who had intentionally betrayed his love and kindness.

I overheard Benjamin maliciously relating even more lies about how good I was in bed, and I slammed my door, nearly cracking the wall. Throwing myself on my bed, I sobbed for hours. I was shocked how my honor had been dragged through the mud by Benjamin and how Jeb, sweet Jeb, had believed his brother over me. My bedspread became soaked with tears as I cried so much.

When I finally became calm, I realized I was not the first person to have lies told about me, and I would not be the last. With my remaining strength, I prayed to my Savior. He surely knew what it was like to have lies told about Him. Because of those lies, he had been nailed to a cross. I hoped He might help me find resolution for my situation and help me understand what I needed to do to set things right.

The next week passed by in an awkward silence. I would catch Jeb's accusatory eyes staring at my back, and his face continued to have an expression of betrayal. Without ever giving me the opportunity to speak the truth, he still believed his brother's lies. Like the day I had arrived, we were back to the beginning, and it felt as if Jeb was holding a shotgun to me. It was as though a redskin, an Indian, couldn't be trusted to tell the truth. His love and trust had vanished with a few lying words from his wicked brother.

Another thing convinced me of Jeb's growing resentment. Benjamin was allowed to stay on in the house, in spite of mistreating me. *What happened to all of the conditions he was supposed to meet?* Behind Jeb's back, his brother continuously smirked with satisfaction, his dirty deed having the results he sought. Every night, I continued crying myself to sleep.

After a week of seclusion and loneliness, I was awake on my bed, wondering what to do. Should I grovel to Jeb and beg him for forgiveness, even though I had done nothing wrong? It was hot in my bedroom as spring had come early. I opened my window to get some fresh air and drifted off in a restless sleep.

In the middle of the night, I woke with a start. A firm, masculine hand was clasped tightly over my mouth to prevent me from screaming, and my eyes flung open in terror, expecting to see Benjamin's evil face close to mine. With disbelief, I heard a voice whisper in Cheyenne, "Sh! Sh! Don't scream, Mokee. It's only me, Tovee."

When I realized Tovee was still alive, tears filled my eyes. He had not forgotten me, unlike Jeb, the man I lived with. With a heart of gladness for his survival, I pulled Tovee into my arms, smelling his familiar outdoor scent. I didn't recognize the feel of his newly muscled chest and powerful arms, however, and I pulled back to gape at him.

Tovee had changed in many ways, not all good. He was no longer a boy, but a man, and he was a good six inches taller and much stronger, but still lean. He was dressed differently than before, wearing what looked like a uniform with a sash of geometric drawings. What startled me most was his cynical expression. His once handsome face had become hardened, and his eyes were no longer innocent or fun-loving, but serious and even deadly. In one look, I knew he was not only a warrior, but a warrior who had killed frequently and faced death. There was a restless edge to him and an air of danger.

"Are you ready to come with me?" he asked expectantly, his long-fingered hand, which I now knew had killed and scalped white men, stroking my face out of habit. A mix of emotions filled my heart. I pictured Catherine and how disappointed she would have been to see me return to a world of violence and war, especially when I had a choice.

Then I thought of Jeb and how I loved him, but he had taken away his love and hadn't believed in me. Instead, Jeb believed his brother's malicious lies. He hadn't thought I was worth fighting for, and the pain of his betrayal and stubborn pride knifed my heart. Fearing Benjamin was going to attack me again, I couldn't think of any reason to stay. I wasn't wanted here.

"If I come with you, Tovee, I'm not sure things are the same as they were before," I cautioned, trying to protect my broken heart. He nodded, knowing he had also grown up in the year and a half since we had seen each other. "I have to ask you to promise me something. Jeb and Catherine were always good to me, and I never want their farm destroyed or them personally attacked or killed (I had decided it was best not to reveal Catherine had died). Do you have the authority to guarantee their safety and that of their farm? Will you make an unbreakable vow to me?" I knew his answer would reveal what his new role was with the Cheyenne. If he was only a lowly warrior without authority, he could not make the promise I sought.

"I will make that guarantee," he said importantly, without flinching. "I will tell the others about this one special circumstance."

With a heavy heart, I realized how deep his involvement was in seeking revenge against the white man. Reluctantly, I said I would go with him. Inside, I was reeling and didn't want to leave, but Jeb had left me no choice. I knew I was trading one difficult situation for another, and it could prove to be the biggest mistake of my life.

With sadness, I looked at my closet full of beautiful clothes Catherine had made and my dresser top filled with stacked books. The Bible was on top, and I had grown accustomed to reading it every day. On the end table by my small bed was the journal Jeb had given me as a birthday present. Next to it sat my inkwell and carefully washed pen.

Regretfully, I tucked the Bible and my journal into a drawer in my nightstand. My eyes opened wide as I saw the braided elk skin necklace in the drawer, and I quickly tied it around my neck before Tovee noticed I hadn't been wearing it. With a sigh, I looked around wistfully one last time. I was leaving my heart here, but Jeb hadn't wanted it and had thrown it away.

Quickly, I went into my closet. With the door ajar, I changed into a pair of pants and a flannel shirt. Because I was no longer the little girl that had arrived at Jeb and Catherine's house, my previous buckskin clothing no longer fit. Wearily, I pushed the closet door open and reentered the bedroom. Not fitting into my moccasins either, I sat on the bed and put on my outdoor boots to climb out the window.

"Is it okay I'll be dressed as a white woman?" I asked quietly, knowing his new comrades might not understand.

"I explained it all before I came to retrieve you," he said impatiently, appearing anxious to get back to his camp.

"Let's go," I said, not wanting to draw out my departure any longer. With effort, Tovee smiled briefly, glad I was coming, but I didn't smile back as my heart was broken. I knew what was ahead for me, and it was a world of violence and war. Sadly, I knew I would be joining Tovee's camp of Hotamétaneo'o, the Cheyenne Dog Soldiers.

In general, pride is at the bottom of all great mistakes.

John Ruskin

Chapter Thirteen

Jeb and Mokee had never had a fight before. After he caught her kissing Benjamin, he had never seen her as angry as when she stalked from the kitchen. *What right did she have to be mad?* Couldn't she understand his shock when he walked in and found her kissing Benjamin? They had been passionately wrapped in each other's arms like there was no tomorrow. If she had chosen his brother over him, so be it. He'd have to accept it, that was all, but didn't he deserve an explanation after letting her stay at his house for nearly a year and a half? After all, he had even told her he loved her. If he remembered right, she had remained silent. *Didn't his love count for anything? How could she betray him like this?*

The past week had been the most uncomfortable of his life. Mokee was in a fractious snit and wouldn't look at either him or Benjamin. Jeb had to admit she didn't act like she was in love with his brother. In fact, when he caught her eyeing Benjamin, it was with a look of loathing and disgust.

Perhaps he had jumped to some premature conclusions, but how was he going to find out? She wouldn't even talk to him. Instead, she clattered the dishes onto the table every night, slopped some food onto the plates, and stormed out to her room, refusing to even eat with them. He also noticed her eyes were swollen as if she had been crying.

One night, Jeb studied Benjamin's narrow eyes as they followed Mokee's noisy departure from the kitchen. What he saw nearly made him sick. His brother's eyes were dark with malice and vengeance, the same nasty look he'd seen when his brother called Mokee a redskin. Maybe there were some problems he hadn't noticed since Benjamin moved back in. The best solution was to try to have a reasonable talk with Mokee to clear the air, even though her answers might break his heart.

Benjamin suddenly threw his chair back from the dinner table and said he was bored and going into Abilene for some action. He also said he wouldn't be back for a few days. Jeb stared at his brother's back as he slammed out the kitchen door. Why would Benjamin go all the way to Abilene to find a woman if he loved Mokee? Nothing was making any sense, and Jeb decided he would have a good night's sleep and try to talk to Mokee in the morning. Surely they could act like two adults about their problems.

The next morning, Jeb got up at the crack of dawn as usual. He sat in the living room, reading a book on naval history and waiting for Mokee to get up and start making breakfast. She was an early riser most days. When his watch read nine o'clock, he started to fidget and wonder where she was. Maybe she wasn't feeling well, he worried, thinking she looked a little pale the past few days. He sprinted up the stairs two by two.

Jeb knocked on her closed door. "Mokee?" he asked in a loud voice, rapping again. There was no reply. "Mokee, answer me. It's Jeb." He was growing impatient at the obstinate woman and opened the door slowly, not accustomed to barging into her bedroom. What he saw made his heart sink to his stomach. The window was wide open, and the curtains were blowing in a chilly morning breeze. Mokee was gone, having fled in the night.

Taking the steps two at a time again, Jeb tore outside, wanting to see if any tracks were beneath her window in the damp, rain-sodden ground. His heart did a flip-flop as he saw the tiny boot prints of her feet and small steps heading toward the tree line. A man's longer stride was next to hers, and he leaned down to examine the footsteps more closely, wondering if Mokee had run off with his brother.

He almost wished it had been Benjamin, Jeb thought angrily. Next to Mokee's footprints were the smudged, soft prints of a large pair of moccasins. They obviously belonged to an Indian, and Jeb was certain she had fled with Tovee. Her former companion would have known exactly which bedroom was hers. As the pair of footsteps reached the trees, there were hoof prints of two horses, which had been tied to a bush. Mokee and Tovee's footprints vanished from the ground as the couple mounted, and the horses headed west and deeper into the Kansas grasslands.

Jeb was heartsick as he trudged back into the house. *Why had she run off?* She hated war and violence, and she had made so many strides learning English and becoming a Christian. His eyes became moist. Was she so mad at him she would give up her new life? *Had he been wrong about her caring for Benjamin? That was impossible,* he thought, stubbornly clinging to his former conclusions. *She was clearly kissing Benjamin.*

Wondering if she had left a note or any clues in her bedroom, Jeb bolted back upstairs. All of her favorite books were still there, but he couldn't locate the Bible she read every day. He started yanking out her drawers. They were full of clothes, which meant she hadn't taken any of them with her. He pulled drawer after drawer out, and each was the same, jam-packed with wrinkled clothes and clutter. *What a messy little pack rat,* he thought with a faint smile.

Next, he flung the closet door open. All the beautiful skirts and blouses his mother had so painstakingly made were neatly hung in a row, as well as a flowing white cotton summer dress and her beautiful blue wool Christmas dress. He saw the gold necklace he'd given her draped carefully over the blue dress, and he was suddenly heartsick again.

The nightstand, he thought, rushing over to the bed. He knew she always kept Tovee's necklace in the nightstand. Jeb noticed the bed was unmade, and her nightgown was on it. It appeared Mokee had slept part of the night. With forcefulness, he pulled the nightstand drawer so hard it nearly toppled on the floor. Just as he had expected, the necklace was gone.

He rummaged around the drawer until he found what he was looking for. There were her two favorite belongings, her Bible and the journal he'd given her. He grabbed them both and strode downstairs, determined to see if she'd left any clues to her whereabouts. Maybe he could even uncover her true feelings for Benjamin among the pages of her journal.

The house was eerily quiet as he sat down on the living room sofa and put his reading glasses on. It was like all of the life whooshed out of the house with Mokee's smile and energy gone. All of a sudden, he felt old and discouraged, and he wondered if he would ever see the beautiful young woman again.

Momentarily, he held the Bible in his hands, and he shut his eyes in prayer. "Please God, keep Mokee safe wherever she is," he said out loud. "And, Mother, if you can hear me, Mokee needs your help and protection," he said as an afterthought. His mother had always said she would watch over them from the other side. If anyone had enough determination to do it, it was his mother. He gently set the Bible aside and opened the journal, deciding to start reading Mokee's entries in the past two months to uncover the truth. Jeb's heart was pounding in his chest as he began.

"I'm really worried Jeb has allowed his brother, Benjamin, to live here in the house," Mokee had written shortly after Benjamin moved back in. "I have seen enough hate and vengeance in my life to know Benjamin hates me, and his goal is to destroy me and Jeb as well. I don't know how to tell Jeb my fears. It is only natural he wants to think the best of his brother. I don't think it is right for an outsider like me to warn Jeb about his blood brother, whom he naturally loves more than me."

Oh Mokee, he thought sadly. Reading Mokee's desolate words were painful, especially when she said she wasn't as loved as his no-good brother. Jeb sighed deeply at her misconception and continued the heartrending ordeal of reading the truth.

"The day Benjamin showed up to stay, I was going to surprise Jeb in the field and help him build the fence. I've been so worried about Jeb, losing Catherine and having to handle all of her business affairs. I've been thinking a lot about what he told me at Christmas, and I've been looking for the right time to tell him I love him. I thought I might try to find the right words while we built the fence. . .."

Oh my God, Jeb thought, breaking down in tears. *Mokee did love him, but Benjamin showed up, and she never got to tell him.* Through the wetness, he read the next entry which was a few days later.

"Jeb's brother Benjamin is stalking me, I'm sure of it. No matter where I go, he's right behind me. The other morning, I went to the barn to get some eggs, and Benjamin followed me. I hid in the first stall just to see what he would do. I saw him go to the loft, and all the while he was saying, 'Where are you, you little redskin? Come out and quit playing games.' I was so frightened, I ran back to the house without the eggs."

"That son of a. . .," Jeb shouted out loud in a burst of anger, his tears suddenly gone. He had been so busy trying to settle his mother's estate and hoping his brother had set his life straight, he had put Mokee in danger by ignoring the obvious.

"When I was on the staircase today, Benjamin hurried to be next to me and nudged me into the wall, rubbing his body next to mine. I told him to leave me alone, but he just smiled that evil smile of his and said, 'Someday, you little redskin, you're going to beg me,' and then he stalked away. I want to tell Jeb so badly, but he's been so distant lately. It's like he doesn't want his brother to know he cares for me. Maybe he's ashamed I'm an Indian, and he's staying away from me because he doesn't love me anymore. I feel so alone and isolated. I wish Catherine were here to help me."

"Oh, Mokee, I'm so sorry," Jeb whispered in anguish. "How could I have hurt you so much? I'm so stupid sometimes. . .."

"It happened again. I was trying to put the sheets away upstairs, and Benjamin came at me from behind, but I sidestepped and he landed against the closet shelves. As I rushed away, I heard him say, 'You're pretty fast for a redskin, but someday I'm going to catch you, honey.' God help me if I'm ever alone with the monster."

Jeb was in shock, but he kept reading with resolve.

"I was alone in the kitchen making pea soup, which Jeb likes so much. I was hoping to show him I cared by making one of his favorite meals. From behind, I felt a hand on my waist, and I thought Jeb had returned from his business appointment. I eagerly spun around to greet Jeb and found it was Benjamin instead. He began roughly attacking me, shoving me against the sharp counter and smothering me with unwanted kisses. I pushed as hard as I could, but I couldn't get him off of me as he was too strong. I took my knee and rammed it into him. Although it stunned him momentarily, it made him roar with anger like an animal, and he assaulted me even more harshly, that is until he heard Jeb coming through the kitchen door.

"All of a sudden, Benjamin, the conniving snake he is, pretended we were kissing romantically, and Jeb, my sweet, kind Jeb, believed him. I don't know which was worse. The fear of being helpless while Benjamin tried to molest me, or the hurt of not being believed by the man I thought I loved.

"I don't know what to do. I'm afraid Benjamin will attack me again if I stay. He knows if I leave, it will hurt Jeb, and revenge has been Benjamin's goal all along. Why can't Jeb see what his brother is doing to us? We were so happy before he moved back into the house. If only Jeb believed in me. I thought when you loved someone, you trusted that person. I've worked so hard over the past year and a half to please Catherine and Jeb, but it seems Benjamin's wickedness has unraveled all of the faith Jeb had in me. He looks at me with coldness now, as if I'm deceitful like the stereotype most white men have of Indians."

Mokee's last entry was short, and Jeb read it with effort. "My heart is very sad. Benjamin has won the hateful game he's been playing. Somehow, I have to find a way to leave, but I don't even know where to go. There's no place I fit in anymore. Worse yet, I know if I do leave, it will only be my physical body going. My heart will always remain with Jeb, loving him although he doesn't love or trust me anymore."

There were ink blots on the final entry, and Jeb didn't know if Mokee had cried as she wrote the painful words, or if the ink had smudged from his own tears, which were helplessly dropping on the journal. He had never cried so much as he did that morning. *Poor Mokee*, he kept thinking. *At the time in her life when she needed him most, he'd let her down.*

After a long, painful morning of introspection, Jeb's tears dissolved. He wasn't sure what to do about Mokee. Would she try to come back on her own, or was she lost to him forever? If he went searching for her, would he even be able to find her? If he found her, would he just be on a suicide mission? He would have to think about the answers to these raw questions and come up with a plan.

There was one thing he could do in the meantime to ease his pain, and Jeb stood up in a storm of rage. He decided to pay his dear, sweet brother a little visit in Abilene.

Chapter Fourteen

With unswerving resolve, Jeb rode the lengthy distance to Abilene at a fast pace. While his own temper was still hot, he was determined to find his no-good brother. It took far less time than he imagined it would to reach the settlement. One of his neighbors, Sam Thompson, was in Abilene, and he unexpectedly came up to Jeb, who was tying up his horse in front of the general store.

"I imagine you're here to see about your brother," Sam said point blank, clapping Jeb on the back in a friendly greeting.

"What?" Jeb asked in confusion, wondering how his friend could possibly know his intentions.

"There was quite a to-do last night," Sam said, enjoying the opportunity to gossip on the beautiful spring day. "Your brother was caught with his pants down, if you get my drift," the man continued with a chuckle. "He was with a married woman he's been seeing off and on over the last year. All of a sudden, the woman's husband got back in town from laying track for the railroad. Guess the husband caught them, well, you know, and he threw your brother half-naked onto the street.

"No one's real sure what happened next, but your brother pulled out a gun and shot the man in the leg. It ended up the man was unarmed, though I heard your brother said he shot the man in self-defense. The temporary sheriff came along and arrested your brother for assault, and he spent the night in the pokey. He's still there. Bet he'll be glad to see you. He's been waiting for someone to bail him out."

"Well, I have to be going if I'm supposed to bail my brother out of jail," Jeb said silkily, giving no indication of his true thoughts. "Thanks for the information, Sam."

"Sure, anytime."

Jeb walked the short distance to the tiny, makeshift jail and took a deep breath before he entered. He was usually not a violent man. In fact, he prided himself on his calm, even temperament. "Sheriff," he said, nodding politely. "I'd like to talk with my brother alone for a few minutes, please."

The sheriff nodded and accompanied Jeb back to the lone jail cell in the back of the building. He unlocked the cell, relocked it after Jeb entered, and disinterestedly padded his way back to the front office. "Yell when you want out," he said gruffly before shutting the door separating the two areas. With a forced calmness, Jeb stood silently with his arms crossed, staring at his pathetic excuse of a brother.

"Bro'," Benjamin said with a pleased smile on his unshaven face. Jeb looked down at his brother's mismatched clothing and realized Sam's story about Benjamin being naked in the street had been true. The sheriff must have loaned him his current pants, which were at least two sizes too big and sagging in his crotch. "Are you here to bail me out?"

"Maybe, maybe not," Jeb said lethally.

"What do you mean?" Benjamin complained with an impatient whine in his voice.

"It depends on what your answers are."

"What answers? Did you get up on the wrong side of the bed or something?"

Jeb ignored Benjamin's questions. "Did you, or did you not, attack Mokee?"

In disbelief, Benjamin blew a gasp of air out of his mouth. "Is that the lie the damn redskin told you? That little woman was hot to trot. She came after me every time you were gone. You know what they say about redskins. You can't trust 'em."

In one swift movement, Jeb charged across the cell, grabbed Benjamin's long, brown hair, which was easy to do as he was sitting on a cot, and punched his face with a forceful right hook. The bones of his nose made a crunching sound, and his nose broke and twisted sideways on his face. Blood spurted out all over the narrow bed.

"That was for Mokee," Jeb said with an unnerving coldness. "And, this one is for me." With the speed of a mountain cat pouncing on its prey, Jeb gripped his brother by the collar with his left hand, and he delivered another crushing blow with his right, shattering Benjamin's jaw into pieces. His brother lay dazed in a pool of blood and teeth.

"You have no idea how good that felt, Benjamin," Jeb said unemotionally, staring without pity at the stranger in front of him. "I'm not a violent man. In fact, I deplore violence. But, you've deserved that for a long time. And, here's how it is. No, I'm not bailing you out. And no, you're not welcome at the house or farm ever again. If I ever see you trespassing, I'll shoot to kill. And there's one more thing. Your inheritance was based on the stipulation you would stay out of jail. As of today, your trust fund is now officially dissolved. As of this moment, I no longer have a brother." There was a moment of silence as the two glowered at each other.

"Sheriff," Jeb bellowed. When the sheriff got back to the cell, Jeb said quietly, "Your prisoner appears to have had a little accident with the wall. It's a pity." After an apathetic glance at the battered prisoner, the sheriff quietly led Jeb from the cell, never questioning what happened. With hatred in his eyes, Benjamin glared at his older brother as he left. Jeb, on the other hand, felt exceedingly good, the best he'd felt all day, although he knew it didn't solve his problem of finding Mokee.

Before he left the jail, he shook the sheriff's hand and said, "I won't be paying his bail or coming here again. The monster you have in there isn't my brother anymore!"

The sheriff nodded in understanding, and Jeb slammed out the door into the sunshine.

Chapter Fifteen

Spring was the busiest time of year on the farm, and Jeb needed to plant his fields for the growing season. As he routinely plowed row after row, he was deep in thought about what to do about Mokee. Sometimes he even tried to pray. After he beat up his brother without regret, however, he was sure God wouldn't listen to him.

Jeb's initial thoughts about Mokee were to let her come back on her own. He decided he would give her a few months to think about their life together and how good it had been. She was an intelligent, logical woman. He was sure she would come to her senses and realize he still loved her, in spite of his momentary anger and distrust. His theory proved to be utterly wrong, however, as she never came back.

The house was lonely and lifeless without Mokee and also without his mother. Jeb read and reread Mokee's journal, shed a few more tears, and then read it some more. The most recent time, he actually studied it, and he realized how perceptive Mokee had been about people and the world around her. She analyzed the war between the white men and the Indians with objectivity, and she seemed to understand the deep misunderstandings both worlds had for the other. When Mokee wrote about violence and man's inhumanity toward man, it was the voice of a witness caught in the crossfire with no place to run.

Because it represented the view from the side the white men called the enemy, Jeb realized Mokee's journal was significant. It truly showed the Indians were intelligent human beings with loved ones, governments, oral histories, spirituality and religion, social structures, clubs and societies, and deep thoughts about the injustice in the world around them. Had anyone ever tried to treat the Indians as intelligent equals? Or, were they continually treated as lesser human beings who needed to be subjugated? If Mokee ever returned, he would talk to her about the importance of sharing her journal one day.

As time passed and she never came back, Jeb faced the fact he would eventually have to go after Mokee, in spite of the danger. *He was damn sure he wasn't going to live without her.* The first thing he needed to do was hire permanent help on the farm. He realized he might have to leave for an undetermined amount of time. After inquiring in Salina if there was anyone looking for work, he discovered one of his neighbor's sons, Donny Webster, a big, strapping teenager with muscles the size of cannonballs, was engaged and looking for work before his wedding. After agreeing to terms, wages, and hours, Jeb gratefully turned over many of his chores to the ambitious young man. Although Jeb was only a few years older than his new hire, he felt positively ancient.

In the first half of 1866, Kansas had been relatively quiet in regard to outbreaks of violence with the Indians, but Jeb knew the times were changing. The quiet was only an uneasy peace before the storm as the Indians regrouped. According to Mokee, the more militant branches of the Cheyenne would continue to seek revenge for Sand Creek, and there would be an intensification of further hostilities and merciless acts of revenge.

He wondered over and over where Mokee could be. Jeb momentarily shut his eyes and pictured Tovee and his wild, angry eyes and belligerent behavior. The young Indian warrior would never have returned to pick up the pieces at Sand Creek or to grovel on a tiny reservation with the older chiefs who wanted peace. No, Tovee would have wanted to be in the thick of the action with the younger warriors, killing white men and possibly even women and children while getting revenge.

With fear pounding in his heart, Jeb came to the devastating realization Mokee's life was in great danger the longer she remained with the Indian warrior. Tovee's choice for revenge would be prowling the countryside with a violent band of Cheyenne Dog Soldiers. Poor Mokee, who hated war, would be trapped with the women of the camp, moving around with the warriors until they were eventually attacked and killed by American soldiers.

Dog soldiers were known to be the most ferocious of Indian warriors, proud, brave, and fanatical as they wreaked havoc on white settlers throughout the Plains. As Jeb sat there without a plan, he knew the Dog Soldiers were probably organizing future strikes along the five hundred mile length of the Smoky Hill and Republican Rivers, which the warring bands defiantly claimed as their hunting grounds. If the basin remained the focus for future strikes, it meant Mokee might still be nearby.

Jeb became frantic. Without further delay, he had to do something. The Cheyenne band could leave for other areas or even head back to the Dakota territory. In that case, Mokee might be lost forever. With panic cascading through his chest like a raging waterfall, Jeb sprinted to the barn and saddled his horse. Filled with a surge of energy, he rode without stopping all the way to Fort Riley, which was just east of Junction City.

When he finally reached the military compound, he inquired at the administration building about hiring the services of a Cheyenne scout and interpreter as soon as possible. He was told to write out his request on a paper and tack it to the bulletin board in the lobby under the category, Services Needed.

Knowing the competition was cutthroat for qualified interpreters and scouts, Jeb listed the location of his farm, the job as dangerous, and the payment for services rendered at a thousand dollars cash, a tremendous amount of money in

1866. For that kind of money, he knew he would have a taker by sunrise, so he made the lengthy ride back home and waited impatiently for morning to come.

At daybreak, a bold knock at the front door announced the arrival of Ma'o'nehe. The visitor was a Cheyenne interpreter from Fort Riley, and he told Jeb to call him Red Wolf in English. Never had Jeb seen such a fierce-looking Indian, his massive size and powerful build downright intimidating. Compared to Mokee's light tan skin, Red Wolf's skin was like sun-baked clay, a rich red, coppery color etched with cavernous grooves.

It was impossible to tell the man's age. He could have been in his late forties as his taut body was strong and muscle-bound. But he might have been sixty or more as his long black hair had a mass of silver streaks, and his face was as deeply lined as a bone dry riverbed. When he spoke in impeccable English, his voice boomed with authority.

After Jeb got over his initial awe, he decided he liked the Indian's no-nonsense, gruff approach, and he invited him warmly into the house. The two sat in the living room and stared at each other momentarily. Then the man took charge and matter-of-factly recounted his lengthy resume as a scout with the military.

Surprising the Indian, Jeb gave him a warm grin. "You're just the person I'm looking for. Would you like some breakfast while we talk?" Red Wolf looked surprised at the invitation and nodded yes. He hadn't eaten in his hurry to get there. Jeb liked the Indian so much he cooked him a huge breakfast, and the two sat around the kitchen table conversing and even laughing like old friends as they ate ham and eggs. Red Wolf was bemused with how the man treated him as an equal, and he served him as if there were no differences between an Indian and a white man. The Indian didn't always get such cordial treatment from his white bosses. They usually maintained some sort of invisible separation from him.

When he heard the white man say he wanted to rescue a Cheyenne woman named Mokee'eso and marry her, he was even more taken aback. Usually white men considered Indians inferior and looked down on them, especially the women. He'd seen firsthand how the common procedure in war was for the white soldiers to go after the women and children first, either using them as human shields or brutally killing them, a practice Red Wolf despised.

It was then the white man revealed the catch in his plan. He needed to rescue the woman from a band of Cheyenne Dog Soldiers. Even worse than that, the white man admitted one of the warriors might also be in love with her and wouldn't want to let her go. *Dag blasted stupid man*, Red Wolf irritably thought to himself. He decided the white man was plumb crazy, and he ought to leave well enough alone and find somebody else to marry.

The Indian tried to dissuade the man named Jeb out of such a foolhardy plan, thinking he didn't understand the danger, but the white man would not be moved. He said his life wasn't worth living without Mokee, which was his nickname for the Indian woman. If he had to, he said he would simply ride into the Dog Soldier camp by himself. At least she would know he loved her enough to come after her, even if he died trying to reach her.

Jeb started telling Red Wolf how Mokee had arrived with her friend, Tovee, after the Sand Creek Massacre, and he and his mother had protected them from the white soldiers who came to the house searching for survivors. He explained Mokee stayed on after Tovee left, and she learned to read and write English and even became a Christian.

With a faraway look in his eyes, Jeb also described how she resembled a little ragamuffin with her chopped off hair when she first arrived. Mokee had grown into a beautiful woman, he continued, and she loved literature and philosophy and writing in her journal. He told about the cruelty of his brother, and how he himself was at fault for driving her away. He hadn't understood the problems his brother was creating, but the worst thing was he hadn't believed Mokee.

By the end of Jeb's brief story, Red Wolf could almost picture the young woman in his mind, a gentle little thing caught up in war and violence she hated. It was then Jeb stared straight into Red Wolf's eyes. With a penetrating look, he asked him the most unexpected question. "Haven't you ever loved a woman so much, Red Wolf, that you'd do anything in the world for her, including die?"

The Indian startled at the white man's directness, and he brought to mind his own sweet wife, Nanomone'e (Peacemaker Woman). Jeb's question struck a raw nerve as Red Wolf painfully remembered how she hated war and yearned for peace, yet died in a brutal attack by the white soldiers. He had never been able to let go of his grief.

Red Wolf wanted to be angry and hate the white man for tearing open his festering wound, and he glared at Jeb with a malevolent look, which would make most men quake. Without fear, Jeb unequivocally stared back, waiting patiently for a truthful answer. *Damn white man called my bluff,* thought the Indian, giving him a grudging respect.

There was no trickery or intention to hurt the Indian in Jeb's eyes, only genuine love for the woman, Mokee. He seemed to have an honest desire to know if Red Wolf had ever experienced the same love, and whether they could forge a bond of commonality between them. *Blast it all! How could he refuse to help this foolish, but straightforward white man?* The man only wanted to help a woman of peace like Nanomone'e. How had Jeb known he had asked the one question that would make Red Wolf accept the dangerous mission? *By helping this white man, could he finally put his own grief to rest?*

If the truth were known, Red Wolf had only come to inquire about the job to trick the man out of the ridiculously large sum of money. After all, he didn't really like white people much at all, although he worked for them. There was something different about this white man though. If ever he wanted to help a white man, it was this man.

Maybe it was the sincere love he saw in the man's eyes for Mokee and the lack of any ulterior motive except to marry her. It might have been because the man named Jeb was apparently colorblind. He had not only welcomed Red Wolf into his home in friendship and made him breakfast, but he had put his life at risk to save two Cheyenne from the white soldiers after Sand Creek.

Little did Jeb know he was hiring the one Indian scout who could actually expedite his search for Mokee. None of the white soldiers Red Wolf ever worked for realized the complete truth about the Indian, and he knew he would never tell Jeb the full truth either. But the fact was he had been a Cheyenne Dog Soldier in his youth and still made contact with their war chiefs in secret. No one in his long career as a scout and interpreter had ever suspected he was playing both sides of the fence to help his Cheyenne people. He had to. It had been the white soldiers that murdered his wife, Nanomone'e, and that was something he could never forgive.

Red Wolf couldn't believe the blasted white man talked him into accepting the foolhardy job, he complained to himself as he left to prepare. It could be a suicide mission for Jeb, maybe even for him if Mokee had joined one of the more radical bands of young rebels. He added a string of silent expletives to his objections. The Indian couldn't believe how he was growing soft as he got older. It didn't even seem plausible, but Red Wolf actually liked this white man named Jeb, and he hoped he didn't get him killed.

PART THREE

Chapter Sixteen

The Cheyenne Dog Soldiers, or Dog Men (Hotamétaneo'o), were aggressively fierce warriors who played a major role combatting American expansion into the state of Kansas and the territories of Nebraska, Wyoming, and Colorado. Beginning as one of six Cheyenne military societies, it evolved into a separate, militaristic group in the late 1830s, and it often opposed the efforts for peace made by the Cheyenne chiefs, such as Black Kettle of the Council of Forty-four.

Originally, the best warriors in each band of Dog Soldiers were honored with sashes, which they wore in battle. The sashes were long enough to be pinned to the ground by one of the three Sacred Arrows they carried into battle. The significance of this act was to show the Dog Soldier was so courageous he would stand his ground and fight to his death to save his people. Instead of a sash, some bands used to pin themselves to the ground by an unusually long rear panel of each warrior's breechclout, which was a brief garment consisting of a waistband and a front and rear panel attached to the waistband.

In a new kind of warfare against the white men, however, older traditions gave way to aggressively organized raids, which were quick and brutal, killing settlers, burning buildings, destroying resources, stealing supplies, disrupting commerce, and sometimes kidnapping victims.

All Dog Soldiers still dressed ferociously for battle, their bronzed skin slathered with war paint as well as their ponies. Many were bedecked in head feathers, which represented war honors, and others wore just a few simple breath feathers. The warriors carried an array of battle accoutrements including well-worn plumed spears, bows and arrows, tomahawks, stone-headed clubs, knives, and thick buffalo hide shields. They also carried more modern weapons, such as revolvers and rifles they had stolen.

Not only were they feared for being so violent, they were bent on revenge for the atrocities done to the Indians by the white soldiers, and they had an unyielding mindset to kill without mercy. To them, peace treaties meant nothing as the whites kept changing the rules and breaking treaties of the past. As the Dog Soldiers assumed a more prominent role in the battle against the whites, they eventually gained more respect in the tribe as a whole, especially after continued efforts for peace failed.

The traditional clan system of the Cheyenne began to collapse as early as the cholera epidemic of 1849, which killed thousands of Cheyenne. At the same time, the Dog Soldiers contributed to the breakdown of the traditional matrilineal clan system, where a newly married man moved to the camp of his new wife's Cheyenne band. The Dog Soldiers began doing the opposite and bringing wives to their own roving camps.

Another thing which contributed to the downfall of the clan system and the emergence of the Dog Soldiers was the Sand Creek Massacre in 1864. Because of so many casualties among peaceful bands, the Dog Soldiers, who weren't there, survived by numbers alone and grew stronger. By moving forward with the massacre, the American soldiers ended up killing many of the true peacemakers. This ironic outcome unintentionally strengthened the more radical branch of the Dog Soldiers.

The Cheyenne Dog Soldiers and its smaller bands of raiding parties sometimes lived in the headwaters country of the Republican and Smoky Hill Rivers in northern Kansas, the southern Nebraska territory, and the northeastern portion of the Colorado territory. As the warrior-like bands became stronger, they roamed east of other peaceful Cheyenne bands to an area between the Platte and Arkansas Rivers. They intermarried with Republican River Brule and Oglala Lakotas (Sioux). Eventually, the Cheyenne, Arapaho, and Sioux would form an informal alliance to fight the United States military on the central and northern Plains.

Because there was an increasing polarity between the Dog Soldiers and the more peaceful Southern Cheyenne bands, they effectively became a third division of the Cheyenne people. In the 1860s, Dog Soldier leaders, including Tall Bull and White Horse and their frequent ally, the warrior Roman Nose, coordinated attacks with smaller bands of Dog Soldiers on white civilians and the United States military.

Tears are often the telescope by which men see far into heaven.

Henry Ward Beecher

Chapter Seventeen

It was August in 1866 by my calculations. It was so hot in Kansas my normally straight, long black hair was frizzing in ringlets, and my wisps stuck out like corkscrews from my unaccustomed braids. I had been gone from Jeb's farmhouse for a little more than three, agonizingly long months. Most of the time was spent traveling around like a homeless nomad with a small raiding party of Cheyenne Dog Soldiers. They were an arm of a larger, more powerful band intent on bringing down the United States government. I hated it because I hated war, but I was stuck and knew it was my own fault.

Every day, I berated myself for leaving with Tovee as I obviously made the wrong decision. I'd had a choice, although I imagined Tovee would have forced me to go with him if I had said no. Why hadn't I thought things through more carefully or listened to my intuition? It kept telling me Tovee had evolved into a killer. Why hadn't I waited on the Lord's answer to my prayers and let Him guide me? I was too busy being hurt by Jeb's anger and the lack of resolution to the problem of Benjamin. I was blind not to realize the alternative of traveling the countryside with a band of ruthless warriors was far worse.

Talk about stupid, I thought. Catherine and Jeb had always praised me for my quick intelligence. I now knew their praise was totally misplaced. The truth was I completely lacked any common sense whatsoever. Worse yet, I missed Jeb's gentle kindness and companionship. In spite of the anger that drove us apart, I realized I loved Jeb, and I always would. It's sad it took a crisis to solidify my love, because the obstacles now seemed insurmountable.

Jeb probably continued to judge me guilty of an affair with Benjamin, all because I ran away. By not being brave enough to face my problems with Jeb and speak up, I gave up my chance for peace and love. Every night, I prayed for Jesus to help me out of the mess I had made for myself and to give me a second chance to make things right with Jeb. But, Catherine never told me whether He helped stupid people who made foolish choices.

I thought back to my first day in the Cheyenne camp. Tovee and I had ridden through the night, and we found his home encampment at dawn's first light. That information meant the camp wasn't too far from Jeb's farm. The small cluster of tepees was hidden in the dense tree line along a tributary of the Smoky Hill River.

Because we had ridden in the black of night, I was disoriented and not exactly sure where the camp was located. I rebuked myself for not paying closer attention in case I needed to escape. My body was aching, and I was exhausted from the lengthy ride. I hadn't ridden much in the past year, and I was out of practice. Although I wanted to tumble onto a sleeping mat somewhere, I thought I should make an assessment of my new home.

First off, I didn't recognize anyone from my original village. My parents weren't there. None of my former friends or any of Tovee's closest friends was there either. Instead, it was a rough, dirty camp of unkempt young rebels from the ages of seventeen to maybe twenty-two. So they wouldn't be caught, the warriors moved their camp after every raid.

It wasn't a peaceful encampment of homes and a friendly community like I had known as a child. The tepees were small and ragged, easily portable and undecorated for warriors on the run. Because the individual tepees were too small to have a cooking fire in each one, all the tepees shared a central cooking pot in a clearing.

Without the presence of older squaws or elders, there was no sense of stability or restraint in the camp. Instead, there were young, dirt-covered girls I call camp followers, seeking the excitement of living on the edge of danger with their wild young warriors, who lived only for each day's battle. I would have guessed there was a greater sense of community in the larger bands of Dog Soldiers, which had older warriors and their families. But, that wasn't the case with this small raiding party. I also noticed Tovee and a few of the other young warriors seemed to be the leaders of the marauding band.

What was I doing here? I knew immediately it wasn't just my appearance that had changed. Even though I was only sixteen and a half, I was no longer a girl, but an educated woman. I had learned about the vast world around me and had become a woman of peace through Christ. Although I could have adjusted to living in a peaceful Cheyenne village like the camp of my parents, I was definitely out of place with those who, through violence and war, sought to reclaim a past that no longer existed.

After our arrival, Tovee possessively dragged me by the hand to his small, threadbare tepee. Many of the young bedraggled girls stared at me when we walked by. I must have looked like a white woman to them in my pants, flannel shirt, and boots, and they watched me warily with distrust.

When I glanced around, I immediately sensed their animosity and jealousy. I was holding hands with Tovee, who admittedly was an impressive-looking warrior with the passage of time. His temperament had changed, though, and it wasn't for the better. I felt like I didn't know him any longer. He was continually restless like a caged animal, a predator that was ready to break loose and attack his jailers.

We hadn't spoken since leaving the farmhouse. As though I was a nuisance, Tovee wearily pointed me at a sleeping mat. Gratefully, I began to sit down, but then I noticed another girl's clothing folded near the mat. I looked at Tovee with disgust.

"Whose clothes are these?" I asked suspiciously, wondering why he had come for me when he was in a relationship with another woman.

"They belong to He'evo'nehe," he said with a bored shrug, ignoring me while he sank down on his own mat. I immediately tried to picture what a girl named She Wolf was like. "Don't worry. I kicked her out," he said harshly.

"What?" I gasped. "You had a girl living here with you, and you threw her out. Where's she supposed to go?" This new, ruthless Tovee was a stranger to me.

"Don't worry about it, Mokee. She knew I already had a woman. Besides, she sometimes stays with some of the others. A lot of them do. It's a very loose camp." As if I were still naïve and stupid, Tovee shook his head at me. I was appalled at the way he was living and rejecting the moral structure of the older camps. Faking a yawn to escape his stare, I struggled to get comfortable on my sleeping mat.

"There's room over here with me," he whispered suggestively, ignoring my complaints about another woman.

My mind was reeling at the mess I had gotten myself into. "No thanks, Tovee," I said abruptly, turning my back to him. I knew my rejection probably angered him, but I didn't care. Help me, Lord, I prayed through my silent tears.

The next few weeks were among the worst of my life. Tovee was eager to have me meet his friends and to show me off, yet I remained aloof and by myself, trying to decide what to do. If it hadn't been so dangerous, I would have tried to escape. The truth was, however, I wasn't sure where the camp was. One thing I did know. There was no way I could sit by the campfire at night and listen to the warriors brag about their killing exploits. When I heard them laugh about their victims' last expressions, especially children they had killed, it turned my stomach.

One night, Tovee had enough of my sulking behavior, and he left the others to find me. Contemplating my mistake leaving Jeb, I was sitting alone in the dark in Tovee's tepee. "What's the matter with you, Mokee? You seem different," Tovee accused heatedly as he sat down next to me on the floor.

I faced him in anger. "You're asking what's wrong with me, Tovee?" I asked with disbelief. "Have you looked at yourself lately? You're a murderer, a killer who laughs about his victims. Remember how awful it was watching the women and children slaughtered by the soldiers at Sand Creek. Yet, you're doing the same thing. You go around the countryside killing innocent men, women and children, the same as the soldiers we watched. Somehow, you justify it and say it's for revenge, or you're saving the Cheyenne people. All you're really doing is stirring up the white soldiers' animosity again, and they'll start killing more Cheyenne, who are basically a peaceful people. Can't you see it's a vicious cycle? The only solution to stop the killing would be to follow our leaders who believe in peace, not those who follow a path of war."

"I'm not a murderer," he declared belligerently. "I'm a warrior defending my people after they were attacked. I'm still Tovee," he said sadly, reminding me of the sweet young boy he once was. For a moment, his flicker of tender emotion drew me in, but I quickly turned away before I gave in to it. Suddenly, his temper flared wildly. "Since you love white people so much, I'm not good enough for you anymore," he said bitterly.

I spun my head to face him. "Tovee, I care for you very deeply. I always have. But I hate killing. You should remember how I used to have nightmares about war and violence when I was younger. It took me nearly a year to stop dreaming about the horrors at Sand Creek. For the first time in my life, I felt safe and at peace with Catherine and Jeb. Please don't make me stay here where I have to be on the frontline of war. Until the war is over, please take me back to their house, or at least take me to where my parents live in peace," I begged. Tears began to fall down my face.

"I think you're in love with that white man," Tovee accused irrationally, his anger growing. "Aren't you? Admit it." Carefully, I stared at him through my tears, trying not to give him access to my heart. Jumping to his own conclusions, he shook his head in disbelief, and his voice grew louder. "I never should have left you there so you could learn their lying ways. You're supposed to be mine. Did you forget our promise to be together?" With disgust, he flipped the end of the braided elk skin necklace I wore into the air.

My mind made an instantaneous decision to appease Tovee. Frightening me, he seemed to be getting more and more agitated and ready to snap. His short fuse was the biggest change I noticed in him since my return. Because there didn't seem to be any hope left for me to get back to Jeb, I had to be careful not to alienate my only ally. Tovee was my only hope for survival in this rebel band.

"Tovee, I am yours. I came with you, didn't I? Let's go away from here together, just you and me, maybe back to our parents or someplace where we'll be safe." My eyes pleaded with him for understanding, but his eyes suddenly went cold and black, devoid of any emotion.

With the quickness of a coiled rattler attacking its victim, Tovee's strong hand painfully lashed out at me and slapped my cheek, toppling me helplessly to the hard ground. I tried to push myself back up, refusing to be intimidated by his harshness. Helplessly, I stared at him in shock, feeling my cheek sting like a hundred tiny needles. He'd always been so kind to me in the past, and I never thought he would ever hit me.

His verbal assault continued. "You're a coward and a traitor to your people," he hissed vehemently. "I don't know why I brought you back here at all. I thought being with me was what you wanted, and what we always wanted. But, you obviously don't love me anymore. I think you love that white man though you won't admit the truth. I am sure of one thing. You don't love your people anymore. You can't even admit we're trying to save the Cheyenne nation from the white man."

As if to emphasize his point, he squeezed my face ruthlessly, intensifying the excruciating pain of my bruised cheek. "I'm going back out with my friends to celebrate our future victory over the white soldiers, but let me warn you about something. They won't have any tolerance of your liking white people, and you're as good as dead if they think you're a traitor. I'd stay away from O'kome if I were you." I immediately pictured the towering warrior, whose name meant Coyote in English. He had a jagged scar across his cheek. "If he even hears you say you like a white man, he'll slit your throat. So, snap out of it and start acting like an Indian, or I'm going to let the others fight over which one gets you to be his bed warmer." With his harsh comments, Tovee stalked from the tent.

I wept for a long time that night, knowing the sweet young warrior I had once loved was gone, and there was a volatile stranger in his place.

When I woke up the next morning, I could barely open my eyes as they were so swollen from crying. As if it were deeply bruised, my cheek was throbbing, so I shifted to my other side instead of facing the wall. I momentarily wondered if my face had a huge purple splotch, but then I realized it didn't matter. Nothing mattered anymore. The life of peace I had hoped for was over, all because of my foolish choice to return with Tovee. I was filled with profound sadness, and I had given up.

"Mokee, come here," a soft, apologetic voice said from across the tepee. I pretended to be asleep, not wanting to face the person I no longer knew or loved. Suddenly, I felt Tovee's muscled body sink down to lie next to me, pulling me against his ribbed chest and stroking my hair.

"I am so sorry," he whispered, tracing the outline of my injured cheek with a string of kisses, like a delicate strand of pearls. "There's no excuse for what I did last night. Please say you forgive me. Please, Mokee. I will never strike you again in anger. I promise."

I wasn't sure I had the strength in my heart to forgive Tovee, but I knew Christ could loan me His strength to help me make a conscious effort. My silent prayer was for Christ's forgiveness to overflow through me and do what I could not. I murmured words of forgiveness to Tovee, which I knew weren't true, and I fell back asleep against his chest, too weary to wake up again in a world of violence.

An uneasy truce followed with Tovee. I began to pay more attention to the world around me, knowing I had gotten myself into this mess, and I would have to get myself out. I observed the men got their orders from a larger, older band of Dog Soldiers, and they were sent on small, inconspicuous raids by the older band every week or so. Usually after a raid, we moved the encampment to a safer place. It was as though the older Dog Soldiers were training the younger ones for when the larger war would come.

Upon the raiding party's return from causing discord, we rapidly moved our camp. There were always raucous celebrations regaling the activities of each raid, especially if there had been any killing, which seemed to be the personal goal of some of the warriors. Because of Tovee's warning about Coyote and his lack of tolerance, I began attending the gatherings, but I always inconspicuously remained in the background. If I focused on silently reciting Bible verses, I could make it through even the goriest details they recounted.

After the raids, Tovee's behavior always worsened. It was as though the violence he participated in permeated every part of his body. He inevitably became more short-tempered with me, so I quickly learned to keep my distance from him when he returned. After studying all of the warriors, I concluded their bloodlust on the raids made them behave like unfeeling animals killing their prey. It was startling to see their humanity diminish a little more each time they went on raids, and my observations made me conclude that peace, not violence, was the answer to life's injustice.

During the intervening time between the raids, Tovee's behavior mellowed and he treated me better, but then the upsetting pattern would repeat all over again. I often reflected on the words of John Greenleaf Whittier, an American Quaker poet who advocated the abolition of slavery. He said, "Peace hath higher tests of manhood, than battle ever knew," but peace didn't seem to be in the mindset of the roving band of warriors I had now unwillingly joined.

As for me, I tried not to say or do anything that would cause controversy or anger. Realizing I was trapped here temporarily, I set a goal of surviving one day at a time, and each day I searched for a window of opportunity to escape back to Jeb.

In the meantime, I acted as Tovee's squaw, bringing him his meals, tending his tepee and clothing, and transporting and setting up his tepee every time the camp moved, which was frequently. I deliberately hid my revulsion for his acts of violence, and I never mentioned Jeb again.

I also pretended to be more accepting of Tovee's affection, and I platonically moved my sleeping mat next to his, sleeping in his arms at night and occasionally kissing him, but rejecting intimacy. He realized I was not the same Mokee as before. I rarely smiled, laughed, or initiated conversation. I could tell he was truly confused how to scale the boundary walls of my heart and achieve any emotional closeness. For now, my truce and minimal affection would have to be enough.

Because I knew it pleased Tovee, I also tried to blend in more with the other young women in camp, helping with the communal cooking and mending the raggedy tents. They seemed to accept me eventually, but I didn't talk much with them. I was afraid anything I might say would reveal too much of my recent experiences. It was important to keep my desire for peace with all people, no matter what color their skin was, close to my heart for my own protection.

If I had to describe this period of my life, I was existing, but not really living, and I was biding my time while I gathered knowledge about my surroundings. I often wondered at night if Jeb was merely existing too.

Just remember –
when you think all is lost,
the future remains.

Robert H. Goddard

Chapter Eighteen

Red Wolf had devised the perfect plan, and he and Jeb had already experimented with the logistics of it at two different Dog Soldier camps. So far, they'd been unable to locate Mokee, but they were definitely getting closer. Basically, the Indian found a secure spot to conceal Jeb for at least a day or two, whether it was under the cover of gnarled tree roots or in the leafy branches of a fallen tree.

Then Red Wolf turned Jeb's horse into a pack animal and went alone into each Dog Soldier encampment. He told Jeb his reputation as a respected interpreter for the white man preceded him, and he was allowed to enter the encampments. Jeb, however, wasn't aware the Indian's reputation as a spy for the Cheyenne was the main reason he was welcomed into the nomadic camps.

Red Wolf stayed at least a day enjoying each camp's hospitality, eventually saying he was searching for a young woman named Mokee'eso, who was the daughter of Paveena'e and Vohpeaenohe, names Jeb had shown him from Mokee's journal. He then went on to say she had disappeared after Sand Creek.

At the last camp, which was larger than the first and had older, more prominent warriors in addition to several war chiefs, Red Wolf ran into an old friend, Taa'evanahkohe (Night Bear). His friend told him there was a small raiding party of very young warriors roaming the countryside and taking orders from them. They were currently in central Kansas near the location of Fort Fletcher before it closed.

Trying to get even more information, Red Wolf said the last person Mokee'eso was seen with was nicknamed Tovee, and he asked if the name sounded familiar. He was told there was a brash, young warrior named Tovôhkeso (Swift Fox), who was one of the leaders of the raiding party along with O'kome (Coyote), and Oo'êstseahe (Shaved Head). Red Wolf knew Tovee would be a logical nickname for Tovôhkeso, and he decided he struck gold at the second camp.

Always cautious, Red Wolf asked his friend, Night Bear, if he might act as a courier for them and bring the younger camp a message or some orders. He thought a legitimate mission might make the camp more readily accept him. Night Bear agreed a message would be a sensible approach with the brash young warriors, and he asked the war chiefs to come up with a specific day and location for the younger camp's next attack.

After retrieving Jeb from his hideout the next day, the two set off toward the west at a fast pace along the Smoky Hill River. The next afternoon, they found the remnants of a previous encampment along one of the river branches. Red Wolf examined the entire campsite from debris to the warm embers of what appeared to be a central cooking fire. It was important to determine how recently the Indians had been there and how many there were. When his conclusion was the small raiding party had left that morning, they quickly took off to the south, leaving the tree line and heading for another area of forests. Within two hours, they spotted a recent trail, and Red Wolf began looking for a good hiding place for Jeb.

They were now in an area of tributaries of the Arkansas River, and the river was unusually low as it was the hottest and driest part of the summer. Where the riverbed used to be when the current was higher, there were many toppled trees left over from spring flooding. With his supplies in a backpack, Jeb eased his way behind a dry clump of massive roots, prepared to wait while Red Wolf left for the next encampment.

In a nonthreatening way, the towering Indian interpreter rode cautiously toward the camp. The older Dog Soldiers at the previous camp warned him a few of the younger warriors at this particular camp were aggressive and unpredictable, and he needed to keep his wits about him. The young warriors might not realize he was a spy. Instead, they might think he was a traitor.

As he rode, Red Wolf began improvising his plan. He already decided he would give the message only to the Indian called Tovôhkeso, pretending those were his orders from the war chiefs. He also made up his mind he would try to find Mokee'eso without mentioning her or her parents. Jeb had described her perfectly, and the Indian knew he was looking for a tiny, pretty black-haired girl with sand-colored skin, making her look almost like a white woman.

He would have to be careful, however. Jeb told him Tovee was smart and observant, and he would be suspicious about even the slightest interest in Mokee. Jeb also warned him against bringing up Mokee's parents. He had said Tovee would probably ask trick questions about them to see if Red Wolf was legitimately seeking Mokee for her parents or not.

When a ring of wild-looking young Dog Soldiers with sashes across their chests encircled him, Red Wolf wasn't surprised. Belligerently, they aimed their arrows directly at his chest, as if daring him to move. He yelled out a friendly greeting, saying he had a message for Tovôhkeso from Taa'evanahkohe. Red Wolf knew Night Bear was a well-known and respected Dog Soldier in the war against the white man. While the young group processed his request, the towering Indian waited patiently. He knew for him to single out a warrior to speak with elevated Tovôhkeso's reputation above the others, undoubtedly making them jealous.

Suddenly, a tall and muscular, but lean warrior stepped forward and said he was Tovôhkeso. Red Wolf nodded at him, sizing him up. The young man was just as Jeb had described, shrewd, suspicious, and uncompromising with continuously shifting eyes. The interpreter was sure he was about to strike pure gold. But just as he was a watchful poker player when playing cards with the white soldiers, he would have to play his cards with precision here.

Pretending as if he believed Tovôhkeso was the leader of the ragtag group, Red Wolf asked him to tell his associates to put down their weapons and let him dismount. The young warrior nodded importantly and gave the order to the others to disarm. Then the interpreter asked him if they could go to his tepee to talk privately, and the younger man nodded again. He wasn't very talkative, Red Wolf observed, but his body language spoke volumes about distrusting the visitor. As Red Wolf walked alongside the man, he wondered how to proceed and gain the trust of the warrior he was certain was Tovee.

As they entered a small, threadbare tepee, Red Wolf noticed a dark-haired, pretty young thing with skin the color of sand sitting on a mat, quietly sewing. She didn't bother to look up. Once again, Jeb's description was perfect, and the interpreter knew he had come face-to-face with Mokee. "Is this your woman?" he asked Tovee, wondering what the younger man would say.

He hadn't meant to stir up a controversy with his words, but he observed the younger man was uncomfortable with the question and wasn't sure what to answer. As if daring him to lie and say she was his woman, the young woman glowered at Tovee. *Amazing*, thought Red Wolf, watching the woman he thought to be Mokee quell Tovôhkeso with one disparaging look. Instead of answering his question directly, the younger man introduced his companion as Mokee'eso. Red Wolf nearly smiled. He had struck the Mother lode!

Now came the hard part. How did he get Mokee alone to tell her Jeb was hiding about an hour away, and they had a plan for her escape? Red Wolf, being an elderly man, decided to have a coughing spell, which he did pretty convincingly. He then asked if there was any place he could get some fresh water to drink after his long ride, and Tovee fell right into his plan by telling Mokee to take the visitor to the creek. Still coughing as he exited with the young girl, he spoke about how he'd had a bad cough most of the summer, even though it was so hot. As he left disinterestedly with Mokee, Red Wolf hoped Tovee overheard his dull conversation.

As they walked further away from camp, the interpreter thoroughly checked the vicinity for possible eavesdroppers. There were none. As they entered the shade of several towering oak trees, Red Wolf began speaking in English in a low, fast monotone.

"Look straight ahead, Mokee, and don't react to what I'm saying. I'm here with Jeb to rescue you. He's an hour from here hiding near a branch of the Arkansas River. Nod if you understand me."

Mokee's face almost beamed as she quickly, but imperceptibly nodded. She continued to stare straight ahead and kept walking.

Red Wolf coughed some more for any distant bystanders. They finally reached the creek, and the interpreter bent down and cupped his hands to drink. Mokee sat nervously on a nearby rock to watch. While he pretended to drink, he continued speaking. "Jeb said to tell you he loves you and to please forgive him for allowing Benjamin to attack you. He promises Benjamin will never be back, and he wants you to return home with him. Well? If you don't want to go, I won't take you back, no matter what Jeb wants," he assured her.

Very softly in perfect English, Mokee said, "I love Jeb, and I forgive him. How are we going to leave though? I'm watched constantly. Tovee will never let me go."

The interpreter coughed and then drank again. "I'm going to send the men on a raid tomorrow. If it all works out, we'll go then." Without waiting for her reply, Red Wolf spun around. As if he were totally bored with the young girl, he began to hike back to camp alone. Mokee followed behind, acting as though she'd done her job and found the man to be a dreary old geezer. Tovee looked pleased the older man arrived back alone, and he noticed Mokee had stopped to talk with one of the other young women. Red Wolf was impressed with Mokee's quick-thinking to throw off Tovee's suspicions, and he marveled at the calm way she had accepted the news.

He began explaining the raid to Tovee for the next day. They were to strike the settlement of Cimarron, which was southwest along the Santa Fe Trail. Red Wolf found himself hoping his carefully arranged plan to rescue Mokee would move forward smoothly. In a rare occurrence while they traveled together, he had grown to respect the white man, Jeb. His first impression of Mokee was that she was a perfect match for Jeb and a clever young woman. In his world of constant violence and killing, it made Red Wolf happy to think he could bring together two people who loved each other in a time of war.

Maybe he was just getting mellow as he got older, but he was growing weary of constant war. Little did the interpreter know, however, he would soon have to rely on his expertise as both a scout and a spy. Things were not going to progress as smoothly as he hoped.

I love you the more in that I believe
you had liked me for my own sake
and for nothing else.

John Keats

Chapter Nineteen

I was stunned at the knowledge Jeb still loved me, and I couldn't believe he was brave enough to try to rescue me from the Dog Soldiers. It was an unheard of thing. No one ever rescued anyone from the Dog Soldiers and lived to tell about it, and the very thought of it was reckless and dangerous.

Who was this stranger, Red Wolf? Why had he gone along with Jeb on such a farfetched plan? He was certainly distinctive-looking and had a powerful bearing, but I had never heard the interpreter's name mentioned in all the time I'd been at Tovee's camp. When they traveled to the older Dog Soldier camp for their orders, I don't think any of the warriors had ever met Red Wolf.

If he had been at the other camp, I'm sure the Indian would have been great fodder for conversation. He was unusually tall for a Cheyenne and even eccentric with his booming voice and flowing, silver-streaked black hair. Almost like a chief, Red Wolf carried himself with complete confidence and authority. He seemed to feel any words from his mouth should be unquestioningly believed, and that he should be treated with the utmost respect and deference. Looking at the others, I could tell they were guardedly suspicious and thought Red Wolf was lying.

The two Dog Soldiers I feared most in camp were Coyote and Shaved Head. Wherever I went, their judgmental eyes followed me with hatred. Like badges of honor, their faces and muscular bodies were sliced with scars from hand-to-hand combat with the enemy, and their hostile emotions were always on the edge of violence, like bow strings pulled too taut. They were Tovee's rivals for leadership of this small band, and the three of them were continually in an unspoken competition to see who could claim the greatest number of white victims. I hoped Tovee was losing the contest.

The greatest number killed sometimes included unarmed women and children, but Tovee defended it by saying the white soldiers targeted women and children first, and the Indians' revenge was just. If one person did something despicably evil, I never could wrap my mind around the logic that it was acceptable for another person to do something equally evil in return. It also was beyond my understanding why entire groups were targeted for the color of their skin. So many innocents were being killed in the senseless war to possess land, and I kept praying a lasting peace would come someday for people of all colors.

As much as I wanted to daydream of peace, I needed to shake myself back to reality. The next twenty-four hours were critical for Red Wolf's plan to succeed. Over the past months, Coyote, Shaved Head, and Tovee all hoped one of the war chiefs at the larger Dog Soldier camp would recognize them for their bravery, and each one was vying for a position of prestige and honor. This competition, I believe, was the motivation for Coyote and Shaved Head to sneak behind Tovee's back to prove Red Wolf's story was false. It was obvious neither one liked Tovee's unmerited recognition of leadership from the compelling stranger.

It seemed peculiar when Coyote and Shaved Head huddled in secrecy behind a tree near the edge of the encampment. When they headed together to the small corral, which was simply an enclosure with a few ropes tied between the trees, I was sure something was up. Cautiously, I followed the warriors at a distance and saw them each saddle their horses, but head in opposite directions out of camp. What alarmed me most was the most vicious warrior, Coyote, was tracking Red Wolf's trail into our camp, and I knew it would inevitably lead him to the Arkansas River branch where Jeb was hiding.

In alarm, I rushed back to Tovee's tepee, hoping to figure out a way to talk to the stranger alone. As good fortune would have it, one of the camp women came running in to tell Tovee a knife fight had broken out between two of the women over one of the warriors. After excusing himself and telling me to be hospitable to the visitor, Tovee sprinted through the camp to break up the fight before there were injuries.

I jumped at my chance to speak, which I did in English. "Listen to me quickly, Red Wolf," I said forcefully. "The warrior, Coyote, with the long scar on his face, and the bald one, Shaved Head, with the scars all over his body, suspect you are a traitor. Shaved Head appears to be riding in the direction of the other Dog Soldier camp, probably to confirm your orders, and Coyote is following your trail from the Arkansas River branch to see if you're hiding something. I'm afraid he's going to find Jeb and kill him." I could feel panic surging through my body, and I was ready to spring into action.

The interpreter's face froze like a stone statue. As if he were used to dealing with critical decisions on a daily basis, he remained calm and unflappable. "That's not particularly good news. Jeb isn't trained to protect himself against a warrior like Coyote."

"What shall we do?" I pressed him. "Please, I want to help Jeb."

"There's nothing we can do, Mokee, but wait and let the events play out. If you want the truth, I don't believe Coyote will kill Jeb if he finds him, and there's always the possibility he won't find him." I looked dubiously at Red Wolf. "All right, then. Let's assume he does find him. What will happen? He'll be excited for sure as he'll think he's caught me in a lie. For that reason, he'll probably want to bring Jeb back alive as proof I'm up to no good.

"If Jeb is captured, let's talk about what you should do. You must not react at all, even if Coyote's beaten him to a pulp. If you react, he'll be killed on the spot. For my part, I'll simply act like I'm disinterested in the prisoner. If either of us were caught, Jeb and I have already agreed we would not give the other away.

"Obviously, if Jeb is captured, Tovee will be the only one to recognize him, and he'll think immediately I'm lying about my true mission and their raid tomorrow. The important thing is for you to convince Tovee by your actions you're not interested in Jeb anymore. It would be even better if you can show Tovee you find Jeb despicable.

"At the other camp, Shaved Head will find out my orders are not only legitimate, but directly from the war chiefs. The camp isn't far from here, though Jeb and I took a circuitous route to get here. Shaved Head should be back soon. The war chiefs won't be happy no one believed a courier they sent, so Shaved Head will have nothing to report except my truthfulness. I'll act insulted I wasn't believed, and I'll demand to speak to Tovee alone with the prisoner, which will confirm my orders were to see him directly.

"If Tovee consents to meeting me alone with the prisoner, then your job is of utmost importance. Not only do you need to persuade Tovee you despise Jeb and don't want to go back with him, you need to remind Tovee about Jeb saving both of your lives from the white soldiers after Sand Creek. Tell him it's only right he spares Jeb's life and protects him from his comrades.

"After you have played your part, I will play mine, something I do all the time, child. I want you to trust me. I will tell Tovee the truth. Jeb paid me extremely well to bring him along, but it is obvious you don't want to return with him. As I had orders to bring from the chiefs, I let Jeb come along for the money. Because I have completed my business of delivering the orders, I would like to be permitted to take the prisoner away with me and return him to his home. I will also remind Tovee since Jeb saved his life before, it would be wrong to kill him now.

"Hopefully, I will be allowed to leave immediately with Jeb. When the warriors go on their raid the next day, I want you to ride as fast as you can for one hour due north from here. Jeb and I will wait near a branch of the Arkansas River. From there, we will head north to your previous encampment and then east. Don't worry about the others finding us or even following you. Their mission will send them much further southwest toward the Santa Fe Trail, and we will be heading the opposite direction.

"All of this is based on Jeb's possible capture, which you seem to believe is going to happen. If Coyote comes back empty-handed, our plan remains the same. I will leave and join up with Jeb. You will leave due north after the warriors ride out of camp for their mission. Well?" Red Wolf finished his lengthy explanation and seemed pleased with the substitute plan he had so quickly developed.

My heart was thudding in my chest with worry for Jeb. "Who are you, Red Wolf, and why are you really here with Jeb?" I wasn't sure I trusted him either, but I had no alternative. The forceful man seemed too smooth and slick.

The Indian smiled at my directness. "It is true Jeb hired me to find you, and he does pay exceedingly well. But, my job is as an interpreter and scout for the white soldiers. When Jeb made it known he was in need of my services, I was temporarily stationed at Fort Riley."

"You said the war chiefs of the Dog Soldiers gave you orders to carry. If you work for the white soldiers, why would the Cheyenne chiefs give you orders?" I countered suspiciously, feeling there was something important I was missing.

Red Wolf chuckled. If I could have seen his thoughts, he was thinking I was as smart and outspoken as Jeb had told him. "No one knows this, and you must promise to keep this a secret, but I am an informer for the Cheyenne."

I gasped. "You spy on the white soldiers for the Indians?" He nodded, his black eyes twinkling at my shock. "You must not like white people very much. How do you get away with it?" He just smiled, not giving me an answer. "So, are you going to double-cross Jeb because he's white?" As I waited for the stranger's answer, I held my breath, not knowing if he would tell me the truth.

"The fact is, Mokee, I like Jeb a lot, so no, it's not my intention to betray him. My goal is to rescue you both. I'm glad you asked that question, though, as I'm going to have to put on a convincing performance and pretend I don't like either one of you very much. I especially need to act like I could care less what happens to Jeb. Will you trust me it's an act?"

"Do I have a choice?" I asked softly.

Just then, Tovee traipsed through the tepee flap. I quickly asked him in Cheyenne how the fight came out and who was involved, and I could see Red Wolf slightly nod at me that my words were a good cover. Then I murmured I would leave so Tovee could discuss business with his guest, and I would also bring back some food. As I walked through the hot, stagnant air of August, I could barely breathe. I realized the next few hours meant life or death for all of us, even Red Wolf.

Chapter Twenty

As I was serving Tovee and Red Wolf a simple lunch of stewed rabbit, I kept one ear listening for any disturbance outside. Enough time had passed for Coyote to have returned from the Arkansas River branch, especially if he had found Jeb and taken him hostage. Shaved Head would also be back shortly. I knew the entire plan, whether Jeb was captured or not, would soon be set into motion.

Silently, I kept praying for Jeb's safety. He was what mattered to me most. When the men had almost finished their meal, I heard sudden hoof beats and people yelling and cursing white people. I knew without a doubt only one thing could have caused such a commotion. Jeb had been captured.

As we followed Tovee outside, Red Wolf and I exchanged anxious glances. There was my Jeb, poor Jeb, half-naked on his knees. He was bound in tight, coarse ropes, and it looked as if he had been dragged back to camp. Coyote had used his face for a punching bag. It was covered with fresh blood and purplish bruises, and one of his eyes was already swollen shut. Looking like a torn map, Jeb's chest was also a mass of raised welts and dried blood.

I almost gagged. It took everything in my power not to cry out or rush to help the man I loved, someone who didn't deserve such inhumane treatment because of his skin color. Remembering Red Wolf's warning, I shuttered my emotions and stared at Jeb with apathy. His one eye flickered in recognition of me, but I quickly looked away.

"I thought you'd be interested in meeting Red Wolf's traveling companion, a white man," Coyote said proudly, spitting on Jeb as if using an exclamation point. I thought Coyote was the vilest warrior I had ever seen. If the mob of erratic young Dog Soldiers got out of control, I even feared for Red Wolf's safety. "What do you have to say for yourself, Red Wolf?" Coyote added with a sneer, acting as though he, not Tovee, was in charge.

As if the Lord stretched down His hand to answer my prayers, Shaved Head could suddenly be seen on the perimeter of the camp. He was riding swiftly toward us. As he got closer, I could hear him yelling, "No, wait. Stop. Red Wolf is telling the truth. He really is who he says he is." The slightly overweight, scarred warrior was out of breath. It appeared he had galloped the entire distance from the camp of the war chiefs.

As everyone turned their attention to Shaved Head, Jeb was forgotten. Coyote's proud stance suddenly deflated, and he looked disappointed at his failure to get one up on Tovee. Tovee, meanwhile, as if sensing the need to stabilize the situation, began to question Shaved Head as if he were the leader, not Coyote.

"So, you rode all the way to the other camp? And?"

"And, Red Wolf was given orders by the chiefs for us to attack a white man's settlement tomorrow. It's southwest from here," the bald warrior said quickly, knowing his information was important. "I have to tell you, the chiefs didn't like it we didn't trust their courier." In unison, all eyes shifted toward Coyote in blame, everyone knowing he was the instigator of the inquiry.

Instead of backing down, Coyote got a smirk on his face and asked harshly, "If Red Wolf is so trustworthy, then who the hell is this white man?" A few glances were exchanged among the bystanders. All of them realized it was a logical question.

All of a sudden, the commanding figure of Red Wolf stepped forward unafraid into the fray, and he stood proudly by Tovee. "As you have found out, my orders from the war chiefs for your next raid are legitimate, and my friendship with the chiefs goes back twenty years at least. Now, I have been directed to speak with Tovôhkeso alone regarding this mission and the prisoner, and I will answer to him alone. Bring the prisoner to his tepee at once," he bellowed at Coyote, even pointing his gnarled finger toward Tovee's tepee. I could tell Tovee was confused at seeing Jeb and even Red Wolf's connection with Jeb, but he remained pleased with Red Wolf's continued recognition of his authority.

As Tovee, Red Wolf, and I marched to the tepee, I was gathering my courage and praying with every step. Poor Jeb staggered along behind us. He was still tethered by Coyote and dragged from the clearing. Once the two were through the tepee flap, Coyote shoved Jeb's brutalized body to inflict even more pain. He skidded roughly across the ground, and it tore me apart inside to hear him groan. Tovee curtly dismissed Coyote, which the warrior didn't like, and all of us awkwardly sat in silence.

It was my time to act. "I can't believe Jeb followed me here," I said disgustedly in Cheyenne. "I'd like permission to tell him in English just what I think of his following me," I said vehemently to Tovee, giving him the impression I was really going to lambast the battered white man. Rarely seeing me so angry, Tovee nodded his approval to speak.

I marched forward in a rage. "Jeb," I yelled, needing to get his attention and knowing Tovee would recognize the word. Sweet Jeb looked up at me through the channels of dried blood on his face. I began my diatribe in English and began stalking back and forth in front of Jeb. "I'm going to yell at you now so someone in this room thinks I'm furious at you. But the fact is, I love you so much, you crazy man, and I forgive you for everything. I hope you forgive me for stupidly running off, and I'm going to do everything I can to escape with you and your friend tomorrow."

I paused and took a deep breath, throwing my hands on my hips in anger. I resumed my yelling. "Your friend is going to act like he hates you too, but he's going to do everything in his power to leave with you today and wait for me. Trust him, and you better be ready for kisses, because I'm going to kiss you like crazy and never let you go." I gritted my teeth. "And, now I'm going to spit on you, you wonderful, foolish man, because I think it's going to look damn good!" With the aim of a marksman, I spit at Jeb's face, and then I whirled around with my unbound hair flying in the air like a woman scorned. I stalked back to where Tovee was sitting and put my hand affectionately on his shoulder.

"Thank you for allowing me to speak, Tovee," I said heatedly in Cheyenne, my eyes still flashing with fire. I think my act was successful as Tovee looked at me in amusement. "You have no idea how good it felt to tell him all that." I huffed and puffed as I tried to settle myself down on the floor. As Red Wolf's face was expressionless and almost bored, it was impossible to read his mind. If I could have read it, I would have seen he was pretty impressed with my acting abilities and even said to himself, "Damn, girl!" Jeb kept looking at the floor dejectedly, doing his part of acting miserable at my pretended rejection.

Red Wolf spoke up after a moment of shocked silence. "I have given you all the information you need for your raid tomorrow, Tovôhkeso, and I will tell the chiefs you are someone they can count on. It is true I brought this white man here. I am a businessman, and he paid me handsomely. However, it is apparent the woman doesn't return his affection.

"When he hired me for the job, the white man told me he saved your life and the woman's from the white soldiers. In repayment of your debt to him, I think you should let me return him to his people unharmed, a soul for a soul." Red Wolf shrugged as if it didn't really matter to him. "As my business is done, I am prepared to leave with him immediately. I think it's wise if I go soon to avoid any more trouble in your camp."

Tovee looked like he was deliberating, but I think he was trying to trick me. "What do you think, Mokee?" he asked with a blank expression. He was probably thinking back to my arrival, and how I had never admitted my true feelings for Jeb. I had only said I hated being on the frontline of war. "Do you want me to kill Jeb or let him go?"

My entire world depended on Tovee believing my answer. I reached deep within and found more anger to bring to the surface. "Just because I'm angry at him for following me, he did save our lives, Tovee, and we do owe him that. I say we let him go back where he belongs." I looked at Jeb with disgust. I knew Tovee was watching me closely, trying to discover any chinks in my armor. I stared at Tovee, shuttering any emotions while I waited for his answer.

Finally, he said, "You may take him with you, Red Wolf, but I suggest you tell the white man, Jeb, if he ever returns here again, I will kill him myself."

Red Wolf nodded. "As you wish," he said with a bored sigh, dropping the subject off Jeb. "Do you have any more questions about tomorrow? The chiefs thought your surprise attack should happen in mid-morning. If you leave at daybreak, you should reach the white settlement by then. They also thought it should be a quick strike like the last one, with as much damage to any buildings as possible.

"Oh, there was one more thing. They suggested you lay a false trail by continuing southwest after the raid and curving around through the prairie to return here." Red Wolf suddenly stood up and yelled, "Jeb, get up. We're leaving." He yanked Jeb's tether roughly, which startled him, and then turned to Tovee. In a demanding voice, he said, "My horses, please."

"Mokee, go get the horses," Tovee ordered, and I nodded and left immediately. I hoped nothing would transpire when I was gone, so I hurried on my mission. Many curious eyes followed me as I crossed the camp with the horses. Within fifteen minutes, Red Wolf and Jeb rode slowly out of camp. Jeb was leaning weakly against his horse's mane, and the compelling interpreter was leading the horse by a long rope. Tovee called a quick meeting of the entire camp to announce he was satisfied with Red Wolf's explanation. He also said he allowed the scout to leave in peace with the white man. Excitedly, he told about Red Wolf's instructions and announced there would be a raid at daybreak, and the camp eagerly began making preparations.

Love is like war --
easy to begin but hard to end.

Chapter Twenty-one

The night before battle was always a time of intense preparation by the warriors, and they assembled their battle accoutrements as they planned to leave at dawn. They also equipped their horses for the morning as well and gathered any personal items needed from the traditional sashes of the Cheyenne's most fearless warriors to their breechclouts, war paint, and head feathers. The women, meanwhile, prepared a communal feast of proportions larger than usual to give their men a grand sendoff, and there was an evening of singing and storytelling, which ended at an early hour.

I was on my best behavior during the festivities, helping with the cooking and trying to act properly enthusiastic, yet not overdoing it as was my usual reticent way. I realized after Tovee and I got back to his tepee, I should have paid more attention to the lustful way he had been watching me. We had just entered the tepee flap when Tovee forcefully dragged me into his arms and kissed me like there was only tonight and no tomorrow, which was always the fatalistic mindset of a camp of violent warriors heading to war.

In my case, I was living for tomorrow and hopefully more tomorrows after that. My heart had been literally singing with joy in anticipation of seeing Jeb in the morning, but I knew my escape would still be dangerous. I needed to walk a very fine line, showing Tovee the necessary affection he expected on the night before battle and staying faithful to Jeb, the man I loved.

I should have expected tonight would be different. After all, I had unexpectedly rejected the man Tovee thought I loved right in front of him. He was convinced my actions meant I was ready to take the next step and make my commitment of love to him. With an iron grip, he pulled me down to his sleeping mat and continued his sensual assault, and I knew if I didn't take hold of the situation immediately, it was a lost cause.

"Tovee," I said with strength, trying to get his attention.

He sighed in frustration. "What is it, Mokee? Now is not the time. . ."

"It is the time," I interrupted, slightly pushing him away to look at his face. "I care for you deeply, Tovee. You know I do. But I cannot bring a child into the world of violence we're living in."

"I'll be careful. There are ways to prevent. . ."

"No, the other women told me it isn't true." I began to cry. I knew he hated tears, and the tears felt cleansing as they washed my face. "If I would be with child and you would go off to battle and die, I-I would be so afraid and alone. Please, Tovee. Don't do this to me. Accept I am here with you, and I'm giving you all I can, but I cannot give you more. I'm too afraid to become with child." My eyes pleaded with him for understanding.

With frustration and even anger, Tovee pushed off of me with his muscular arms. I could see he was annoyed by my refusal to make love and discouraged by my continued tacit rejection of the vagabond, unsettled life of a Dog Soldier. The other women seemed to accept it without complaint. "I'm going outside for a walk. Go to sleep." Heatedly, he marched out into the stagnant night air.

When Tovee returned much later, I pretended to be asleep, and he sank down beside me and scooped me into his arms to hold me while we slept. Briefly, I wondered if he had been with another woman, but then I realized it didn't matter to me anymore. My love for Tovee was gone, although I still had feelings for him and wanted him to remain safe. On that last night, I was filled with great sadness, and I listened to the steady, methodical beat of his heart until I fell asleep.

It wasn't only Tovee who was wrong to keep pursuing the senseless and violent war between the white men and the Indians. It was the white soldiers as well. While I drifted into an uneasy sleep, I prayed for God's mercy on Tovee. I had loved him once, and I felt great regret for what might have been in a world of peace.

Let a joy keep you.
Reach out your hands
and take it when it runs by.

Carl Sandburg

Chapter Twenty-two

The morning's light came quickly, and it was another hot, oppressive summer day. I accompanied the other women to the corral to see our men off to battle, and it was a fearsome sight to behold. The Dog Soldiers, fully armed, feathered, and masked with bright war paint, galloped away in a cloud of trail dust.

As I watched Tovee go for the last time, I swallowed a lump in my throat. He had been my first love, and I knew he was not a bad man, just misguided into thinking revenge would bring peace. His biggest mistake was he had surrounded himself with people who were filled with hatred. Without realizing it, he was becoming more like them every day.

Although I was polite to the other camp women, I had never been one to socialize, nor did they expect it. I slowly walked back to Tovee's tepee, pondering the best way to make my escape. I straightened the tepee and found the original pants and shirt I had worn when I had first traveled to the camp. I also found my boots. I slipped everything into a parfleche along with some buffalo jerky of Tovee's.

With a hammering heart, I untied the braided elk skin necklace Tovee made for me long ago. I laid it gently on his sleeping mat, hoping he would understand it was my way of saying good-bye. I had no idea how he would interpret my leaving, or whether he would be angry and seek revenge on me or Jeb. As the English poet Lord Byron once said, "Hatred is the madness of the heart," and I knew Tovee was suffering from that madness toward all white people. I hoped he would accept I left because I hated war, not him. I wished there had been a way to let him know I loved him once, but perhaps some things were better left unsaid.

There was a spare bow and quiver of arrows in the tepee. If anyone asked, I prepared an explanation about taking my horse and going hunting near the camp. I made my way to the corral by a path skirting the border of the campsite, but it really wasn't necessary to hide my actions. Most of the women had already gone back to their tepees to wait for the men, and the corral was unguarded. Many of the horses were gone for the day, and I easily saddled the mare Tovee had brought to Jeb's. She seemed more than able to make the long journey ahead. It was barely an hour after daybreak when I made my way north from camp toward the distant tree line.

I never looked back.

Although it was already sweltering, I rode as fast as I could. I hoped I didn't wear out my horse for the long journey later on, but I was anxious to get to safety before someone spotted me. It took me about an hour and fifteen minutes to reach the banks of a large ribbon of water, which was part of the Arkansas River. Being a member of a constantly moving Cheyenne band was a great advantage. I had grown used to changing campsites frequently and paying attention to landmarks. With a good sense of direction, I quickly found the designated spot for our rendezvous.

The only problem was it appeared to be empty. Unless they ran into difficulties, Red Wolf and Jeb would have to be hiding close by. I suddenly wished I had the ability to do a bird call like some of the warriors. Instead, I asked myself where I would hide, and the answer came to me quickly. The best place to find cover would be under the fallen trees on the arid, cracked riverbed of the shrunken river.

After tying my mare to a sheltered bush, I crept to the grassy rim overlooking the drought-stricken stream of water, and I sprawled on my stomach, looking in every direction for any movement. There was nothing, not even a breeze! I was suddenly growing apprehensive. Could they have gone on without me, or had something happened to them?

All of a sudden, I heard a twig break behind me. A low, masculine voice spoke in English, "Well, what's a pretty little thing like you doing here all by yourself?"

I spun around, my heart in my throat, thinking I would have to defend myself from an attacker. Instead, my eyes beheld the most beautiful sight I'd ever seen in my entire life. It was Jeb standing sturdy and tall and handsome in the scattered rays of sunlight streaming through the leafy trees. His face was still bruised and purple, but the dried blood had been washed away. A huge crooked smile made his face glow, and he held out his arms in welcome.

Without any uncertainty, I leaped up from the ground and raced across the space separating us, diving into Jeb's arms and encircling his waist with my legs. Unable to help myself, I shrieked with joy and kissed him over and over again, covering his lips and cheeks, and even his eyebrows and eyelids. My heart sang with the words of John Keats, "Beauty is truth, truth beauty, that is all ye know on earth, and all ye need to know." I was blessed in the most beautiful moment of my life to know the truth and beauty of Jeb's soul.

"Mokee, Mokee, you are so brave and so wonderful. I don't deserve you, but I love you so much," Jeb managed to say in between my crazed kisses and flowing tears. I couldn't get enough of the touch and feel of him. It was a miracle he was alive and had rescued me. *Thank you, Lord, thank you, Lord,* I kept saying in my mind.

"Jeb, I'm so sorry. . .," I managed to say out loud between my silent prayers and gasping breaths. I took a deep breath to calm down.

"No, don't say it. Never say that. If anyone should be blamed for your leaving, it was me," Jeb said softly, wiping my sudden tears with his fingertips. His eyes gazed into my face with love and wonder. This long-awaited moment was real, and we were together again and alive. "Because I wanted to think he'd changed, I didn't understand what Benjamin was trying to do. I was a fool. But, I promise you this, Mokee. I will spend the rest of my life making it up to you and showing you how much I love you, if you let me. Even though I'm one of those blasted white men you lambasted in your journal, will you marry me, Mokee?"

I nodded happily through my tears, my joy so great it was pulsating inside my chest and threatening to burst it. "Jeb, I'd marry you if you were a blasted purple man," I whispered. My lips sank onto his with emotion. Jeb's kisses equaled mine with hunger and passion, and I realized I never wanted this beautiful moment of reunion to end. I was home.

All of a sudden, a low, male voice cleared its throat grouchily. Having totally forgotten about Red Wolf, Jeb and I both guiltily spun around to see the formidable Indian guide grinning broadly, but growing impatient. After untangling myself from Jeb's arms, I rushed over to the massive Indian and threw myself into his surprised arms. I gave him a gigantic hug, and I kissed his chiseled cheek. "Thank you for giving me my life back," I said meaningfully, referring to his bringing me Jeb and keeping him safe. The tears of joy were still washing down my face, and I looked at the interpreter through new eyes of respect.

"You're welcome," he said in his low voice, and I could tell he meant it. I wasn't sure, but I thought his eyes had grown a little moist. All at once, he was all business, shoving his emotionalism aside. "I hate to break up this lovey-dovey party, but we've got a very long ride ahead of us. Did you bring any clothes that don't make you look like an Indian?" he asked brusquely.

"I have old pants, boots, and a flannel shirt, but I think the shirt's too hot," I answered quickly. Red Wolf nodded and retraced his steps around a barrier of bushes. He led his enormous black stallion forward. Going into his saddlebag, he found a small, short sleeve shirt he had anticipated I would need. "Go put the pants, boots, and shirt on and wear your hair straight, no braids. Hurry up," he demanded irascibly. While I changed behind a bush, Jeb retrieved both his horse and mine and when I returned, we quickly mounted.

"I've decided we're going to ride to one of my home bases, Fort Larned, which is northeast of here," Red Wolf announced efficiently. He always had a plan, and I was growing to trust him implicitly. "The raiding party was sent in the opposite direction to the Santa Fe Trail, so there's no danger of running into them again. However, I do think it's important we cover our tracks immediately. Since the Arkansas River is so low this time of year, I thought we'd ride in the water as far as we can. It'll be slow going, but I think it's the safest thing to do. We'll spend the night at the fort. In the morning when we're refreshed, we'll head north to the Salina area, and I'll head back to Fort Riley. Are there any questions?"

Red Wolf looked at each of us authoritatively, and we nodded our agreement with his well-thought out plan. His stallion also appeared to be in accord as he was already prancing in a circle, ready to go.

Chapter Twenty-three

When America was expanding westward in the 1800s, the Kansas plains had many United States Army forts. Some only survived a short time, but eight played major role. The more important forts included Leavenworth, Scott, Riley, Harker, Larned, Hays, Dodge, and Wallace, although some had name changes in their early years.

Contrary to common thought, forts were not built like fortresses to protect the army from warring Indians. Instead, the main reason for constructing forts in the first place was to keep peace among the different tribes and to prevent encroachment on native lands. When the Santa Fe Trail opened in the 1820s, the expansion of trade was opposed by many tribes, and the forts added a new purpose of protecting commerce along the trail. Some forts also served as Indian agencies and distribution points for annuities given to peaceful tribes in treaties.

The growth of the United States was a pattern of continued expansionism and moving Indian tribes further west off of their traditional lands. The number of emigrants increased with the Pike's Peak Gold Rush and Kansas opening for settlement in 1854. New trails also began being used for mail and stage routes, and railroad construction took place through former tribal lands. With more settlers, buffalo herds began to be slaughtered. All of these combined factors were perceived by the Indians as a threat to their way of life.

In 1863, Congress authorized President Lincoln to move forward with the extinction of all Indian land titles in Kansas and to move the displaced Indians to lands designated as Indian territory, which was located south of their traditional lands in the Oklahoma territory. As the government increasingly failed to uphold the original lands granted to the Indians in earlier treaties, the Indian tribes grew hostile. A period of Indian Wars broke out in Kansas from 1867 to 1869, and all of the eight Kansas forts became military supply depots and headquarters for the troops during this period.

All mankind love a lover.

Ralph Waldo Emerson

Chapter Twenty-four

I was surprised how established Fort Larned was. The three of us arrived at the military facility well before dark, and we were escorted into the compound by a captain, who was a friend of Red Wolf. Several other officers shouted out their greetings to the Indian as we passed by. I'd never seen anyone so well-known or respected as the imposing Indian. Not wanting to be in the way and needing to get the kinks out of our legs, Jeb and I left the others and strolled hand in hand toward a quadrangular parade ground.

Red Wolf went inside the officers' quarters to announce our arrival and make arrangements for the night, and we had no idea what reason he made up for Jeb and I being with him. In addition to the officers' quarters, Jeb and I saw an expanse of buildings on our walk including a hospital, a combination storehouse and barracks, a bakery, a guardhouse, soldiers' quarters, blacksmith, carpenter, and saddler shops, a meat house, and two laundresses' quarters.

Most of the structures were made of crumbling adobe, though the soldiers' quarters and the bakery were dug into the riverbank. When Red Wolf rejoined us and saw our interest in the buildings, he said Congress had appropriated money to rebuild most of the fort with stone and timber buildings, which would better stand the threat of a large-scale Indian war. We noticed some of the new construction had already begun. He also said many of the original buildings weren't constructed very well, and there was plenty of vermin infestation in all of the buildings.

Red Wolf was continually surprising us with his connections and expertise in dealing with the military. He had arranged for rooms and asked if I would like to freshen up before dinner. I nodded and followed one of the officers, and I heard Red Wolf say he wanted to talk with Jeb. My room was tiny, but clean, with a narrow, rustic wood bed and a small dresser with a pitcher of water, a large bowl, and a few towels. After the grueling ride in the summer sun, it felt wonderful to wash the grime off my face and body. I even rested momentarily on the bed, waiting for Jeb to get me for dinner.

When I heard a knock, I rushed to the door and eagerly flung it open. It was Jeb, and he was smiling happily. He softly closed the door behind him and then eagerly pulled me into his arms. Although he was weary from the ride and still in pain from his beating, his kisses were enthusiastic and hungry, but sweet and growing so familiar. His kisses meant I was home. He pulled back to look at me searchingly with his gentle blue eyes.

"I have something to ask you, sweet Mokee," he said with a secretive smile.

I was puzzled by his excitement. "What is it, Jeb?" I asked curiously.

"Remember how you said you'd marry me," he began to explain quietly, his eyes continuing to look lovingly, but questioningly into mine. "I know you won't be seventeen for four more months, but life is so uncertain as we're both finding out," he continued, not exactly making sense.

He exhaled and tried again. "You know how Red Wolf is a master at organizing things. Oh hell, let me just say it, Mokee. I love you, and I want to marry you. . . now. Is it too soon for you? Red Wolf says there's a chaplain here who can marry us. Do you want to get married tonight?" Jeb was so nervous his forehead had started to break out in beads of perspiration.

I couldn't help but smile impishly at dear, sweet, vulnerable Jeb. Did he actually think I would turn him down? He was my life. I loved him so much, and my heart had not only forgiven him for our misunderstanding, but I had also forgiven myself. Where would I ever find another man who would bravely go into a Dog Soldier camp to get me back?

"Of course, I'll marry you tonight," I said after a moment of suspense, reaching up and kissing his cheek. He sighed with relief. "I can pretend to be seventeen, and I can even be Hannah Smith from Boston again if you want."

Jeb chuckled, remembering our deception in Junction City and even at his mother's funeral. "I actually think that's not a bad idea, Mokee, as we don't want any questions from the soldiers about where we've all been. I'll tell Red Wolf about your new identity." He smiled contentedly. "I know this is sudden, but I can take some time off from the farm, and we can go on a honeymoon later," he said.

"I'm not sure I know that word," I answered, thinking about the strange combination word. "I know bears eat honey. Will we eat honey and look at the moon?" I was thinking white people had strange traditions.

Jeb started laughing so hard he almost cried. If I could have read his thoughts, he was thinking he never wanted anything so much as to marry his Indian princess. . . me. He pulled me to him and kissed me thoroughly, barely letting me up for air, which I admit I didn't mind at all. Who needed air anyway? Reluctantly, he moved back from me.

"I was told to tell you there are some fresh clothes you can wear in the dresser. It doesn't matter to me if you change. I think you look beautiful in your pants and shirt. But, see if you like anything, and meet me in the main room in about fifteen minutes. Red Wolf has taken charge of everything, so I need to get cleaned up too." Jeb left the room shaking his head and smiling, still thinking about eating honey under the moon.

I was surprised to find a lovely white silk blouse and a long black skirt in one of the drawers, both in a small size that would fit me. There was also a pair of slip-on black shoes, which were a good fit, and I even found a brush and comb set. Within minutes, I was ready, though I wished I could have washed my hair with Catherine's berry shampoo. I eagerly left the room, ready to face my future and feeling very blessed I even had a future to face.

In the main lounge of the officers' quarters, a small group of soldiers in uniform waited for us. Red Wolf came over and surprised the soldiers by giving me a kiss on the cheek. He whispered in my ear, "You look lovely, Hannah."

With love in my eyes, I smiled mischievously at the impressive Indian. "Thank you for everything," I said with sincerity. Jeb came over and comfortably put his arm around my shoulder, telling me softly I never looked more beautiful. He also was wearing a white shirt and black slacks and in my eyes, there was not a more handsome man. The chaplain came over, and Red Wolf introduced us all, with my name being Hannah Smith. As there were no women at the fort, one of the soldiers stepped forward to be a witness. I guess if there had been a woman present, she would have been a maiden of honor. Jeb had asked Red Wolf to be our best man, although a few of the soldiers looked a little surprised at our choice.

"Oh, I almost forgot something," Red Wolf said gruffly, walking to a table in the corner. He brought back a bouquet of wild daisies he had picked earlier. "Every bride needs a bouquet," he said in a husky voice, handing me the flowers. If clay-baked skin could have blushed, I could have sworn he turned a deeper shade of red. I was starting to think Red Wolf, under his steely composure and bluster, was an old softy.

As if it were a misty dream, the beautiful candlelight ceremony went by with promises to cherish one another and kisses. Jeb whispered he had Catherine's engagement and wedding rings at home for me, and I realized I would be going with Jeb, my brave, precious husband, to our home. I could feel the glow of Catherine's approving smile, and I prayed a silent prayer of thankfulness for the night God led a frightened little Indian girl to the safety and love of Jeb and Catherine's home. God does love all of his people, I said to myself in benediction.

It wasn't often joyous occasions happened at forts in the middle of Indian country. So it pleased the officers to have a simple wedding reception with ham, potatoes, and corn on the cob, where we had to nibble our way across an ear of corn. Because I was so messy, I probably embarrassed Jeb, but he didn't seem to mind as he was also pretty messy.

One of the officers, Lieutenant Joe Phillips, got out a little metal instrument he put to his lips, and he blew through the air holes and made music. It was called a harmonica. The men liked to sing, and they wistfully sang songs about the Civil War, one of which was *When Johnny Comes Marching Home*.

As I sat there with my hand in Jeb's strong, calloused hand and I listened to the sometimes melancholic music about war, I realized all men missed the love of their families. In their hearts, all men wanted peace, even these white soldiers. The problem seemed to be no one could find the narrow path leading to understanding.

Instead, it was as though the hotheaded emotions of men, both white and red, caused them to fanatically jump into a raging river of revenge and to let the current mindlessly sweep them along. None of them could hear the small, steady voice of God over the roar of the river as He beckoned them to swim against the current and find His path of peace. Imagine what would happen if everyone joined hands in the river and stood their ground, refusing to be swept away by the misguided emotions of hatred any longer. Maybe all it would take would be the bravery of a few to speak up for what was right.

"Do you want to go upstairs?" Jeb asked quietly as the hour was getting late. His question startled me out of my deep thoughts. I had spent my entire life searching for the path of peace, and tonight was no different. My lifelong quest still eluded me, but I could feel the answer was getting closer. I nodded to Jeb I was ready, and we went around the room together thanking each of the soldiers, and especially Red Wolf, for the beautiful ceremony and reception.

After setting the oil lamp on the dresser and quietly shutting the door to the small bedroom I had used before, Jeb held his arms open for me, and I happily flew into them. His lips met mine with strength and love and surprisingly, vulnerability, and I realized Jeb's kisses reflected the many dimensions of who Jeb really was. I was humbled God had blessed me with the love of this kind and honorable man, who loved me for myself and was colorblind when it came to a person's worth.

With heated kisses, we toppled on the bed, and my heart was filled with joy. Jeb and I were together at last. Who could ever find as brave a husband? He had risked his life to travel across Kansas to rescue me. I had never felt so much love, and time seemed to crystallize and hold this one moment in perfect stillness. Although he didn't say it, I could tell Jeb was both pleased and surprised I had never been with Tovee. It brought me great joy to bring the gift of myself to Jeb alone as it was the only gift I had to give.

Maybe love was the harbinger of peace and the true path, I said to myself in a moment of illumination as I later dozed off in my new husband's arms.

Chapter Twenty-five

We heard an insistent rapping at the door and then a deep voice saying, "Rise and shine Jeb, Hannah." I groaned, being absolutely contented where I was in Jeb's protective arms. I looked at him sideways through my disheveled hair. Who could have dreamed of a night so perfect and filled with love? Jeb smiled in his endearing way and kissed me through the mass of thick, black hair sweeping over my face.

"The boss speaks," he complained, his eyes shining with love.

"I know," I grimaced selfishly. "It just seems like I waited so long for last night."

"Me too, sweetheart," he said softly. "There were times I thought last night would never even happen."

Although we wanted to stay where we were, both of us knew it was important to leave the area as soon as possible. Tovee would soon realize he had been deceived. Although I didn't want to share it with Jeb, I was worried about Tovee's reaction to my leaving him. His entire demeanor had drastically changed over the past year, and his emotions were unstable and explosive. I hoped I would have the opportunity to speak with Red Wolf privately about my worries. If Tovee sought revenge, I feared not only for my life, but for Jeb's as well. I also thought Tovee might someday seek retaliation on Red Wolf for instigating the plan.

Reluctantly, Jeb and I dressed in our old sweaty traveling clothes, and we met Red Wolf in the main room for a fast breakfast. After our quick good-byes and expressions of thanks, we once again began the demanding ride across the hot, flat prairie to the north central part of the state. Good fortune was with us as the skies were overcast, and the gray, smooth clouds kept the temperatures slightly cooler than the previous day. It was still unbearably humid, however, and the sweat rolled in beads off of my body.

As we rode across the monotonously horizontal grasslands, there were two things I thought about, well maybe three things. The first thing was the likelihood of a late afternoon thunderstorm. Menacing black clouds were steadily rolling in from the distant west, and I hoped we would be home before the storm struck. Second, I thought of the wonderful bathtub at Jeb's house, now my house once more. I wondered if Jeb would allow me the luxury of having a relaxing bath tonight. I wanted to soak away the painful memories of the past few months, when I thought everything I treasured was lost.

My third thought, which was more of an afterthought, was of Jeb himself. Although Indian men prided themselves in their prowess as warriors and according to the other women, lovers, Jeb was a warrior in his own way. I smiled secretly, indulging in a few of my more vivid memories from the past night, wondering if tonight would be the same.

We finally reached the banks of the Smoky Hill River and took a brief respite to water our horses. Still recovering from his beating, Jeb collapsed under the abundant shade of an elm tree for a quick nap, and I nodded at Red Wolf hoping he would take my hint and walk with me a ways. When we were out of hearing distance, I poured out my fears about Tovee's vengeance. I asked the Indian if he remembered the elk skin necklace I wore around my neck at Tovee's camp. When he said he did, I told him Tovee had made it for me long ago, and I had placed it on his sleeping mat as a way to say good-bye. Bluntly, I asked Red Wolf if he thought Tovee would come after Jeb, or even me, in a jealous rage. I explained Tovee felt I was his possession.

Red Wolf couldn't hide the brief flicker of alarm in his eyes. Then his eyes glazed over in an undecipherable, blank expression. Attempting to be reassuring, he told me he would report a specific threat in the area near the farmhouse and have soldiers regularly patrol there in the future. I knew in my heart Tovee wouldn't be deterred by the presence of a few soldiers. He would simply kill them.

When Red Wolf saw my doubting look, he put his massive arm around my shoulder in a fatherly way. He said perhaps I should convince Jeb to spend the month of September in the city of Topeka for a belated honeymoon. Red Wolf also said Jeb was able to take time off now as he had hired someone to help with the farm. The trip would safely keep us out of the area for a while, he added, and surely Tovee would give up with our continued absence.

I didn't know if I believed his assumption about Tovee ever giving up, but the thought of going to a city named Topeka intrigued me. For Red Wolf to have even heard about it, Topeka must have been a wild and rugged city with a lot of bears eating honey.

Topeka wasn't particularly wild or rugged, nor did bears run through the streets with their pots of honey. Jeb finally let me in on the joke about the honey in the honeymoon, and I was finding him to be a very ornery, fun-loving, and incredibly lovable husband. My life was overflowing with joy as I complied with Red Wolf's advice. After traveling about a hundred miles east by stagecoach, Jeb and I spent an entire month in the growing city of Topeka.

Topeka was chartered as a city in 1857, and its name was an Indian name of the Kansa and Ioway tribes meaning "to dig good potatoes," the potatoes being prairie potatoes, not the kind of potatoes Jeb grew on his farm. As an addition to the Oregon Trail in the early 1850s, there was also a new military road, sometimes called the Fort to Fort Road, going from Fort Leavenworth through Topeka and then on to Fort Riley, making Topeka more easily accessible.

The first mayor of Topeka was also the founder of the Atchison, Topeka & Santa Fe Railroad. Jeb was interested in finding out when the railroad tracks would be completed as far as Junction City and also Salina, and he had meetings with the owners of several railroads, including the Union Pacific, to hear their plans. I know Jeb was hopeful of expanding his wheat farming business the next year, especially if he could find a way to transport the wheat to eastern cities by rail.

When we were exploring Topeka, he also looked into the possibility of using steamboats to transport wheat. There were many steamboats on the Kansas River, which flowed through the city, and the steamboats brought lumber, meat, and flour and left for eastern cities with corn and wheat. When Jeb and I were walking around the well-appointed city and shopping in little specialty stores or dining in restaurants, Jeb shared his dreams for his farm with me, or as he called it, our farm. I was shocked how much land a thousand acres really was. It was an area big enough to house several bands of Indians. Because of the lack of transportation to the markets, however, he was currently only farming a small portion of it.

Jeb also surprised me by taking Catherine's engagement and wedding rings out of his breast pocket and taking me to what was called a jewelry store, which was filled with nothing but necklaces, rings, broaches, money clips, pocket watches, and something called cufflinks, which fastened sleeves shut. There was even an apparatus called an assaying scale on the counter, and the jeweler weighed pieces of gold for prospectors returning from the gold fields.

Catherine's engagement ring was unusually beautiful with an oval, milky-colored opal, which was surrounded entirely by diamonds. The matching wedding ring was a plain band of white gold, and the jeweler said he could have both rings sized within a week, which I found meant making them smaller to fit my tiny ring finger. Jewelry is unimportant to me, but because Jeb's face was shining with such happiness at giving me his mother's rings, I acted joyful also.

The 1860s saw Topeka become a commercial hub with many Victorian era luxuries. Victorian era, Jeb explained, referred to Queen Victoria of the country of England, which was across the ocean, and the prosperity her land was experiencing under her rule. After Kansas became a state in 1861, Topeka was eventually named the state capital, and a state capitol building began being constructed in 1866. Though a drought in 1860 and the Civil War slowed the growth of Topeka, the year of 1865 saw a return to prosperity and a doubling of the population.

I was amazed at all there was to see and do, and every day we spent time walking around the city and enjoying what it had to offer. This was only the second city I had visited, and I was overwhelmed at its size. There was a sawmill, a number of different kinds of stores, three hotels, a blacksmith shop, a tin ware factory, a brickyard, a post office, several new bridges, multiple schoolhouses, a college, sidewalks, three churches, business blocks with offices, single family dwellings, and a meeting center called Constitution Hall.

Jeb purchased several newspapers to read and even told me about a literary society in the city. There was also a fort on the waterfront and a ferryboat to cross the wide Kansas River. Stagecoaches ran regularly to Atchison, Kansas City, and one which we took to and from Junction City. In January of 1866, the Union Pacific Railroad had reached Topeka. Jeb found out it was in the process of laying tracks westward through Fort Riley, Junction City, Abilene, and eventually Salina.

As I walked the streets of Topeka with my new husband, the thing I thought about most, besides my deep love for Jeb, was how misinformed the Cheyenne were about the strength and numbers of the endless mass of white people coming west. The Indians mistakenly believed if they killed a few settlers, the white people would be discouraged and quit coming west. They had no idea how vast a nation the United States was becoming, filled with countless emigrants from all over the world and booming with new technology and industrialization. As I saw Topeka, one truth filled my mind. The white people were unstoppable.

As I walked hand in hand with Jeb, I also thought of the miracle of being rescued from the violent life of a roving band of Dog Soldiers and to be suddenly and unexpectedly blessed with a time of love and peace. *Why? Why did God rescue me when countless others were trapped in war and violence? What could His purpose be for my life?*

Chapter Twenty-six

As I would think all honeymoons are with two people in love, my honeymoon had been perfect and blissful. It felt good, however, to finally settle in the familiar, welcoming rooms of Jeb's farmhouse in October. For most of 1866, life had been painful for me, starting with Catherine's illness and death, then Benjamin's assault and Jeb's anger, and finally my biggest mistake, running away with Tovee. Although I had been trapped with his roaming band of Dog Soldiers since the middle of April, I discovered something important about adversity. First, no matter where I was, Christ was always with me and ready to help. And second, Christians are not exempt from difficulties and hardships.

Toward the end of August, I also discovered another truth during my brave rescue by Jeb and Red Wolf. Miracles do happen, and nothing is impossible for God. He does answer prayers. It barely seemed I blinked after my rescue than I found myself married to the most wonderful of men. Then I was blessed again to be tucked away in Topeka for all of September, getting to know my new husband and gaining a better understanding of the white people's culture.

Reality was here again, and I had to face my fears whether Tovee would seek vengeance on me for leaving him. It was so easy to fall back into the easy routine of living at the farmhouse. I loved it, and I felt like I never left. Instead of sleeping in the little bedroom that had once been his sister's, this time I shared a beautiful, wood paneled bedroom with Jeb. There was still a great sadness for me missing Catherine, but I felt her spirit blessing my marriage to her son, and it would have to be enough.

Jeb and I resumed our old, comfortable habits of rising at daybreak. Before Jeb went to work with his new farmhand, Donny Webster, I always cooked him a huge breakfast of eggs, potatoes, ham, and biscuits. I liked Donny a lot as he was very mannerly and even a little shy.

On the first morning after Jeb left for the fields, I moved my clothes, so beautifully sewn by Catherine, into Jeb's bedroom. He had thoughtfully made room for my things in his large closet and rustic wood dresser. On other mornings, I tried to be disciplined by writing in my journal for at least an hour before heading back to the kitchen. Both Jeb and Donny usually came for lunch at about noon, and they were both tired and starving. I usually had a huge pot of soup or stew simmering on the stove to tide them over until dinnertime.

During the afternoons, I would do any work needing to be done at the farmhouse from laundry or mending to cleaning. Then I got dinner started. Jeb always came alone for dinner. Donny still lived at his parents' house nearby and ate his breakfast and dinner with them.

Conversation at dinner was always animated, and Jeb tried to share everything about his day, especially funny things. He always asked about my day as well. Because he didn't want me to be bored around the house, he said he'd love it if I joined him in the fields some days, just to sit and watch or write in my journal.

My favorite time of day was always after dinner as Jeb and I sat in the living room, just as we used to do in the evenings with Catherine. Jeb loved to read books on history and military campaigns, and he also subscribed to several newspapers. It was important for me to keep track of where Indian raids were taking place, but I also loved to read literature, poetry, and the Bible. Both of us would settle against each other on the wide leather sofa, reading and sharing what we read, and sometimes kissing which inevitably led us upstairs. Life was very good and very peaceful. It seemed war was no longer my shadow.

It became early November, and the harvest was almost done for another year. Jeb was preoccupied, however, making big plans for next year's planting and harvest. When we were in Topeka, he had secured promises from the railroad executives of the Union Pacific Railroad. The tracks would be laid at least as far as Junction City and possibly even Abilene and Salina by the end of next summer. Not only was Jeb intending to develop half of his thousand acres and plant additional wheat, but he hired two more permanent workers and made Donny Webster his foreman-in-charge.

For many years, Jeb had used an old Buffalo-Pitts thresher his father had purchased for his one-man operation. Basically, the thresher was an endless belt studded with pins, and it threshed and cleaned the wheat grain. The machine had advantages for a small farming operation. It was efficient, inexpensive, and small like the size of an upright piano. It also used a team of horses to drive a shaft, which was attached to the gears.

Because Jeb had decided to expand his wheat and corn production with the coming railroad, he purchased a combine harvester, which was going to be delivered in the spring. A combine harvester merged three separate operations of reaping, threshing, and winnowing into one single operation. Wheat and corn weren't the only crops which could be harvested with a combine. If he decided to expand his production to other crops, Jeb would also be able to use the harvester on oats, rye, barley, soybeans, or flax. Excited about his new equipment, Jeb went into town one morning in early November to check on the expected delivery date and to purchase a few supplies for the upcoming winter.

I had a leisurely morning, and I decided to dress a little nicer than usual for Jeb and even fix my hair. When I was looking for Catherine's pearl-handled hairbrush, I remembered I had last brushed my hair in the little bedroom, which had been her daughter Margaret's. When I entered the tiny room, the hair stood up on my arms like I'd seen a ghost, and I immediately felt a wave of anxiety rush over me.

It was then my eyes focused on the white lace-trimmed bedspread. Conspicuously, right in the middle of it, was a bouquet of gruesome dead flowers. The jagged stems had been deliberately sawed in half, and blackened leaves and petals were methodically strewn all over the bedspread. How they'd gotten there was a mystery. When I brushed my hair the day before, the flowers had not been there. Because I didn't want to jar the flowers, I sat down near the pillow. I was shaking with fear. Who could have played this nasty joke, if it could even be called a joke?

Only two people would do something so disgusting. One was Benjamin, who had vanished after Jeb banned him from the house after I ran away. Jeb eventually revealed his brother had been in jail, and he had beaten him up before he disowned him. I always knew Benjamin was vengeful, and it was obvious he blamed me for the loss of his inheritance. So, dead flowers might be his gift.

Shuddering, I decided Tovee was a more likely suspect. His roving band of Dog Soldiers could be in the area for the winter, and I knew he viewed my running away as a betrayal of the unspoken promise between us. His gift of dead flowers would be to torment me and show his anger. It could also be a threat, a visual warning hinting Jeb and I might soon be as dead as the flowers.

If it were Tovee, what would alarm me most was the ease with which he got in and out of the house. It seemed logical he would place the flowers on the bed I used to sleep in. He had no way of knowing I was married now and had changed bedrooms.

All of a sudden, I heard a slight scraping sound in the closet, and my eyes spun to the wooden door, which was ajar about an inch. My heart pounded in my chest with panic. I realized too late I should have run from the room when I had seen something was wrong. At the very least, I should have screamed. Instead, I sat frozen like an ice statue near the pillow, my voice not working and my eyes getting wider as the closet door edged opened. The dark eyes within the closet met mine with vehemence, and the door suddenly crashed open against the dresser. It was Tovee, and he was enraged.

"Well, look who's here," he sneered, taking a muscular arm and callously sweeping the dead flowers off the bedspread onto the hardwood floor. The brittle petals broke in tiny pieces, making a huge mess. "Did you like my gift of flowers?" he asked with a malicious innocence. "You should know I liked your gift. I especially like how you honored your promise to be with me."

All at once, he thoughtfully fingered the elk skin necklace he wore around his neck. There was no mistaking it was mine. I still hadn't found my voice as I was so frightened, and my silence seemed to make him even madder. He seemed deranged as his eyes were fluidly shifting from thing to thing in the room.

Suddenly, he took out his hunting knife, and he began flipping the blade into the air with ease and catching it by the handle. "Scared, Mokee?" he asked nonchalantly, still tossing the knife like he was thinking of using it on me. "Do you want to know how many white people I've scalped with this knife, or how many I've killed?" He laughed out loud. "It's too bad the white man, Jeb, isn't here. I'd like to cut his heart out and give it to you." He snickered like he'd made a joke. "He deserves it for stealing you away to live here. But, I guess I'll have to wait for another time to kill Jeb. I saw him go into town."

His threats about Jeb jolted me into reality, and I jumped defensively to my feet. "You leave Jeb out of this. I left you because I had to, Tovee. If you had taken me to a different camp, I was willing to stay with you. After Sand Creek, you of all people know how I hate war and killing. I couldn't live my life on the warfront any longer." My voice caught as I tried to soothe his hurt feelings. "Please understand, Tovee. I didn't want to hurt you. I still have feelings for you. I-I just couldn't live with all the violence. If we had returned to the peaceful band of our parents, things might have turned out differently."

All at once, Tovee hurled his knife angrily into the wall. It slammed into the wood and vibrated wildly, nearly breaking in two. In almost the same motion, he brutally yanked my forearm and spun me into his powerful arms. "I can't believe you're Cheyenne," he growled like a rabid dog, holding me in a hurtful vise. "Here I am, killing the white man to help the Cheyenne people."

"If you're killing, you're doing it for yourself, Tovee. It's not going to help our people, can't you understand? It's only going to make more of them be slaughtered like at Sand Creek," I interrupted loudly, trying to plead with him to listen to reason.

My words enraged him even further, providing him the excuse he needed to do what he had been intending to do all along. Viciously, he flung me on the bed and threw his muscular body on top of mine, lashing out at me with vile, punishing kisses. I struggled against him, flinging my head one way and then the other, but it was useless. His body had become unbelievably strong in the past year. All at once, he grabbed my hair painfully at the scalp, rendering my head immobile on the bedspread. I could feel my eyes smart with pain. With the look of an animal contemplating its prey, he pulled his head back from mine and tilted it from side to side.

"You can make this hard, or you can make this easy, Mokee," he said in a hiss like a venomous snake. "I'm only here to take what's mine. And you're mine. You lied to me and deceived me, and you deserve to pay. You know what I've come for, and I'm going to take what's mine one way or the other. I don't really want to hurt you, but if you fight me, I will. I'm into hurting people, remember? That's what you always thought of me. Kiss me back, Mokee, and act like you like it. Pretend you care for me like you said you did. If you don't, I promise you after I'm done with you, I'll find the white man, Jeb, and kill him." His black eyes glittered with hate and jealousy, and I knew he spoke the truth.

Praying silently for God to help me and protect Jeb from harm, I lapsed into spirit and faked kissing Tovee. I don't remember much else as I focused on the goodness of God and His promises. In my mind, I recited every Bible verse I could remember. I could almost feel Catherine's presence, encouraging me to be strong and endure. Tovee quit hurting me with my cooperation, but I felt dirty and violated. Stoically, I withstood his attack in silence, thinking of other women in wartime, both white and red, who had suffered a similar fate. No matter what Tovee did, he couldn't touch my soul, which was Christ's. Holding Jeb's beautiful face in my mind, I silently kept saying over and over three words, *"Keep Jeb safe. . .Keep Jeb safe . . .Keep Jeb safe. . ."*

When he was finished, Tovee hastily stood up. He was disinterested in me any longer. He'd gotten what he'd come for and as he stared down at my crumpled body on the bed, he masked his thoughts. "That wasn't bad, Mokee, but I think you can do better in the future. I'll be back someday soon. If you expect me not to kill the white man, Jeb, I expect even better treatment. Understand?"

I nodded, hiding my emotions and fighting my hatred. This wasn't Tovee, the sweet boy I used to love. After his harsh reprimand, he retrieved his knife from the wall, leaving a noticeable gash. Before he could be discovered, he sprinted from the house. Although I was in shock at what had transpired, I had survived. Mentally, I was still frightened but physically, I was not harmed.

As quickly as I could, I cleaned up the dead flowers and straightened the room. Tovee had angrily torn the outfit I had so carefully dressed in for Jeb, so I wadded it in a ball and hid it in the bottom drawer of Margaret's dresser. I fixed myself up as best as I could for Jeb, determined not to tell him what happened. I knew Jeb would go after Tovee to kill him, and he would probably be killed himself.

Later that night, I asked Jeb if I could have a hot bath. Being the sweet man he always was, he prepared it for me willingly without any questions. I soaked as long as I could, wanting to wash away any memory of Tovee. Afterward, when we sat reading and discussing his new combine and maybe taking a trip to Junction City in December, I silently thanked God for Jeb's goodness, and I became overwhelmed with love for him. I made a surprise kissing attack at him right over the top of his book. He seemed so pleased with my spontaneity, he suddenly scooped me up in his arms, and we headed up the stairs. As I had hoped, all thoughts of Tovee finally vanished.

By the middle of December, I was positive I was pregnant. Though I hid it, I was nauseated, especially in the afternoon, and I had missed my monthly time. I wished there was someone I could ask, but I didn't have any women friends. There was a huge problem with my pregnancy, however. I didn't know if the father was Tovee or Jeb.

Thinking I might give birth to a baby with the dark bronzed skin and chiseled features of Tovee nearly paralyzed me with fear. What would Jeb think if we suddenly had a very Cheyenne-looking baby when my coloring was so light? There was only one person who could help me with my crisis, and that was Red Wolf. I needed to ask him for advice about Tovee, and I was going crazy not having anyone to confide in.

Telling Jeb I missed the Indian scout, I suggested we should invite Red Wolf for Christmas. Jeb thought it was a great idea, and we decided to go see him at the same time we were in Junction City. After Jeb finished his business transactions and we did a little Christmas shopping, we headed to Fort Riley.

Luckily, we caught our Indian friend at a good time. In the middle of January, he was scheduled to leave with a battalion of soldiers for Fort Hays in the central part of the state. He had the rest of the month of December and also part of January off, and we insisted he come and stay with us for a while.

Only I knew Red Wolf's cover as a spy for the Cheyenne might have been compromised when he rescued me, and I doubted Red Wolf would ever risk going back to the Dog Soldier camps again. I was sure Tovee made sure everyone knew the Indian scout couldn't be trusted. Red Wolf continuously surprised us with his resourcefulness, however, and perhaps his connections to the Cheyenne world were still intact.

The three of us set off for Salina by horseback. Jeb and I were genuinely looking forward to having the Indian as our guest, especially me as I was desperate to talk with him. A few days after his arrival, I found the opportunity to be alone with Red Wolf. Jeb had excused himself from breakfast and said he had to meet Donny and the other workers in the fields to discuss next year's planting schedules. As soon as the door slammed shut, I stared at Red Wolf, tears welling helplessly in my eyes.

"Child, what's wrong?" Red Wolf asked perceptively in his low voice. I could see he was genuinely concerned.

"I told myself I wouldn't cry, but I just don't have anyone else to turn to, and I think of you like my father," I said, starting to sob. Red Wolf quickly shoved his chair back and took me by the arm into the living room. We sat together on the edge of the leather sofa, and the massive Indian patiently held my hands until I regained my composure.

"I-I'm pregnant," I began.

Red Wolf smiled. "Well, that's. . ."

"No, let me finish," I said quickly. "I don't know if the baby is Tovee's or Jeb's."

"Child, you haven't seen Tovee since August. . ."

"No, that's not true," I said more forcefully. "Tovee assaulted me here in the house in early November, while Jeb was in town. He threatened to kill Jeb if I didn't cooperate, and there was nothing I could do. H-He said he's coming back, and he'll kill Jeb if I don't cooperate again. I'm scared, Red Wolf," I said softly as tears splashed down my cheeks.

Red Wolf was so mad he looked ready to explode. "Does Jeb know any of this?" he bellowed.

I sighed, trying to control my emotions. "I couldn't tell him, because he would have gone after Tovee and probably gotten killed. He's no match for an Indian warrior," I said with a slight smile. "Red Wolf, I love Jeb so much. I tried to show him the same night, but. . ." My voice trailed off.

"But what, Mokee?"

"But, I got to thinking later when I found out I was pregnant, what if my baby has dark bronzed skin and chiseled features like Tovee? My skin is so light Jeb will suspect something's wrong. He's seen Tovee, and he'll know right away if the baby looks like him."

"Child, you could have a dark-skinned baby with Cheyenne features because of your ancestors, not Tovee, and the baby could still be Jeb's," he explained gently, patting my hands to reassure me.

"I suppose you're right, but there's something else I'm worried about even more than the baby's appearance. I almost think I should run away again," I said seriously.

"NO running away!" the Indian thundered and then realizing his harshness, he softened his tone.

"I shamed Jeb by being with someone else, even if it was forced," I continued, ignoring Red Wolf's protest. "Worse yet, if I continue to stay here, I'm endangering Jeb's life. Tovee vowed to kill him, and it's my fault. Tovee believes I'm his woman, no one else's."

"That's enough, child." Red Wolf kept holding my hand reassuringly. All at once, he smiled his broad, confident smile, and it made me feel like he could solve all of the world's problems. "After everything Jeb and I went through to get you back, you're not going anywhere, young lady. You understand?" I nodded with uncertainty, still thinking it was best if I left.

He continued speaking. "The first thing is it doesn't matter whether the baby is Jeb's or Tovee's. You and Jeb love each other, and you'll be wonderful parents. You will both love this baby regardless of its appearance. Secondly, you've let yourself get rundown with worry, and you need to take better care of yourself and start eating and resting more. You're not the first woman to be attacked during war, and it's sad to say you won't be the last. For the sake of the baby, you need to pick yourself up and go on. You have a lot to live for and being assaulted doesn't reflect on you as a person. And I, meanwhile, am going to have a little fatherly chat with Jeb, and he and I are going to come up with a plan to keep all of you safe. And then, I myself will figure out what to do about Tovee."

"You aren't going to. . ." I could barely say the words "kill him." I had mixed feelings about Tovee, but I didn't want to see him hurt.

"I have access to a lot of information with the military on the location of the different Dog Soldier bands. I can keep track of where Tovee is, and maybe even have the war chiefs send Tovee's band further west into Colorado for raids. You let me worry about that part of it. Have I ever disappointed you before, Mokee?"

I smiled through my tears. "Never," I said softly. Somehow, I knew Red Wolf would solve my problems.

Later that evening, I went to bed early as I wasn't feeling well. I was so exhausted I felt I could sleep an entire week. It felt good, however, to have finally shared my troubles with another person, especially one so competent at resolving challenges. Little did I know Red Wolf decided to have an immediate talk with Jeb.

"How are things with Mokee?" Red Wolf asked conversationally. The two of them sat in the living room with a crackling fire in the fireplace. The Indian was staring into the dancing flames, trying to decide what he was going to say.

"Things are wonderful," Jeb answered contentedly, glancing up from his newspaper. He'd been reading about a new farming supply store. "I couldn't be happier. And, it's all thanks to you, Red Wolf."

"I can see you're happy," the Indian continued. "But what about Mokee?"

Jeb gave his friend a suspicious look. The Indian had his attention now. "What are you getting at, Red Wolf? Did she say something to you?"

"I'm just curious whether you can tell me what Mokee's been thinking about today."

"Well, she's happy you're here, that's for sure. And, she's thinking about Christmas, of course," Jeb said, positive he knew his wife's mind. "She loves Christmas, you know. It's her favorite time of the year."

There was a moment of silence. "Look, Jeb, it's like this," Red Wolf said with his normal bluntness. "I'm going to tell you some things that will make your blood boil, but I want you to promise me you're going to sit here quietly until I'm through. Well?" Jeb nodded uncomfortably, his heart beginning to sink to his stomach. "That little girl upstairs is going to have a baby, and she's scared because Tovee raped her last month when you were gone from the house. She's worried it might be his baby."

Jeb nearly lurched off the sofa to run upstairs to Mokee, but Red Wolf forcefully shoved him back on the cushions. "I'm not done with you yet, Jeb. You promised you'd hear me out. Because Tovee threatened to kill you, Mokee let him attack her. She felt the only way she could protect your life was to give in to him." Jeb's eyes nearly popped out as he listened, but he tried to be quiet.

"Mokee thinks you won't want her anymore if you hear this. She thinks you'll be disappointed she was with someone else, even though Tovee forced himself on her, and she feels soiled and violated. She also has another fear. If she has a baby with dark copper-colored skin or Cheyenne features like Tovee, Mokee thinks you won't want her or the baby. I hope she's wrong, Jeb, because it would mean I'm a poor judge of character, and I don't like to be wrong." Jeb was growing angrier the more he sat still and listened to Red Wolf's harsh rebuke. He was ready to kill Tovee with his bare hands.

"Her worst fear is this. Tovee said he's coming back to attack her again, and he's vowed to kill you if she doesn't give in. Mokee thinks she can save your life by running away again, an idea I strongly opposed." Jeb was fidgeting all over the sofa and ready to bolt, and the Indian restrained him with his powerful forearm. "Now calm down, and just listen, Jeb. Mokee told me she thinks of me as her father. As her honorary father, I have the duty along with you to protect her so she gives birth to a healthy baby in a home where she and the baby are loved. Are you with me?" Jeb nodded weakly, sick with worry at the newest revelations.

"Now, I think you and I need to come up with a plan to make this house secure with locks on the doors and windows. Maybe the new foreman, Donny, can live in sometimes and protect Mokee when you have to be gone. One thing's for sure. She's never to be left alone again, you hear me, even to go outside or to the barn. You and your workers need to be armed at all times, and we need to figure out a secure place where she can hide if Tovee does make it inside. As for me, I'm going to try to work through the military to track Tovee and keep his raiding party out of central Kansas." Red Wolf looked squarely in Jeb's face. "You can talk now, Jeb. I can see you want to say something."

"I ought to punch you for accusing me of being prejudiced against Indians. I can't believe you think I wouldn't love Mokee if she has a dark-skinned baby. That could happen even if the baby were mine. And hell, you're one of my best friends, and you're not exactly white as snow, you know," Jeb ranted, fuming with anger.

The towering Indian grinned slyly at his friend, glad to see he took offense. "I wouldn't punch me, Jeb. I'd squash you like a pitiful fly."

"I know you would, you ornery old coot. I'm not a fool, even though you seem to think I am half the time," Jeb said defensively.

"I don't think you're a fool. But I do think you get preoccupied and when you do, you aren't very observant. If I had one wish for you, *son*," Red Wolf smirked, "I would hope you and your little wife, Mokee, would learn how to communicate better on a daily basis. Then she wouldn't have to bottle things up inside and drag her dear old *father* in to fix things." The two glared at each other for a moment and then they both smiled, their friendship still intact. Jeb knew his cantankerous *father* was right, and he sighed in defeat.

"Are we in agreement we have to make the house more secure?" Red Wolf asked. Jeb nodded. "That'll be my job while I'm here visiting, and I'll get on it in the morning. I think your job is to go upstairs and reassure your bride you love her more than anything in this world. You especially need to tell her it wasn't her fault Tovee assaulted her. And it wouldn't hurt to say she could have a baby with purple and green stripes, and you would love the baby as much as you love her. Also, reassure her you and I are going to do everything we can think of to prevent any more attacks. Go get at it, *son*."

Jeb stood up, suddenly nervous at the prospect of letting Mokee know he knew the whole story. Then he took a deep breath, thanked Red Wolf for being such a good friend, and slowly walked up the steps like a man going to the gallows. Red Wolf watched him go, confirming in his mind Jeb and Mokee were like children to him, especially since he never had children of his own. Just like he knew months ago when he first met Jeb, the white man was one of the few he actually liked and called a friend. Then he thought of how Mokee had confided her problems to him and cried in his arms. Here he was, nearly sixty-five, and Red Wolf had discovered the most amazing thing. *He suddenly had a family.*

Chapter Twenty-seven

Christmas was beautiful this year. Occasionally, it snows in December in Kansas. But this year, we were surprised with a white Christmas, and the house looked lovely draped in a snowy party cape. There was even a herd of deer padding quietly through the silver dollar-sized snowflakes, reminding me of the frozen white paradise of the mountain forests where I grew up.

I felt a bit nostalgic this Christmas, even a little weepy, which I guess is normal for someone who's pregnant. I truly hoped my parents were alive and safe, and I wished I could share the news with them about becoming grandparents next year. Red Wolf said he would try to find them when he resumed his travels with the military in January. If anyone could find my parents, he could.

When I confided in him earlier in the month about my pregnancy, and my worries about Tovee and whether Jeb would still love me, Red Wolf took charge. Before long, everything was better. That same night, Jeb overwhelmed me with his pledge of love and support for our baby, no matter who the baby looked like. He even asked my forgiveness for his preoccupation with his work and for leaving me unprotected in the house.

Instead of looking at me like I had shamed him or was somehow soiled, Jeb said he was unworthy of me as I had so unselfishly given myself to Tovee to protect his life. By morning's light, the bond between Jeb and me was unbreakable, and I knew with certainty I would never think of running away again from his steadfast love. He made me promise we would both learn to talk about our problems together, and I should never be afraid to speak up again, no matter what it was about.

When I looked into Jeb's gentle blue eyes and saw his compassionate smile, I felt God's blessing wash over my entire body with cleansing and forgiveness. My healing was so complete I began to pray for Tovee's soul and for the strength to forgive him.

Red Wolf took his job seriously as honorary father to me, and he began energetically working to fortify the house like it was Fort Knox. I knew all about Fort Knox from a book Jeb had shown me, and I started to think we had bars of gold hidden in the floorboards. Every window had new locks, and the outside doors had huge bolts on the inside. There were even ways to lock interior doors from either side, such as closet or bedroom doors, either to keep someone out or keep someone in.

Deciding we needed a safe hiding place if Tovee or other Indians were spotted, Red Wolf devised a way to lock the root cellar door with a bolt from the inside, not just with the bolt on the outside. Even if the house caught on fire, the cellar was so deep within the ground we knew we would be safe. It was also the ideal place to hide during windstorms called tornados.

Red Wolf seemed to think of every possibility of attack, even putting a sturdy board in the corner of each room to grab and use as a weapon. He next constructed a metal, fireproof door on the kitchen floor, and he concealed it under a rug, which was permanently fastened to the top of it. It provided an interior entrance to the root cellar, which could be locked from the cellar side. If we entered the root cellar through the kitchen, the outside cellar door in the yard could remain locked, and it would look like no one was in there. Then, we could lock the inner bolt of the outside door, making us even safer. He also made sure the root cellar had enough supplies for at least a week as well as oil lamps and blankets. Red Wolf took his job as a protector very seriously.

One day, the Indian said he had to return to Fort Riley for a few days, but he would be back before Christmas. When he returned, Jeb and I were shocked to see he had a pack horse with both a crate of ammunition and a crate of Henry rifles, which were made by the New Haven Arms Company in 1860.

"Do you think he stole those?" I whispered to Jeb, looking askance at the quantity of rifles.

Jeb raised his shoulders as if he didn't know, and he didn't want to know. With Red Wolf, sometimes not knowing was best. Always fascinated with weapon designs, Jeb whispered to me the powerful .44 Henry rimfire had been used by the Union army, and Confederates had called the Henry "that damned Yankee rifle that they load on Sunday and shoot all week!" He said the rifles could fire an amazing 28 rounds a minute.

In the crate, there were also a few newer Winchester rifles, Model 1866. Jeb said they were the latest model and really hard to come by. They used the same cartridge but were built on a bronze-alloy frame with an improved magazine and a wooden forearm. I nodded, not understanding a word.

"This is your Christmas present," Red Wolf said gruffly, unloading the rifles. We traipsed after him as he hid a few strategically around the house along with the cartridges nearby. The rest he took down to the root cellar with Jeb's help. "Hope you like your present. I thought we'd have some shooting lessons tomorrow, and then after I'm gone, you can teach your workers how to use the rifles. When I was at Fort Riley, I found out things are looking poorly for settlers in this part of Kansas, and you've got to be prepared for random Indian attacks."

Jeb, Donny, and I all learned the basics of shooting a repeating rifle. Jeb and Donny were fascinated, and even lunch couldn't get them off the shooting range. As for me, I knew I couldn't kill anyone as I hated violence. Even if Tovee came after me again, I would never shoot him. His mind was confused right now. Because he was so obsessed with revenge, he couldn't see he was becoming like the white soldiers he hated. I felt sorry for the kind young boy he had once been, and I continued praying for him every day.

Red Wolf didn't like it when I avoided rifle practice. While he and I were setting up lunch in the kitchen, he asked me the question, "If Jeb were on his knees, injured and bleeding, and an Indian was standing over him with a knife, ready to stab him and take his scalp, could you shoot the Indian?"

I hated his question, and I told him so, but it did make me think all through lunch. Later on in private, I told Red Wolf I would shoot an attacker to save Jeb's life. Surprising Red Wolf, I also said I would shoot an attacker to save his life. I gave him a sweet smile and added that he and Jeb were the only two I would use a gun for. Then I tossed my hair in the air and walked away, leaving him standing there with his mouth open.

Christmas had become my favorite time of year. I had actually gotten used to having a tree in the house, though Red Wolf seemed to find it a bit odd. It was hard to believe Catherine had been alive a year ago, and Jeb had kissed me for the first time and given me my first journal. I remembered the joy of decorating the tree and singing *Stille Nacht*. So much had transpired since then, and so much innocence had been lost. I was seventeen now, a married woman, a Christian and one day soon, a mother. But some things didn't change. Just as when I was a child, I still thought about war.

Jeb and I tried to decorate like Catherine had done so beautifully. We unpacked each ornament very carefully and had Red Wolf help us trim the tree, lighting the candles when we were done and singing as we stood by the fire. As Jeb set up the nativity scene, he retold the story of the first Christmas to Red Wolf and me. I wondered if Red Wolf had ever heard the story before.

We decided to exchange gifts on Christmas Eve this year, rather than Christmas Day. When we had been in Topeka for our honeymoon, Jeb and I found Red Wolf a unique Meerschaum pipe in a specialty store. Believed to be the best pipe of the time, it was ornately carved and similar to Cheyenne peace pipes, which were thought to be sacred. Red Wolf loved it, and I enjoyed the leathery, comforting scent of pipe tobacco.

In addition to a beautiful gold locket with room for a future picture of our family, Jeb gave me a first edition book of love poems by Elizabeth Barrett Browning. After seeing all the papers Jeb was accumulating with his farm purchases, I gave him an initialized leather briefcase to hold his important documents. As I gazed around the room at two people I loved with all my heart, I knew the gifts we had just exchanged were only symbols. We, ourselves, were the true gifts to each other, just as Christ was God's gift to us all.

Red Wolf was in charge of hunting for Christmas dinner, and he brought home a good-sized goose, which we roasted along with potatoes, carrots, and chestnuts. It was indeed a wonderful Christmas and seventeenth birthday for me.

As January came, it was time to say good-bye to Red Wolf. He was rejoining several regiments of troops heading to Fort Hays. About a week and a half after Christmas, we watched his stately silhouette ride off in the long shadows of the setting sun. A feeling of sadness came over me as I prayed for Red Wolf's safety, as well as the safety of our small, but growing family. My heart pounded anxiously over what 1867 would bring and whether war would still be my shadow.

PART FOUR

Chapter Twenty-eight

After our Christmas together, it had been difficult to say good-bye to Red Wolf. My heart was very thankful for his intervention in our problems. If not for his help, I might have done something irrational, like running away again. Jeb and I both really missed the Indian since he left for his new assignment at Fort Hays. We knew he wouldn't write, but we prayed for him every day as Kansas was becoming more violent with escalating Indian raids.

As far as Jeb and I could determine, our baby was due in early August. Jeb's compassion and understanding about our continuing problems with Tovee made it easier to get excited about the new addition to our family. Unless Jeb was fooling me, and I would never believe that of him, I was convinced he would be a loving father no matter who the baby looked like. I no longer worried who the actual father was and only hoped Jeb and I would have a healthy baby. Because of my new happiness, I found myself taking better care of myself and eating healthier.

Realizing we had very little protection before Tovee's assault, we were grateful Red Wolf had secured our house like a fortress. Every time I read the Junction City and Topeka newspapers, I learned of more settlers being attacked in nearby counties. No place seemed safe.

My biggest worry was Tovee might try to kill Jeb in a jealous rage. While Jeb thought he was protecting me from Tovee by being home more and always being armed, I was secretly protecting Jeb by paying closer attention to the patterns of raiding activities. With both of us being constantly vigilant, hopefully we would remain safe.

Not wanting to be a hostage to fear, Jeb and I began discussing what we could do to improve the house for our growing family. Although I always thought it was a lovely home, the four bedrooms were very small. Because money wasn't an issue and Jeb had time before spring to work on a project, he decided to remodel the house before the baby's birth.

Jeb did a lot of the work himself, though he did hire a construction crew for any structural changes. Because there were so many new settlers in the area looking for work, Jeb had no trouble finding a competent crew of builders. I also thought the daily hubbub of activity and hammering sounds would be a deterrent to an Indian raid or the likelihood of Tovee showing up. The workers could be seen milling around the exterior of the house most weekdays, and Jeb armed them all with rifles.

Our projects started with the upstairs. We decided to make three bedrooms out of the four, knocking out a wall of Margaret's tiny bedroom and combining the room with Catherine's previous bedroom. It became a spacious nursery and sitting room area with a white crib, a beautiful hooked rug with daisies on it, a comfortable needlepoint rocker, a man-sized leather easy chair, a sizeable brick fireplace, and a fully stocked bookshelf. We also blocked off the small fireplace from Margaret's sliver of a room, and I was glad to be rid of Margaret's twin bed and the memories of Tovee's attack. The new nursery was a spacious place where we could sit and enjoy the baby in comfort. The best part was we wouldn't have to go all the way downstairs to spend time together as a family.

Jeb's and my room was already perfect, but he completely cleaned out anything in Benjamin's old room which had belonged to his defiant brother. Although Jeb stored his brother's things in the barn, we never thought Benjamin would return. Then we decorated the room as a guest room, and one day we hoped to use it as a bedroom for more children.

Our most ambitious project was to have a long, rectangular room built on the first floor. The huge space ran alongside the living room and shared a fireplace with the living room on the inner wall. The new room had an enormous cedar closet and when the area was completed, we bought a spacious feather bed, a soft wool rug, a roomy oak dresser, and a big leather easy chair.

Laughing to ourselves, we justified the expense of the addition by saying if Donny had to stay over, he'd have decent place to sleep. Our unspoken hope, however, was for Red Wolf to consider staying with us permanently when he retired, and it could be his private room. The only problem with our plan is we weren't sure what Red Wolf would think of it. In the living room next to the new bedroom, Jeb ordered a large Oriental rug from Boston to make the hardwood floor warmer and the room more inviting in the winter.

In front of the house, we decided to expand the size of the wooden porch to include the area in front of the new addition. Overtop, we added a slanted roof for protection from the rain, and a white painted railing ran along the entire porch length. The finishing touch was four large white wood rockers, which I knew would appeal to Red Wolf and make our idea to have him stay be more tempting.

Jeb's final project for the house was to move the outhouse closer for more convenience and safety. He designed a new, secure door off the back of the bath closet. It led down a short, wooden path to the outhouse, and the entire structure was redone with thicker lumber to keep out drafts. Not wanting to leave the barn untouched, Jeb had the construction crew begin to build an extra shed at one end to house his new combine harvester, which was expected to arrive in the spring.

Donny was becoming Jeb's closest friend, and the young worker was maturing and becoming more competent handling the farm machinery and overseeing the farmworkers. It didn't surprise me to see construction begin on a good-sized log cabin over the bluff and within walking distance from the main house. Jeb was a generous employer, and he decided it would be advantageous to all of us for Donny and his fiancée, Bethany, to have a house near us. It became our wedding gift to the new couple.

I was very excited at the prospect of having my first woman friend, and I found Bethany to be a kind, bubbly woman about my own age. Without even telling Jeb, it amazed me how he sensed I was missing the companionship of other women. In the spring, a simple wedding was held for Donny and Bethany at his parents' farm nearby, and Jeb and I attended. My pregnancy had started to show, and all of the women were very nice to me, expressing interest about when the baby was due and where I was from. Until the Indian troubles were over, Jeb and I decided we would temporarily stick with the story about my being Catherine's niece from Boston. I was introduced as Mokee, however, as Jeb told everyone it was my nickname.

No longer just employer to employee, Jeb's relationship with Donny continued to grow. All of us began doing things as a foursome, sometimes getting together for meals or going to the celebration of the new railroad in Salina. My joy was made full when Bethany became pregnant soon after her wedding, and I anticipated the future time when our children would be friends. Life had grown very peaceful for me, but with peace came letting down our guard.

My pregnancy seemed to be progressing well according to Doc Hutchinson, who was determined to attend the birth in early August. By late July, I was in shock at how a little person like me could be so huge with a child. I waddled like a fat duck or spent most of my time rolling around like a prize-winning watermelon on the sofa. The living room seemed to be the coolest room during the sweltering days of summer, and I rarely moved off the sofa except to eat, and then to eat some more because I was always hungry.

Jeb had kissed me good-bye after lunch, telling me he and Donny had to go into town to pick up a replacement part for the combine. He assured me the construction crew was still hard at work on the barn addition and if I needed anything, I should tell one of them. He also said I should try to get some much needed sleep. I was sleeping very poorly at night as it was so hot. Without much effort, I drifted into a deep, restful nap on the cool leather of the sofa.

All of a sudden, I felt two soft lips touch mine. I smiled, thinking I was having a pleasant dream. The lips pressed a little harder, and then a quiet voice whispered, "Mokee, it's me." The words were in Cheyenne, and my eyes sprung open with fear to see Tovee's bronzed face inches from my own. He looked haggard and unkempt, and there were huge circles under his eyes from lack of sleep. I shuttered my expression. Since I was already discovered, there was nothing I could do, and I needed to keep him calm to protect my baby.

"What is all this?" he asked in disbelief, the hand which had killed countless people splayed across my overgrown belly. "Whose baby?" he asked harshly, daring me to tell the truth. As if he were debating whether to let me live for my betrayal, his black eyes narrowed angrily.

"Whose do you think?" I countered with as much calmness as I could muster, not admitting anything. I stared at him.

"I'll kill Jeb," he vowed, hastily jumping to the conclusion Jeb was the father.

"No you won't," I said quickly. "Tovee, don't you even remember what you did to me last fall?" I snapped back quickly, hoping to make him see it was entirely possible the baby was his. It was the only way I could protect Jeb from his jealous anger.

All at once, recognition passed through Tovee's eyes. "Oh," he said with sudden awareness. His eyes swept over my over-inflated belly and then back up to my face, and his expression changed swiftly like a kaleidoscope. First, there was shock, then pleasure, then masculine pride, then anger, and finally regret. "I'm sorry," he uttered quietly, surprising me there was still compassion underneath his harsh exterior. He stroked my hair distractedly. "When are you due?"

"I'm due now, Tovee, and Jeb is taking care of me. I have a doctor who will deliver the baby, and I'm staying here, away from war," I announced firmly, not wanting him to get any wild ideas about kidnapping me. Because I didn't want Tovee to know I had been married for a year, I also kept any mention of Jeb vague. Tovee would have killed me on the spot if he knew I had married someone else.

"You can't come with me anyway, Mokee. It's too dangerous right now. We don't stay in any one place for more than a night now. Our band and others are creating a reign of terror," he said proudly. "I'd rather you stay here where you're safe, if it's okay with Jeb." It was one of the few times he had ever said Jeb's name without disgust.

If only he knew how okay it was with Jeb, I thought to myself worriedly. My heart shuddered. Careful not to give any emotion away, I simply nodded it was acceptable with Jeb. All at once, I had another thought. "You better go. Jeb will be back from town soon, and there are workmen in the back."

"I won't be seeing you for a while, Mokee," Tovee said with guilt. "We're heading west." He paused for a moment, staring in wonder at my stomach and amazed he was going to be a father. "Be safe having our baby." His eyes wavered back and forth over mine, and I nodded again. Unlike our last brutal encounter, Tovee gently kissed my forehead and then rose to leave.

I saw he was still wearing the elk skin necklace he had made for me long ago. Without losing eye contact with me, Tovee pulled the necklace to his mouth and kissed it, as if reaffirming his commitment to me and our baby. He quickly spun around and sprinted out the front door, carefully hiding from the workers, who were in the barn behind the house.

Although I had hidden my emotions when Tovee was here, I suddenly began sobbing hysterically, gasping for air between sobs. Tovee was never going to let me alone, especially now he thought I was having his baby. What had I done by letting him believe the baby was his? Tovee would be back some day to kidnap me and the baby, and he would probably kill all of us if he ever found out the baby was Jeb's.

With anguish and worry, I began panting in short breaths, and unstoppable tears began washing down my face. All at once, I felt a sharp stab of pain in my abdomen, and then it circled to my back in a sinking feeling. The pain was severe, and I cried out for help, although I knew the house was empty. Perspiration dripped down my face until the pain gradually subsided, and I struggled to a sitting position and then collapsed on the sofa arm.

Jeb found me a few minutes later when he returned from Salina, and his face was etched with panic as he saw me doubled over, drenched in sweat, and weeping uncontrollably. Tovee's surprise visit had thrown me into early labor.

A baby will make love stronger, days shorter,
nights longer, bankroll smaller,
home happier, clothes shabbier,
the past forgotten,
and the future worth living for.

Chapter Twenty-nine

Love took my breath away for this beautiful little baby in my arms. She was perfect in every way from her pale white, velvety skin to the brown dusting of hair on her head. From her dimpled little hands to her pudgy toes, she was a miracle and a precious gift from God.

Catherine Naomi Preston is her name, 6 pounds, 5 ounces, and she was born July 31, 1867. The name Catherine is for the most kind, elegant, and lovely woman I ever met, Jeb's mother, who generously welcomed a scared little Cheyenne girl into her heart and life and showed her the way to God. Naomi is short for Nanomone'e meaning a woman of peace, wife of Red Wolf, the man who will be my child's honorary grandfather, and the man who will always be my hero. He is the one who saved me from myself. And, Preston, the surname of her father, the beautiful man who is my husband, a man who, through his love and compassion, continually makes the world a better place.

Precious little Catherine surprised us with her birth a week early. When he found me alone and hysterical in the first stages of labor, Jeb nearly fell apart. But he quickly went into action, sending Donny at a mad gallop to fetch Doc Hutchinson and gently carrying me up to our bedroom, where I would give birth. Jeb hurriedly covered the bed with an enormous thick cotton bedspread, which his mother had used for births. Nearly a week before, he had prepared a table with various sizes of clean cloths and bowls. After making me comfortable through another contraction, Jeb bounded down the steps to prepare a large bowl of water to keep me cool in the blistering July heat.

As far as births go, and I know very little about births as I was an only child, Doc Hutchinson told me mine went very well and without any complications. My labor was only six hours, shorter than most, but that was actually good as I was burning up from the heat. Jeb wasn't the least bit squeamish about being in the room the entire time, and he continually sponged me off as he tried to keep me comfortable. The most amazing thing he did was assist Doc Hutchinson with the actual birth, even cutting the umbilical cord. I never cease to be dumbfounded by Jeb. He is so steady under pressure and so reliable.

Several days after the birth when I was feeling a little better, I knew I needed to talk to Jeb about Tovee's surprise visit. Remembering Red Wolf had told me to always speak up rather than run from my problems, I initiated the difficult conversation while I was nursing Catherine on our bed.

"Jeb, the reason I went into labor early was because Tovee had been here," I said bluntly, not knowing how to say it any other way.

"Oh my God," Jeb said with a look of shock and alarm. His face turned ashen white. "Are you all right? He didn't hurt you, did he?" He immediately jumped to the conclusion I had been assaulted again.

"I'm okay. He didn't hurt me," I said quickly. "We really do have a problem though. He obviously saw I was pregnant, and he jumped to the conclusion the baby was yours. He threatened to find you and kill you. To distract him, I asked if he remembered what he did to me, and it was then he realized the baby might be his. I'm sorry I misled him, Jeb, but it was the only way I could keep him from going after you or harming me and the baby." Once again, I felt sad at all of the problems I continually brought into Jeb's life. Sometimes I thought he would be better off without me.

With a look of love, Jeb gently touched my face. "You did what you had to do, Mokee. If he thought the baby was mine, he might have killed you and baby Catherine."

"He doesn't know we're married, Jeb. In fact, he thinks you're letting me stay here because you feel sorry for me. I don't know what we're going to do," I whispered painfully. "He said he's going to be away for a while, but I know he's going to come back and try to take me away with him again, especially since he thinks Catherine's his."

"All he's got to do is take one look at her, and he'll know she's not."

"That's the worst possible situation," I said frantically. "He'll know I lied, and he'll probably kill her and me too. What are we going to do, Jeb?" I asked, starting to cry softly. "Our problems with Tovee never end. He thinks I'm his. You never should have married an Indian."

Although I was still nursing the baby, Jeb put his arm around me and held me close. "How can you say I shouldn't have married you when you look at this beautiful baby?" He softly touched Catherine's cheek while she suckled. "Besides, I married the woman I love. She just happens to be a Cheyenne, and one day I hope she'll be able to be open about her heritage and be proud of it. But whether my wife's Indian or white is totally irrelevant to me. Mokee, there's nothing we can do about the situation with Tovee except pray and trust God will protect us and our baby."

I smiled through my tears, knowing his words could have been spoken by his mother, Catherine, our baby's namesake. Yes, Catherine would also tell me to trust God, and I would have to grow in that trust.

I've often wondered why times of joy pass by so quickly and times of suffering go by agonizingly slow. I remembered my time in Tovee's Dog Soldier camp and how I used to sit in discouragement and practically watch the moss grow on the trees. How different this time was. Jeb and tiny Catherine made it a time of great joy, and morning only began than it melted into dusk again. Each little thing Catherine did, from her first crooked smile like Jeb's to her grabbing my finger, brought Jeb and me such pleasure and pride. I continually thanked God for the momentary peace He had brought into my life.

Sadly, there was not peace elsewhere, however. About a month after Catherine was born, there was an Indian raid on a nearby settlement, and several settlers had been killed. The townspeople were armed and fought off the Indians, and the people very cleverly hid in a roundhouse, which housed the new train. Later, the train conductor smashed right through the wall of the building in pursuit of the Indians and rode toward Salina. Everyone had been talking about the bravery and quick thinking of the settlers, and the story even reached the newspapers in Junction City and Topeka.

Momentarily, I wondered if Tovee's small band of Dog Soldiers had caused the havoc, but then I dismissed the thought from my mind. If he had still been in the local area, he would have done anything humanly possible to see what he thought was his new baby. It was a relief to think he had moved further west like he had said, but Jeb and I and all the other settlers were still at risk from whatever rogue Indian raiding parties continually focused on our area of Kansas.

Aside from the raids, there was good news. This was a banner year for Jeb's wheat farm. He and Donny, with the help of their new crew of workers, had implemented a plan to put five hundred acres into wheat production and an additional hundred acres into corn. What a difference it was from the past year when Jeb only grew enough for himself and the local area.

The new combine harvester ended up being a good investment as it was a boon to harvesting the crops. A new fleet of wagons made transporting the crops quick and easy to the recently opened rail yards. The wheat and corn was then loaded into freight cars and transported to markets in Junction City and Topeka. Jeb was even talking about expanding production the following year to all of his thousand acres and sending the crops even further to markets in Missouri.

Although Jeb had inherited great wealth from his mother's estate, it was apparent he was a shrewd businessman. By working hard, he was turning an incredible profit from the new investments in his farming operation. With pride, I realized everyone who worked for him not only respected him, but liked him as he was generous to a fault and honest. I also began to understand more about this new America. It was being forged from the blood of both white settlers and Indians, and it was a growing land of opportunity for anyone who was willing to work hard. How I wished my Indian brothers might be given those opportunities as well, especially since they had been Americans for thousands of years.

It was with optimism Jeb and I began to read about the negotiations for peace and the signing of a new peace treaty in October of 1867. We wondered if Red Wolf was involved in his role as an interpreter at the negotiation site near Fort Larned. The newspaper articles brought back a lot of memories, some good and others painful, and we reminisced about our surprise wedding and reception at Fort Larned and how our wonderful friend, Red Wolf, had arranged everything and also saved our lives.

We missed Red Wolf so much. Although we hadn't heard a word from him since he left for Fort Hays a year ago after Christmas, it was amazing how he had become such an important part of our lives. Jeb and I wished there was a way we could contact him and at least invite him for Christmas again, but we didn't know exactly where he was. He may have moved on to another fort by then. I wasn't sure whether Red Wolf had an address, so a letter might not be the best way to communicate with him. His empty room was still waiting if only we could think of a way to find him.

Christmas was a joyous occasion again this year as we had a houseful of friends to celebrate our Lord's birth. Donny and Bethany came for dinner with their new month old baby, Joshua, and Donny's parents also joined us. Everyone brought something to share, and it was a bountiful feast as Jeb shot a wild turkey, which was at least thirty pounds.

Little Catherine competed with Joshua to steal the show, and the two of them were happily bounced from lap to lap. I never adopted any of the Cheyenne traditions of binding a baby in a cradleboard. It seemed Jeb and I always wanted to hold Catherine and play with her, and he was a very hands-on father.

Catherine had mastered sitting but, thankfully, not crawling. Most of the time, she sat contentedly playing on the soft Oriental rug. She was encircled by the new wooden toys St. Nicholas had placed in her stocking. With the smell of freshly cut evergreen permeating the house, it was warm and cozy inside with all of the fireplaces crackling with fresh wood. Our indoor Christmas tree was also gaily lit with candles. Did I mention I was glad Catherine wasn't crawling yet?

Although I always wistfully thought of my parents and Jeb's mother, Catherine, at Christmas, they were gone, and we needed to accept that and go on. What we couldn't accept, however, was not knowing where our friend Red Wolf was. Jeb and I both wanted the man who had saved our lives and who was Catherine's honorary grandfather back with us.

Because Red Wolf was torn between two cultures and didn't really fit in with either, we were both sure the Indian didn't have a permanent home. But, we were afraid both pride in his self-sufficiency and stubbornness were keeping him away, and it was a constant dilemma to figure out how to find our friend and coax him here. I continually prayed for his safety and worried he was on the frontline of the battle still raging between the white soldiers and the Indians. Although the newspapers printed optimistic articles about a new peace treaty, I knew better than to believe peace would come that easily.

Jeb and I were beginning to have a Christmas joke about one of his gifts for me. Because I was so prolific with my writing, he began to give me a blank journal every time there was an opportunity for a gift, like Christmas or my birthday. The top row of the bookshelf in the nursery was filled with my completed journals, and I always kept one in progress with me as I walked around the house. Even on my eighteenth birthday this year, there was a lovely new journal with butterflies painted on the cover and, of course, another jar of ink. I had a whole shelf of empty ink jars in the root cellar, which I think I kept for my own amusement to remind me how wordy I was.

The year of 1868 began to pass by, and life was increasingly good for Jeb and me. Catherine was like a beautiful flower, blossoming each day, first crawling and then walking by her first birthday, and eventually talking at every opportunity. Where I was constantly writing, my precious daughter was constantly talking, and Jeb laughingly said each of us had to express ourselves continuously.

Over the course of the year, we had begun to attend church with Donny's family at their Presbyterian Church. Although Jeb had grown up a Lutheran, we all found the Presbyterians to be a welcoming body of believers focused on loving God's son, and we eventually became members and had Catherine baptized.

Every Sunday, Donny, Bethany, and Joshua would ride with us in a large buggy into town. Although I still tried to read the Bible every day, it became a wonderful thing to hear the Bible preached. We usually made an entire day of Sunday, either getting together at Donny's house or ours to eat after church. The children played together as they usually did, and Bethany and I talked about the things we had in common. The men could usually be found in the barn. One thing white men seemed to have in common was their love of equipment. I suppose it was like how Cheyenne men loved horses.

The best part about church was I found many new friends and like-minded people who loved God and wanted peace. Although it continually surprised and pleased me, I discovered there were many good people who had settled in Kansas, not just the ones who sought revenge on the Indians. It would be wonderful if someday these friends and neighbors would realize there were just as many good Indian people. Many of my people loved God in their own way and wanted peace, and they were not the ones who kept seeking revenge for the

Sand Creek Massacre. It was my constant prayer for those who loved peace to find each other.

Although Indian raids continued in Kansas throughout the summer, more skirmishes were reported from the western border of Kansas near Fort Wallace and also in the Colorado territory. The railroad stretched clear across Kansas now, and the final tracks were being laid in the Fort Wallace area, something the Indians were desperate to stop. Although I told myself Red Wolf was still safe at Fort Hays, I had a nagging feeling he was no longer there. *What if he was in the middle of the hostilities on the western border?*

Another concern I had was for Tovee, but it was a concern I couldn't share with Jeb as I thought it would hurt his feelings. For whatever muddled reasons, I was worried for Tovee's safety. It made no sense to me. My Christian heart wanted to forgive him very badly. I felt I had finally reached a point of understanding how violence and revenge could eat away at a man's soul and not reflect the goodness of a person within. When Tovee left after thinking I was carrying his baby, I had seen a glimpse of the Tovee I had once known shimmering through the harsh surface of hatred. It was that Tovee I wanted to reach out to and forgive, but I had let the moment slip through my fingertips. I had an aching feeling inside of me I was too late.

Toward the end of September in 1868, our newspapers began reporting a devastating armed conflict between the Indians and the military in the Colorado territory. It seemed a battalion of fifty volunteers had pursued a raiding party of Indians after it kidnapped two white women. A massive number of Indians attacked, and the battalion sought refuge on an island, where they survived until reinforcements showed up. Although the reports varied on the number of Indians killed, one newspaper account said it was close to a thousand.

It was a dramatic story, and everyone was talking about it after church. The two women had been captured in the Solomon Valley, and the volunteers had marched all the way from Fort Harker to Fort Hays, and then eventually to Fort Wallace. I knew Jeb felt my hand turn icy cold as the news made me shiver. Pulling him aside, I told him I was worried about Red Wolf's safety. In the silence of my heart, I also knew I was anxious for Tovee. I asked Jeb if there was anything he could do to try to track down Red Wolf. With a matching expression of concern, he reassured me he would do what he could.

For the next few weeks, Jeb contacted everyone he knew in the military to ask about the location of a Cheyenne interpreter and scout named Ma'o'nehe, or Red Wolf, but the only information he could piece together was the Indian was no longer at Fort Hays. Nightly, Jeb and I held hands and prayed together for the safety of our friend and in silence, I also prayed for Tovee's safety.

Chapter Thirty

Fort Hays was a blasted place, Red Wolf thought to himself as he struggled to make his large frame comfortable on the army issue cot. He pulled a thin wool blanket up to his neck. The few buildings the fort had were drafty and falling apart, and they were filled with vermin from when the fort was abandoned in the first part of 1866.

I'm too old for this, the Indian grumbled to himself, as he thought of little Mokee and Jeb. *Maybe I should retire and find a small place near them*, he thought, and he realized he couldn't help but think of them as his family. He had a lot of work to do in the meantime, most importantly to keep an eye out for Tovee and keep him away from Mokee, especially while she waited for her baby's arrival.

Red Wolf looked disparagingly around the God-awful room. He yearned for the days of living in a tepee and being at one with the land and the stars. Since coming to Fort Hays, he'd learned the fort, which had originally been named Fort Fletcher in 1865, was built to protect the stage and freight wagons of the Butterfield Overland Dispatch, which traveled along the Smoky Hill Trail to Denver.

Because the troops spent most of their time away from their post guarding the stage stations, the original fort had fallen into disrepair. Not only had the army been undermanned at the time, but the funds to maintain the post dried up. After the Indians temporarily forced the stage line from its normal route, the fort was abandoned altogether. It had just reopened in October of 1866, only three months before Red Wolf had been assigned there. It was now renamed Fort Hays for a Civil War general killed in battle.

The fort's new mission was expanded to include protecting military roads, guarding the mails, and defending the construction gangs on the Union Pacific Railroad, which was laying track across Kansas. Fort Hays would also serve as a major supply depot to ship supplies to other army posts in western and southern Kansas. *It might as well be Fort Nowhere*, Red Wolf complained to himself, before finally drifting off to sleep.

The period between 1867 and 1869 would one day become known as the Indian Wars in the state of Kansas. It was a perilous time to be a Kansan as more than a hundred white settlers were killed in 1867 by Indian raids, usually along the Smoky Hill Trail and the settlements in the valley between the Solomon and Republican Rivers. Every time Red Wolf heard of another attack, he worried about Jeb and Mokee, but he knew he had done all he could to keep them safe.

He often wished he was still stationed at Fort Riley. He would love to see Mokee round with a baby, and it hardly seemed possible she would be a mother soon.

The gossip at Fort Hays in the spring of 1867 was all about a future show of force by the army to let the Indians know who was boss. Before he left on a military campaign against the Indians, Major General Winfield Scott Hancock decided to move the fort nearer the railroad, which was following a route further north of the old trail. Fort Hays also had a frequent problem with flooding, and the fort's original location was on a floodplain, which was another reason for the relocation.

Red Wolf was part of the exodus. The entire encampment moved and was rebuilt in the typical frontier settlement style like the other forts, which meant no true fortification or wall around the post, its only defensive structure being a blockhouse. The new Fort Hays was designed like other forts to be a base for supplies and troops, which could be dispatched quickly when Indian resistance suddenly appeared.

Shortly after the camp moved, General Hancock left and began his campaign to show the superior strength of the United States Army. Before the general's expedition, Red Wolf observed Indian outbreaks in Kansas had been sporadic. It soon became apparent the general's plan to show the army's superiority backfired and instead of scaring the Indians into seeking peace, he ended up provoking an all-out war. All eight Kansas forts were on high alert to serve as military supply depots and headquarters for troops during this period, and Red Wolf continuously went out with his military bosses to investigate the increasing number of Indian raids throughout the area.

As time went on, Red Wolf heard more details about Hancock's show of force, which even used artillery. It seemed Hancock hoped the Indians would be frightened into a permanent peace. With six companies of infantry and artillery, Hancock marched to Fort Leavenworth and then to Fort Riley, where he was joined by Lieutenant Colonel George Custer with four companies of the Seventh cavalry and one company of infantry. At Fort Harker, the expedition added two more cavalry troops and marched to Fort Lamed, arriving on April 7, 1867.

The Cheyenne and Sioux were camped in an area known as Pawnee Fork about thirty miles from Fort Larned. When the Indians refused to come in to the fort and declare their intentions for peace, Hancock decided to march on their encampment. On the 11th of April, his regiment moved forward. Before reaching the encampment, they were met by a large body of Indians bearing a white flag. The chiefs said they wanted peace instead of war, but Hancock's troops ignored them and continued to move forward to make their own camp near the Indian village.

The Indians, fearing another Sand Creek Massacre, fled during the night.

Custer went after them the next day, but the Indians, after first raiding an Overland Stage Company station on the Smoky Hill Trail, scattered. Hancock burned what was left of the Indian village on Pawnee Fork and then marched to Fort Dodge. After several days, his troops headed back to Fort Hays. Red Wolf was shocked how Hancock's campaign had changed the entire picture in Kansas. It seemed every time he hoped for peace and retirement, Red Wolf found war was the inescapable outcome.

Custer and his Seventh cavalry remained in the field still pursuing the Indians, and his pursuit extended northward into Nebraska, which was now a state. The hostiles continued to refuse all overtures of peace and several times turned on Custer, becoming the pursuer instead of the pursued.

It was then Red Wolf learned of an event known as the Kidder Massacre, which occurred on June 29, 1867. Second Lieutenant Lyman Kidder, an Indian scout, and a party of ten enlisted men were sent with dispatches for Custer by General William Sherman from Fort Sedgwick, Nebraska. At the time, Custer was thought to be camped along the Republican River.

When the group arrived and saw Custer's camp had moved, Kidder mistakenly headed south toward Fort Wallace, the westernmost fort in Kansas. The fort was right in the middle of Indian country along the Colorado border. Along the way, Kidder and his party were killed in an ambush by an Indian war party, thought to be Sioux and Northern Cheyenne, in Sherman County in northwest Kansas. After the massacre, Custer's expedition returned to Fort Wallace in July, having failed to gain a decisive victory over the Indians in Nebraska.

The Kidder Massacre was only one example of the atrocities escalating after the failed Hancock campaign. In June of 1867, Indians also attacked Henshaw Station, a stop on the Butterfield Overland Dispatch about nine miles east of Fort Wallace. The Indians killed four men and stampeded the horses, but at the time the station was guarded by only ten soldiers and two stock traders. Pursuit of the Indians was impossible, and by the time a larger force arrived from Fort Wallace, the Indians had disappeared.

Later in 1867, another raid occurred at a small settlement called Brookville near Salina. When Red Wolf heard about it, he almost bolted on his horse to make sure Jeb and Mokee were safe. When a large body of Indians attacked the town, the settlers rushed to the roundhouse and threw up a barricade. The Indians surrounded the building and piled railroad ties against it, trying to set the structure on fire.

Railroad crew members jumped onto a steam engine, crashed it through the doors of the roundhouse, and headed for help. This action caught the Indians off guard, and they fled. When the engine reached Salina, a dead Indian was found lying on a wheel. Because the year of 1867 was turning out to be one of the bloodiest in Kansas history, most Kansans who wanted peace had to be armed and prepared for the worst.

The United States government finally lost its patience with Indian tribes being at war and in July of 1867, Congress established the Indian Peace Commission to negotiate peace. The commission's goal was to separate peaceful Indians from hostile ones and remove all Indians to reservations, which would be maintained away from the routes enabling expansion of the country.

In the fall of 1867, Red Wolf accompanied his military bosses to Fort Larned on the 11th of October for peace negotiations. He vividly remembered his stay there with Jeb and Mokee after her harrowing escape from the Dog Soldiers, and it made him happy to think how he'd arranged their marriage. Much of the new construction had been completed at the fort since his last visit, and it was jam-packed with soldiers with more scheduled to arrive. Red Wolf's skills as a translator were in demand as preliminary meetings were ongoing with tribes already camped in the area.

One of the Indian chiefs present was Black Kettle of the Cheyenne, whose encampment was attacked in the Sand Creek Massacre three years earlier. He and the chiefs of the Arapaho and Kiowa insisted any meetings be moved from Fort Larned to a traditional Indian ceremonial site at nearby Medicine Lodge Creek.

The Medicine Lodge Treaty would become the title for three separate treaties signed from October 21-28 in 1867. The first treaty was with the Kiowa and Comanche, the second with the Kiowa-Apache, and the third with the Southern Cheyenne and Arapaho. All three treaties basically diminished the size of reservations promised in the Treaty of the Little Arkansas of 1865 and moved tribes to an area known as Indian territory, which was located south of Kansas in the Oklahoma territory.

The rhetoric of the commission was conciliatory. It admitted the government had not acted with honesty in past treaties, and it apologized for General Hancock's ill-conceived destruction of the Cheyenne and Sioux village at Pawnee Fork in April of that year.

Words and more words, Red Wolf muttered, as he knew each new treaty basically took more land. The Medicine Lodge Treaty was no different. The new treaty cut in half the lands designated to the Southern Cheyenne and Arapaho. As he listened to the one-sided peace process unfold, Red Wolf thought about how many treaties had been signed over the years. Essentially, the Indians gave away most of what they had and every few years, the government asked for more land.

Red Wolf also knew the Dog Soldiers would not be appeased by a concession saying tribes could hunt north of the Arkansas River as long as the buffalo remained. Because the Dog Soldiers were not involved in the peace process at all and were still actively conducting raids across the state of Kansas, the war continued even as the Indian chiefs and government officials falsely guaranteed peace.

Red Wolf knew another major fallacy of the Medicine Lodge Treaty was it required the approval of three-fourths of the adult males on a reservation for any cessions of land. This approval was never obtained, thus making any treaty invalid from the start. Perhaps the most glaring problem, however, was the refusal of the Northern Cheyenne to join the peace process at all. Instead, they were allied with Chief Red Cloud and the Oglala Lakota (Sioux) in a continuing war against the United States.

In one of the most moving speeches Red Wolf had ever heard, Chief Ten Bears of the Comanche said, ". . . My people have never first drawn a bow or fired a gun against the whites . . . It was you to send the first soldier and we who sent out the second. . .You said that you wanted to put us upon a reservation, to build our houses and make us medicine lodges. I do not want them. I was born on the prairie where the wind blew free and there was nothing to break the light of the sun. I was born where there were no enclosures and where everything drew a free breath. I want to die there and not within walls. I know every stream and every wood between the Rio Grande and the Arkansas. I have hunted and lived over the country. I lived like my fathers before me, and like them, I lived happily.

"When I was at Washington, the Great Father (president of the United States) told me that all the Comanche land was ours and that no one should hinder us in living upon it. So, why do you ask us to leave the rivers and the sun and the wind and live in houses?"

It was a good question, Red Wolf realized, and one for which he had no answer. *Why were the Indians asked to leave the land which had been their home for thousands of years?*

Sweet is the memory of distant friends!
Like the mellow rays of the departing sun,
it falls tenderly, yet sadly, on the heart.

Washington Irving

Chapter Thirty-one

The weather had gotten colder, and another winter was approaching. There was even snow in the air. Red Wolf had been hoping to get some time off and make his way back to see Jeb and Mokee. That little girl must have had her baby by now, and he hoped her delivery went well, and her baby was healthy. He wondered if they had a boy or a girl, and then he laughed out loud at his speculation. *Why should he care*, he thought. Yet, he did care.

As he took his Meerschaum pipe out of his pocket and began packing it with tobacco, Red Wolf smiled wryly. He did care more than he wanted to admit, and he didn't like caring. After his wife Nanomone'e died, he gave up the futile exercise. So why did he, all of a sudden, care so much? If he were being honest with himself, he loved Mokee and Jeb like family, he who never needed anyone.

The Indian leaned his head back against a smudged, cracked wall, and the scent of leathery tobacco wafted pleasantly around his nostrils. He remembered how surprised he'd been when Jeb and Mokee had given him such a fine gift last year for Christmas. Red Wolf shook his head. *What made those two kids so damn likeable?* Then another thought crossed his mind. *What if they got all tongue-tied with each other again, and Mokee ran away?* After all, they didn't have his calming influence around to make them act like adults. *Calming?* The thought made him laugh as he knew he sometimes resembled an active volcano spewing molten lava. If he didn't know any better, he was sounding like a doting parent, only he and Nanomone'e could never have any children.

He took another puff and blew a few aimless circles at the ceiling. Maybe that was what was wrong with the world. There were too many jaded adults and not enough young dreamers. Red Wolf knew one thing for sure. He was way past being an adult or a dreamer. He was just plain getting old and tired, and his limbs had begun to ache with every step, especially with the frigid temperatures.

Why had he even accepted this new tour of duty and traveled all the way to Fort Wallace near the Colorado border? What he wanted to do was retire and sit on a porch rocker with his feet on a railing, and he wanted to tell stories to his new pretend grandbaby of Mokee and Jeb's. But, he knew he couldn't barge in on those two young kids and interfere with their lives. They couldn't possibly have meant it when they said they wanted him to think about staying there a while. They were just being polite, he decided.

Hell, he was used to being a loner and an outcast, and it was probably for the best. He really didn't fit in with either the Cheyenne or the white people anymore. Everyone held him at an arm's length. It was as if people were afraid of him. Maybe it was why he felt so comfortable with Jeb and Mokee. They just seemed like ordinary people, and they didn't seem to particularly fit in either.

Red Wolf still hadn't made any progress tracking down Tovee, and that was part of the reason he decided to take the new assignment. After all, he had promised Mokee he would try to keep Tovee from the Salina area, and he took his promises very seriously as he didn't make many of them. The Dog Soldiers were more active than ever, and the worst part was Fort Wallace was right in the heart of hostile Indian camps. Because it was so prone to being ambushed at its old digs, the fort even had to move its site a year ago.

Ever since he arrived, there was all that damn hammering of new construction. First, a new quarters was built and then a permanent hospital. There was even a dam put up across the Smoky Hill River, but constant Indian attacks kept bringing the construction to a standstill. Even the building supplies couldn't reach the fort because of the Indians. It was easy to forget he was an Indian. Red Wolf was starting to blame them for his discomfort in this blasted cold. Eventually, the hostilities stopped long enough for supplies to reach the fort, and construction resumed.

Now he discovered there was a huge, brainless problem with all of the new structures. Red Wolf was glad he could blame something on the white soldiers for a change. The commanding officer, because of negligence or whatever, maybe stupidity, forgot to have any doors put on the new buildings. The damp winter air continually seeped through the massive openings, something a paper-thin, army issue blanket didn't help. Thinking about the lack of doors suddenly made him shiver, and Red Wolf yanked his blanket tighter around his shoulders.

Since Red Wolf arrived, troop assignments and manpower at Fort Wallace was steadily increasing, mainly because of the civilians arriving to lay track for the new railroad line. It was supposed to connect up in the next year. *Wouldn't it be something to take a train all the way back to see Mokee and Jeb?* Red Wolf shook his head at the direction his thoughts kept going. What the hell was wrong with him for being so sentimental?

Fort Wallace was going to be the toughest tour of duty he'd had yet as the fort had more Indian fights than any of the other forts combined. He knew most of the Indian attackers wouldn't know who he was and would consider him a traitor and enemy along with the white soldiers. So, the odds of his staying alive through this tour of duty weren't especially good. He would have to try to be more watchful this time and pay more attention to his surroundings. *Only one more year*, he kept thinking. If he stayed alive that long, maybe he'd retire.

Because he was a translator and in on most meetings, Red Wolf was privy to most secret information crossing the desks of his commanders and discussed in strategy sessions. That was how he found out several large bands of Dog Soldiers, along with their war chiefs, were thought to be just over the border in the Colorado territory.

The officers argued back and forth about the necessity of sending a scout to track the Dog Soldiers' impending movements, and it was finally decided the information would be important for planning upcoming military missions. Although the camp had a number of qualified scouts, all of them younger than Red Wolf and eager to make a name for themselves, Red Wolf abruptly volunteered his services for the mission. To lessen the chances he'd be spotted by the Cheyenne, it was decided he should head out alone the next morning.

Red Wolf made ready his preparations before bed, grousing the whole time. He really didn't feel like traipsing across the countryside and sleeping on the rocky ground like a teenager. His bum knee was really starting to bother him. Plus, he wasn't thrilled at the thought of living in the wilds again. He'd gotten used to mess hall fare, and Fort Wallace had the best food he'd had at any of the forts. But he also knew this might be his only opportunity to make good on his promise to Mokee, and he needed to see what he could do about getting Tovee sent away from north central Kansas.

He journeyed for days into the Colorado territory and noticed nothing unusual. Red Wolf was almost ready to change course and head north. All of a sudden, good fortune was with him, and he spotted traces of a former camp. Changing his mind, he decided to continue southwesterly for a day or so and sure enough, he spotted the impressive cluster of camps at the juncture between the Arkansas and Purgatoire Rivers. It was only about a day's ride from where the Sand Creek Massacre had taken place.

Mounting a white flag on a timber, Red Wolf rode majestically into the camp on his black stallion. He knew his appearance was as commanding as usual, but he also knew he was plumb tired and felt like curling up and taking a nap. He hoped he would see his old friend, Taa'evanahkohe (Night Bear), as he was the one who had come up with a mission for Tovee's band of warriors.

Before long, Red Wolf was greeted with a few spears directed toward his chest. Then he heard someone shout, "It's just Ma'o'nehe." All of a sudden, the spears disinterestedly went down, and the Dog Soldiers, as if bored with "just Ma'o'nehe," went about their business. Before the last one left, Red Wolf called out and asked where Night Bear's tepee was, and the warrior motioned with his head before walking away.

Soon, Night Bear and Red Wolf were having a grand reunion. The two hadn't seen each other in more than a year. Although he was perhaps twenty years younger than Red Wolf, Night Bear had suffered a lot more battle injuries over the course of his lifetime. Not only did he have a limp in one knee where he took a bullet, but he had a scar stretching from one shoulder to his wrist, which he got from hand-to-hand combat. While they feasted on buffalo stew prepared by Night Bear's squaw, they laughed heartily about their aches and pains, and they vividly remembered the lust of their youth. When she was done serving the meal, Night Bear's squaw left to give them privacy.

It was time to get down to business. Red Wolf explained he was on official business for the military to track down their camp. He said he would take back whatever information the war chiefs wanted the military to have, and Night Bear nodded, saying he would have to discuss it with the chiefs.

Then Red Wolf said he wanted to speak with Night Bear about some unofficial business. "Remember when I came to see you the last time? I received a mission from you to give to a small band of Dog Soldiers, which is an arm of your organization."

"I remember," Night Bear said. His face was unreadable.

"What I did not tell you at the time was I had been handsomely paid by a white man to bring him along. He was in love with a young Cheyenne woman. She had been taken from his home by a member of that band."

"I heard something along the lines saying you were a traitor and seen with a white man," Night Bear confirmed.

Red Wolf had known the story would make the rounds, and he laughed delightedly. "You of all people know I am a businessman, and I take paying jobs from time to time."

Night Bear nodded with an understanding smile.

"I rescued the young Cheyenne woman, whose name is Mokee'eso by the way. If Nanomone'e and I would have had a child, she would have been just like Mokee, which is what she's called. I have come to think of her as my daughter, and I am very protective of her. She's now married to the white man she loves, who's a farmer in Kansas, and they are very happy. She became separated from her parents during the Sand Creek Massacre, and she's had a hard life. I want her to find happiness.

"Here's the problem. There's a Dog Soldier named Tovôhkeso who refuses to let her alone. Not only did he keep her with the Dog Soldiers against her will, but he came back about a year ago and raped her in the farmhouse where she now lives. I don't think he knows she married the white man, but he did threaten to kill him if she didn't cooperate." Red Wolf scowled ferociously, and his low voice became incensed. "My little Mokee's a mother now, and she doesn't deserve abuse by one of her own people. I want her to be left alone by Tovôhkeso, who is obsessed with her and believes she is his. He is treating her with disrespect."

As if ascertaining whether Red Wolf was telling the truth, Night Bear stared at his friend. He could see no hint of falsity. "What is it you want me to do?"

"The Dog Soldier band is under the control of this band, and I want them directed to make their raids as far away from Salina, Kansas as possible. I'm not having Tovôhkeso attack my little girl every time he gets in the area. She doesn't deserve that kind of treatment. I swear, I'll kill him myself if you don't keep him away from there." Red Wolf paused, trying to bring a calm tone of respect into his voice. "I haven't taken any action yet, as I defer to your direction. Tovôhkeso is obviously an effective warrior for the Cheyenne cause, and that is the reason I have shown restraint in dealing with him. This has nothing to do with the war, however. If you had a daughter being attacked, what would you do?"

"I would do as you have done, my friend," Night Bear said quietly. "I would go to the person who could take care of the situation in an impartial manner, and I would trust the situation would soon be resolved."

Red Wolf accepted Night Bear at his word, and the matter was dropped. He enjoyed his old friend's hospitality for the remainder of the day and night. In the morning, after receiving instructions on what to tell his commanding officers, Red Wolf began the long ride back to Fort Wallace. He hoped he wasn't too late in taking care of the matter with Tovee.

He that cannot forgive others breaks the bridge
over which he must pass himself;
for every man has need to be forgiven.

Thomas Fuller

Chapter Thirty-two

Summer finally came. At least his aches and pains got a little better during the hot summer months. Red Wolf was sure he had what the white man called arthritis. Some mornings, he could barely get off his cot as his joints were so stiff. Every day, he reminded himself he could retire in a few months after his stint at Fort Wallace was done. Because he really didn't have a home anymore, he wasn't sure where he was going to go when he quit. He thought he might briefly go see Jeb and Mokee and their new baby. It was important for his peace of mind to see they were still safe, especially after all the raids he'd heard about in Saline County.

The past few months had seen a lot of fighting at Fort Wallace. Indian raids by the younger warrior societies were in full swing, and Red Wolf knew there was a schism developing between the young rebels and many of the older Cheyenne warriors, who wanted to live out their lives in peace. One had only to look at the signatures on the Medicine Lodge Treaty to see they were the names of the older chiefs, and yet the war continued unabated with the more virulent Dog Soldiers.

Hancock, the general who was criticized for burning down the village at Pawnee Fork and trying to scare the Indians into submission, had been replaced by General Philip Sheridan. After nearly eighty settlers were killed in raids in the Colorado territory, the acting governor asked Sheridan for assistance. During the summer of 1868, Sheridan patrolled near the Arkansas River as well as northern Kansas.

The most recent attack by a group of raiding Indians was on group of settlers in the Saline and Solomon River valleys in Kansas. They captured two white women after killing the other settlers. Because Sheridan was so enraged by the kidnapping, he ordered Colonel George Forsyth of the Ninth cavalry to form a volunteer company at Fort Harker to pursue the raiding party. His aide, Lieutenant Frederick Beecher of the Third infantry, hand selected experienced frontiersmen, ex-soldiers, and scouts for the mission. They marched to Fort Hays and finally to Fort Wallace, a distance of almost two hundred miles.

It was at Fort Wallace Red Wolf became involved with supplying the volunteer army with ammunition, rations, pack mules, and a few horses. He knew the group would most likely come face to face with Night Bear's experienced band of Dog Soldiers, though it was unlikely the band had attacked the settlers. The band was extremely large and well-organized with its war chiefs, and Red Wolf had a pang of regret for the ragtag bunch of volunteers, who were probably on a suicide mission. He knew the small raiding party of Dog Soldiers responsible for kidnapping the women had long vanished, though it was possible the band had been assimilated into the larger band. The odds weren't looking good for Forsyth and his group, however, as they were sure to be outnumbered.

Nonetheless, the motley group headed off from Fort Wallace on the 10th of September with orders to stop a raid on the Kansas Pacific railhead and possibly on a wagon train near Sheridan, Kansas, which was about thirteen miles to the east. Later on, Red Wolf learned the troops followed the tracks of a raiding party north to the Republican River and then westward into the Colorado territory to the Delaware Creek, which was also called the Arikaree River or Arikaree Fork. Although they saw no Indians, the soldiers were positive they were in the vicinity. The troops made a camp opposite a sandy island, which would one day be called Beecher Island, and they chose it as a safe place of retreat if they were surrounded by the enemy.

After being notified by their scouts about the location of the white soldiers' camp, the Cheyenne, Arapahoe, and Sioux attacked en masse at dawn on the 17th of September. Forsyth gave the order to reach the safety of the island, and the sudden retreat of the soldiers surprised the Indians. When Forsyth divided his fifty troops to opposite ends of the island, the Indians advanced in disorder. They were met with volley after volley of gunfire from the soldiers, who had dug shallow pits in the sand. Although far outnumbered, the troops picked off many Indians, including two chiefs who were advancing in the tall grass.

The famed warrior, Roman Nose, took command after the demise of the chiefs, and he entered the fray. It was said he was also shot and killed, and the attack temporarily ceased until Chief Dull Knife of the Sioux brought reinforcements. Upon Dull Knife's death, the battle ended, but the Indians stayed on to mourn their dead. Although they no longer attacked, the Indians' plan was to starve the remaining white soldiers, who were hunkered down on the island.

There were many wounded troops, including Colonel Forsyth and Lieutenant Beecher, and any soldiers who survived were severely dehydrated. Because the troops had lost their pack mules in the initial fighting, all they had to survive on was muddy river water and one dead horse. Although it was perilous, two of Forsyth's scouts managed to escape through enemy lines to reach Fort Wallace for help on the 20th of September.

Red Wolf joined a large group of scouts which headed out with the Tenth cavalry regiment, also known as the Buffalo Soldiers, under Brevet Lieutenant

Colonel Louis Carpenter. Although it was a long, exhausting ride to the Arikaree River in the Colorado territory, Red Wolf had roamed these prairies for most of his life, and he knew every shortcut and possible ambush spot. The Indians, who were still camped on the riverbank, fled as soon as they spotted the arrival of more troops on the 25th of September.

While Forsyth's badly injured troops were tended to by the reinforcements, Red Wolf pensively scoured the tall grasses and fields for the dead bodies of Cheyenne warriors he may have known. He hoped he wouldn't find Night Bear's body. A week had passed since the battle, and the bodies remaining were bloated and rancid. Red Wolf kept moving, though, in a silent benediction for his lost brothers. They never understood the resources and sheer numbers of the white men were endless and unbeatable.

In the distance around the perimeter of the battlefield, there were clusters of scaffolds silhouetted against the oddly peaceful blue sky. A few dead bodies rested on top, the height of the platforms protecting the corpses from being eaten by wild animals. Red Wolf decided he would pay his respects later on to those fallen warriors, who had been honored by their wives in death. He knew for certain any fallen chiefs and the warrior Roman Nose, who was rumored to have been killed, would be honored by being laid to rest on a scaffold.

Red Wolf kept walking, not knowing why he did but mesmerized by the carnage of what appeared to be from seven hundred to a thousand Indians. The fallen warriors, many of them Dog Soldiers, were so young, some even teenagers, and their lifeless bodies had no one to venerate them in death. Many had been alone in life, fighting for revenge that never came and dying in hatred. *What a waste*, he thought sadly. Red Wolf was just about ready to make his way back to the others when he saw him. Almost in a trance, he edged his way forward through the tall grass. It was Tovee.

As he knelt down beside the almost unrecognizable body of the young Dog Soldier he hated, Red Wolf's heart pounded. Here was the body of the young man who had defiled his precious Mokee and almost destroyed her happiness. He wanted to despise this body, and he even wanted to kick it and scream out loud at it.

But suddenly, it was pitiable, and tears of remorse began to stream from his eyes. This was a young man who had loved only one thing in his life of hatred and revenge, and that was Mokee. Tovee's life was too brief to understand love couldn't be forced and brutalized, only treated with gentleness and respect for the rare gift it was.

All at once, Red Wolf understood what Jeb had said about forgiveness on Christmas nearly two years before. In recounting the first Christmas, Jeb had said the Great Spirit of love had given all of mankind a gift of love, His only Son

Jesus. Likewise, Jesus gave mankind His gift of love, dying on the cross so we could be forgiven our sins. Jeb had asked how we could give our gift of love to each other. It was then he said the phrase Red Wolf always remembered. He said the true path of life was forgiveness, not seeking revenge or being overcome with hatred. We would someday have peace only by forgiving as God forgave us.

Red Wolf sighed heavily as his misty eyes took notice of something around Tovee's swollen neck. It was the soft elk skin necklace Tovee had made for Mokee when they were young. She had worn it around her neck until the day she left Tovee. A few more tears slipped down his cheeks. Red Wolf reverently removed the necklace and tucked it in his pocket. Although Tovee had not done right by Mokee in life, he had loved her unto death.

Nearly collapsing with emotion, Red Wolf gently closed the young Indian's eyes. His voice was gravelly as he said, "May you find peace in death, Tovôhkeso, brave warrior of the Cheyenne. You are forgiven." After uttering the words of forgiveness he never thought he could say, Red Wolf pushed his weary body up off the ground, and he slowly walked away.

Chapter Thirty-three

Blasted horseflies, the Indian thought as he pulled his sleeping roll up around his chiseled face. He groaned as he got into a more comfortable position on his side, and then he cut loose with a barrage of expletives as his arthritic knee got jabbed by a sharp twig. Who would have thought early October would be so damn hot and the woods filled with pesky bloodsuckers?

Red Wolf thought he would never get rid of the stench of the dead bodies rotting in the sun. Every time he took a deep breath, it seemed he was back on the riverbank by the Arikaree River, smelling the decay. He was sure the horrifying sight would haunt him forever. When he closed his eyes to sleep at night, he saw nothing but swollen bodies strewn over a landscape of blowing grass. What good had it done for his Cheyenne brothers to seek revenge? They were gone now, never to fight again. Worse yet, he couldn't get Tovee's wide-eyed, petrified face out of his mind.

That's why he quit. As soon as his regiment got back to Fort Wallace, he marched into the commanding officer's headquarters and said two words, "I quit." It was plain and simple. He left with the clothes on his back, a few bucks of back pay, his horse, and his sleeping roll and saddle. He was too old to lie around in bunkers and fend off Indian attacks. His joints were in too much pain to sleep on the ground for the rest of his life, and his heart was too grieved for his Indian brothers, who all lay dead for a useless cause. Nothing made sense to him anymore, or maybe everything made sense to him for the first time. He was tired and old. War was nothing but hell and in his last days, he wanted peace and comfort and maybe a hot bath now and then.

He struggled to get off the ground, rolled up his sleeping bag, and mounted his horse. Red Wolf was almost there. He'd passed Fort Hays more than a day ago, and he decided he would pass through Jeb and Mokee's place on his way to nowhere. Nowhere was sweet. He would just fade away and make them think he had a destination. But the fact was, there was no destination for him but a plot in the ground. Red Wolf knew he wouldn't make the young couple deal with putting up with a crotchety old man for the last years of his life. He did have one last thing to do, though. Red Wolf had to give Mokee her elk skin necklace and tell her that Tovee had died. It might be the hardest thing he ever did.

We sensed him before we saw him. It was an early fall evening and because the weather was unusually hot for October, we were sitting on the front porch rocking. Catherine was already asleep in her crib, but her window was open above us. We could hear if she needed anything. The sun was just getting ready to set when we saw the lone, towering figure riding slowly toward us on a massive black stallion.

"Well, I'll be damned," Jeb exclaimed with shock in his voice.

I stared at the distant figure across the expanse of prairie grass and then started saying, "Oh my God. . . oh my God. . ." Before even finishing my garbled words, I was off and running across the grass barefooted, my white cotton dress flowing in a breeze as tears of joy splashed down my face. Jeb was right beside me, matching me stride for stride and telling me he was worried the Indian might be injured as he was moving toward us so slowly.

Exhausted, Red Wolf looked up from his horse. He had ridden with determination, wanting to reach Jeb and Mokee's by dusk. If the two people he loved more than anything weren't running to greet him, he might not have recognized the blasted house. A porch as long as a railway car draped the front with a row of white rockers. *Jeb must be doing well with the farm*, he thought to himself, pleased for his friend.

Then he saw cute little Mokee, her figure as tiny as ever in her white summer dress. A feeling of coldness swept over him. *What if she had lost the baby? They weren't holding a baby.* He panicked and nudged his horse a little faster.

"Well, if you aren't a sight for sore eyes, Red Wolf," Jeb said emotionally. He went forward to help the Indian down from his horse. As soon as the older man got his footing, Jeb hugged him like a son hugs his long lost father. I could tell Red Wolf was touched as his eyes were wet with tears.

"What about me?" I said impatiently, giving up trying to wipe away my flowing tears. I flew into Red Wolf's burly arms, pressing my face so tightly against his I almost smashed my cheek. "We missed you so much, Red Wolf," I said, holding each side of his face with the palms of my hands. Then, I surprised the heck out of him by giving him a huge kiss. His pleased grin was worth it.

"Why don't you take Red Wolf in the house, Mokee, and I'll put his horse in the barn," Jeb said, giving me a secretive look. I knew I wasn't to say anything about our plan to have him stay permanently. By the time Jeb got back from the barn with Red Wolf's things, I had seated my favorite Indian at the kitchen table and was feeding him leftovers from a ham and scalloped potato casserole we'd had for dinner. He looked content, but years older than when he left. His manner was unusually quiet, and he looked haunted by something. Even his hair had turned a silvery gray since we saw him last.

I was sure Jeb noticed the difference in Red Wolf's demeanor as he seemed a little puzzled how to make him comfortable. Suddenly, out of nowhere, Jeb said, "Red Wolf, it looks like you've been traveling a mighty long way. How would you like a nice hot bath before I take you to your very special new bedroom?" Jeb gave a crooked, toothy grin hardly anyone knew how to resist, especially me. "After all, you want to be fresh in the morning when you meet somebody special who lives here now."

I heard Red Wolf breathe an audible sigh of relief, and it was then I realized, because I was so tiny again, he thought we'd lost the baby. Reassuringly, I patted his arm and said, "Yes, you don't want to miss a very special surprise in the morning!" I rose from the table and walked over to Jeb and kissed him on the lips. Then I returned to Red Wolf and leaned over behind his chair to hug him and give him a kiss on the cheek. "I love you, Red Wolf. You need to enjoy a nice hot bath and a good night's sleep, and I'll see you in the morning. Have fun, boys." With a wave, I went upstairs to let Jeb get our friend used to the house once more.

Red Wolf never had a white man treat him with the respect and kindness of Jeb. Without a complaint, Jeb heated pot after pot of water for the most indescribably wonderful bath he'd ever had. The Indian rested in the tub until the water practically turned cold, soaking away not only the trail dust from his lengthy trip, but hopefully the stench of dead bodies infusing the pores of his skin. He lathered his body and shampooed his shoulder length hair with a strange soap smelling like berries, and he even held his breath and stuck his head under water, hoping the scent of death in his nostrils would rinse clean.

When he was through, Red Wolf dried himself in the softest bath towel he'd ever felt. *I could get used to hot baths*, he said to himself, and then quickly shrugged the thought from his mind. He'd stay a day or two, no more, he decided, as he wrapped the towel around himself until he could find his sack of clothing.

As soon as the door to the bath closet opened, Jeb was right there asking him how his bath was. Red Wolf looked at Jeb sideways, knowing his friend was up to something. Jeb was yakking on and on about all the improvements they'd done to the house since he was gone, and he couldn't wait to show Red Wolf in the morning. Then Jeb went on about how he was going to share one of the surprises with him tonight.

While the younger man was running off at the mouth, he'd been ushering the towel-wrapped Indian slowly across the living room, which was brightly lit by an oil lamp. Suddenly, they reached a double door made of wood. Red Wolf didn't remember a door on the side wall.

"Now, I've got a surprise for you, Red Wolf, and I want you to keep quiet about your surprise as we'll talk more about it in the morning," Jeb said, pushing open the wooden doors. Beyond the doors was the most beautiful room Red

Wolf had ever seen, longer than all get out and all lit up in oil lamps. There was a massive four-poster bed, a big leather easy chair, a dresser, and a soft rug under his feet.

"Mokee and I had this room built special for you, Red Wolf, because we love you, and you're a part of our family. We want you to live with us. Now, I know you're going to be difficult and because you're a proud man, you won't take handouts. I've decided you can work for me and take care of the horses and sometimes even the farm equipment in return for room and board. I don't want your answer tonight, because I think you should sleep on it. But I want you to know you're going to break Mokee's heart if you turn her down. Don't forget, she thinks of you as her father.

"Oh, there's one more thing. You might get a little visitor in the morning, and I don't think you should sleep stark naked tonight. I know the thought of wearing a white man's clothes is going to make you shiver in your moccasins, but tonight I'd like you to sleep in pajamas so you won't frighten your little visitor. Understand?" Jeb finished with a smirk on his face.

"I should have squashed you like a fly long ago," Red Wolf grumbled with a scowl. "Damn white man!" He wanted to say, "Damn white man he loved like a son," but he thought it was a bit melodramatic, even though it was true.

"You know, I'm getting pretty strong from working so hard on the farm," Jeb said proudly. "Maybe I'd squash you instead."

Red Wolf made a sound of disdain. "There's a fat chance of that ever happening, Jeb. Are you forgetting who rescued your butt from the Dog Soldiers?"

"I'll never forget who rescued me, ever," Jeb said sincerely, touching the Indian on his shoulder. "So, enjoy your new digs. And by the way, it's good to have you home!" Jeb gave a mischievous grin as he left the room and shut the doors.

"Blasted white boy," Red Wolf hissed, stroking the smooth wood of the dresser with his hand. "I never should have rescued him in the first place." The Indian shrugged his massive body into the God-awful striped sissy pants and shirt and crawled between the crisp white sheets of a torturously soft feather bed. His weary body sank down in heavenly delight. Red Wolf had never felt so comfortable, and his eyes moistened with emotion. Not only was he glad he rescued both Jeb and Mokee, but he was glad to be home.

Forgiveness is the fragrance that the violet sheds
on the heel that has crushed it.

Mark Twain

Chapter Thirty-four

"Now, Mommy, please," the little voice of Catherine pleaded. I looked at my talkative 15-month-old and then glanced at Jeb. Jeb returned my look of confusion as neither of us knew whether it was too early for Catherine to surprise Red Wolf. Finally, we both nodded, and the tiny girl with the pale brown curls and big blue eyes charged across the living room.

"Wake him quietly, Catherine," I whispered, opening the doors to the large bedroom. I could see Red Wolf's huge form still huddled in the sheets. Jeb and I stood at the door, holding hands worriedly, wondering what the Indian's reaction would be to his tiny visitor.

Catherine tiptoed up to the bed and put her face on the sheet right in front of Red Wolf's face. Jeb and I could see his eyes flutter open, and we watched him study the serious little face so close to his own.

"Hello, Grandpa," she said shyly in her sweet voice. She gave him her best smile and then turned to Jeb and me. "Mommy, Daddy, Grandpa's awake," she shouted. Then she turned back to Red Wolf and said, "Lift me up, Grandpa. I want to sit with you."

We saw the Indian's giant form shrug out of the sheets in his striped pajamas, and he gently picked up the little girl and put her on the bed. "Thanks," she said, staring at his face. "Can I touch your face?" she asked, putting her dimpled hands on his cheeks without waiting for an answer. "You're a pretty color." Red Wolf laughed, totally disarmed.

"Will you eat breakfast with me, Grandpa? I'm having oatmeal today." He said for her to go on ahead, and he would be there when he got dressed. Carefully, he set her back down on the floor. Before she left, she turned to him. "Are you going to live here with me, Grandpa?" she asked innocently. Jeb and I rolled our eyes at each other as she wasn't supposed to say that yet. Catherine was what poker players called "our ace in the hole."

"C'mon Catherine," I said quickly, taking her hand and walking her from the room. "See you at breakfast."

Jeb stayed in the room, and he and Red Wolf stared at each other momentarily.

"She's a beautiful little girl," the Indian said, stretching out his limbs. He felt a whole lot better this morning.

"I know. We're very blessed. And, I know she's hard to resist. Did I tell you Catherine's full name?" Jeb asked conversationally. Red Wolf shook his head no. "Her first name, Catherine, is for my mother as Mokee and my mother loved each other very much. Her last name is, of course, Preston, which is my name. It's her middle name I thought you'd be the most interested in."

"Spit it out, Jeb," Red Wolf said suspiciously.

"Mokee decided to name her Naomi, which she said would be a shortened version of your wife's name, Nanomone'e. She said it would help Catherine grow into a woman of peace like her grandmother."

"Damn, but you don't play fair, Jeb," the Indian grumbled with a scowl.

Jeb smiled as he turned to leave. "By the way, I never said I played fair, Red Wolf. You should know me by now. I'm just a typical white man."

Red Wolf chuckled to himself as he got dressed in his buckskin pants and a short sleeved tee shirt Jeb set on the bed. For the first time in a long time, he was genuinely looking forward to his day, and he hurried from the bedroom to get acquainted with his new granddaughter.

Jeb was convinced Red Wolf needed to have a man to man talk. Although the Indian affectionately put up with Mokee's excited chatter about motherhood and all the wonderful changes they had made to the house, Jeb could see their friend was distracted and pensive, especially when he thought no one was looking. There was definitely something troubling him, and the Indian was deliberately vague about his whereabouts for the past two years.

When Mokee was putting Catherine down for her afternoon nap, Jeb suggested he and Red Wolf take a walk around the farm, and he could show him some of the new fields. The day was a little cooler as the skies were partly cloudy, but it still was too warm for a long walk. Instead, Jeb led the Indian to the tall oak tree where his mother was buried, and then he urged Red Wolf to sit down on one of the two benches he had built there to make it a place of reflection. After a few moments of silence and enjoying the shade, Jeb said, "I'm a good listener, Red Wolf."

After a brief moment of hesitation, the Indian began pouring out his heart. He told Jeb about his time at Fort Hays and the sham of the Medicine Lodge Treaty. Then, he recounted how he had been transferred to Fort Wallace and what a hellhole it had been until it was rebuilt. He spoke of the constant fights with the Indians, who were trying to stop the railroad from being built, and eventually the Battle of Arikaree Fork.

By this time, Jeb had moved next to Red Wolf and rested a comforting hand of encouragement on the Indian's shoulder. Red Wolf wept while he told about his Cheyenne brothers and also the Sioux and Arapaho rotting in a field of grass, mud, and dried blood. He said he couldn't get the stench out of his nostrils and the horror of their dead bodies out of his mind.

"Why should I continue living while my brothers are all dead?" Red Wolf asked Jeb in a gravelly voice. "Nothing makes sense to me anymore. My brothers died trying to save their way of life from the white man. Yet you, a white man, want me to live with you and be a grandfather to your child. I can't grasp it, Jeb. Why is it so important to you?"

Jeb was quiet for a minute as he thought about the question. His thoughts suddenly congealed in a moment of enlightenment. "It's important because you and I will be a living example to others. We will show people a white man and a red man can live together in love, respect, and peace. You and I, by our actions, will show others that the God who created us all is colorblind, and the gift of his Son and His death on the cross for our sins was for everyone, no matter what color a person's skin is.

"It's not going to be easy for you if you decide to live with us, Red Wolf. One day, after the Indian raids stop and there is peace, I'm going to convince Mokee to share her journals and her heritage. It may be rough for a while, and there might be prejudice against us in the community. We'll really get to know if we have any true friends. But just as I'm proud to be a white American, I want Mokee to be just as proud to be a Native American, who lived in this great land first. With every step I take, I want to help, in my small way, to heal the wounds which have divided this country. My steps and Mokee's aren't very big or important, but if we influence just one or two other people to follow a path of forgiveness, then our lives will have meant something."

There was a long moment of silence. "Jeb, Nanomone'e and I weren't able to have children, but if I ever would have had a son, I would have wanted him to be just like you," Red Wolf said staunchly.

"My father died when I was a teenager, and we weren't very close. So, I consider myself lucky to get to choose my father, and I choose you, Red Wolf, to be my father, that is if you'll have me. I know I'm a little older than you thought a son would be and a little paler in my skin color," Jeb said with his crooked smile.

The two men stared at each other. "Aw, blast it all," the Indian suddenly exclaimed in his most crotchety voice. "I'm staying until you kick me out. You knew I would, just admit it! Somebody's got to protect you and Mokee from the world, and I guess it's going to be me. I can be pretty awesome when I put on my war paint."

"That's all we need," Jeb said, rolling his eyes at the thought of their own resident Dog Soldier. He'd never let Red Wolf know Mokee had told him about the Indian's colorful past. "Seriously, Red Wolf, I'm really glad you've decided to stay."

Red Wolf nodded, too choked up to say anymore. After a few minutes of a comfortable father and son silence, Jeb asked if Red Wolf wanted to go back to the house for something cool to drink. Surprising Jeb, the Indian said he had one more thing to talk about. Out of a pocket, Red Wolf extracted a simple elk skin necklace and rested it on his knee. When Jeb saw what it was, a cold chill swept through his body, and he felt a mixture of emotions.

"Tovee's dead?" Jeb asked, realizing the meaning of the necklace immediately.

Red Wolf nodded. "It was the strangest thing, Jeb. I kept walking through the field of dead bodies at the Arikaree River until I found him. It was as though his spirit wanted me to find his body and return the necklace to Mokee. When I saw him, I was filled with all kinds of feelings of hatred and anger. But in the end, I wept over his body and told him I forgave him."

Jeb took a deep breath. "Tovee surprised Mokee one last time before he went west to the Colorado territory. She was nine months pregnant and was asleep on the sofa in the living room. It was my fault she was there unprotected. There were workmen outside, and I thought no one would get past them. At first, Tovee was furious, thinking Mokee was pregnant with my baby, but she convinced him it was his. She said he was filled with mixed emotions, but left without harming her and said he would be back. The last thing he did before he left was kiss this necklace as a sign of his commitment to her. The whole experience upset Mokee so much she went into labor that afternoon and had Catherine a week early."

"I just want to warn you about something, Jeb. Don't be surprised if Mokee grieves for a while. You're an understanding man, and it isn't a sign she loves you any less by grieving. But she has many conflicting emotions about Tovee, just as I had when I saw his body. Give her space and time. She needs to come to terms with her grief and realize all of us are both good and bad. He was her first love and though he abused her love, she needs to be able to forgive him for her life to be whole."

"You'll tell her then?" Jeb asked hopefully, not wanting to tell her himself.

There was barely a pause before Red Wolf spoke. "Of course I'll tell her, Jeb. After all, I'm her father."

Later that night, I was sitting in the living room alone, reading a book of Jeb's about the American Revolution and the founding of the country. For some reason, Jeb said he had a couple of things to do in the barn, and I was alone for only a few minutes when Red Wolf padded into the room and asked if he could join me. I welcomed him with a broad smile.

"I guess you heard the news by now. I'm staying as long as you don't get tired of me," the Indian said self-consciously.

"Then I guess you're staying for good. We're never going to get tired of you, Red Wolf."

"You say that now, but I can be pretty cantankerous sometimes," he admitted. "I just want to say I'm mighty humbled by your kindness, Mokee, and Jeb's too. Thank you, child."

"You're welcome." My heart felt light and airy like it wanted to sing.

"I have something painful to talk to you about." Red Wolf cleared his throat gruffly. I looked at the Indian with uneasiness, wondering if he might be ill. He slowly extracted an item from his pocket, and then he placed it reverently on my lap. My heart skipped a beat as I touched my necklace, and I grasped the significance of it instantly. Somehow, I had known for weeks now Tovee was dead, and I had been praying for his soul ever since he rode away the last time, thinking the baby was his.

As I stroked the softness of the elk skin, Red Wolf recounted his gruesome memories of the aftermath of the Battle of Arikaree Fork and how many Indians had bravely met their death that day. He wisely told me it was okay to hold the beautiful memories of Tovee when he was younger in a special spot in my heart. Red Wolf said he was young once, and the innocence of first love is a special gift and not to be forgotten. He also said anytime people choose to love, they are made better by the experience, even if it doesn't work out. Lastly, Red Wolf told me people are both good and bad, and the most important thing was to hold onto the good and forgive the bad.

I asked Red Wolf if Jeb knew about Tovee's death, and he told me he did. I sighed. I had already put Jeb through so much in our brief life together.

"Child, Jeb knows you need to grieve as he knows you loved Tovee once. Take your time to feel sad, as much as you need. Then forgive Tovee with the Great Spirit's help and move on. You have a beautiful life with Jeb and a growing family. Put your anguish, disappointment, and heartache to rest, and live in the present, what is, not what you wanted life to be," said Red Wolf wisely. "Well, I think I'm going to go to bed, child. I'm sorry to have had to bring you more pain in your life." With those words, he stood and bent over to kiss me on the forehead, and then he shuffled despondently off to his bedroom.

As the oil lamp flickered and made shadows against the wall, I sat on the sofa and thought about all Red Wolf had said. He was a wise old man. I didn't tell him, but weeks before when the Battle of Arikaree Fork was recounted in the newspaper, I cried for an entire day. Somehow, I sensed in my heart Tovee had been killed.

I reached on the end table for a book of quotations by American authors and hastily, I thumbed through the index to find the page I wanted. Finally, I found my favorite words by Washington Irving. He once wrote, "There is a sacredness in tears. They are not the mark of weakness, but of power. They speak more eloquently than ten thousand tongues. They are messengers of overwhelming grief. . . and unspeakable love."

As I reflected on his words, I realized my life had been an endless path of tears, too many tears. Watching the slaughter of women and children at the Sand Creek Massacre made me shed my innocence, but watching the brutal revenge of a few of my people senselessly killing white women and children nearly made me lose my soul's direction. What was the answer, I kept crying out to the universe? Was it more killing and the spilling of more blood upon the beautiful land God had made?

The answer came to me in a simple elk skin necklace. Bravery wasn't killing another victim with hate, and bravery wasn't dying for the cause of hate on a lonely battlefield. True bravery was acting with unspeakable love and taking one solitary step to forgive another person, no matter how inequitable the transaction seemed. It would only be as each solitary step joined another in a march of forgiveness that the heart of a nation could be healed.

Epilogue

With Tovee's death, the tension in our household lessened considerably. I wasn't constantly on guard, waiting for another surprise attack or fearing for my child's life. Although there were still Indian raids along the Smoky Hill and Republican Rivers, Jeb and I both felt more comfortable with Red Wolf in the house.

Part of the reason we felt more protected was he had served in the military. The other reason, which Jeb always found hard to believe, was Red Wolf really had been a Cheyenne Dog Soldier when he was younger. That was certainly a secret we would keep. In spite of our resident Dog Soldier, we still used caution as did all the settlers, but life became easier with Red Wolf living with us. Since Catherine and I were always safeguarded by Red Wolf at home, Jeb felt more comfortable going into town on business.

Donny and Bethany and his parents unquestioningly accepted Red Wolf's presence in our home as someone who had done Jeb an enormous favor, and Jeb was repaying the favor. They even played along when Catherine called Red Wolf, Grandpa, until one day their son, Joshua, who had started to talk, called him Old Red, and the name stuck. I didn't know whether my honorary father missed the appellation Wolf or not, but no one called him Red Wolf anymore from that day forward.

Another Christmas came and went, and Old Red became more and more Americanized. Jeb got him an entirely new wardrobe of cotton pants and dress slacks, flannel and short sleeved shirts, sweaters, a dress shirt and tie, a wool jacket, leather shoes (which he balked at), underwear, socks, and a suit jacket. He looked pretty spiffy by the time I trimmed his whitening hair in a manageable length.

Whenever we went on an outing as a family, we always took Old Red along. Everyone was impressed with the ease he fit in from his years of traveling with the military as an interpreter and scout. From my perspective, it was important for Indians to be accepted one by one. I knew Old Red's favorable reception would make it easier one day for me to reveal my hidden origins, that I also was a Cheyenne. I had not yet been brave enough to come forward with the truth. There was still a lot of sentiment against the Indians, especially in the newspaper accounts of continued killings and kidnappings.

Old Red enhanced our household as he was a delightful, but irascible old cuss. The biggest surprise was he became a fixture in the community as well.

There was no one who didn't like him, and he did more for Indian relations than all the peace treaty gatherings I read about over the years combined.

Although it was definitely not his favorite thing to do, Old Red would dress up in a tie, white shirt, suit jacket, slacks, and shiny black shoes every Sunday, looking very debonair with his white hair flowing to his collar. Then he would accompany us and Donny, Bethany, and Joshua to church, and we would all go out to lunch afterward. One thing which really strengthened my faith in the goodness of most white people was how warmly he was welcomed at church. Jeb appreciated it too, and we knew we had found our church home.

Jeb's farming business was thriving with the rail system, and he put all of his thousand acres into wheat. More wheat meant more workers, and more employed workers meant a growing community needing schools, a library, a fire department, stores, and more churches. It was an endless circle of opportunity and an exciting time to live in Salina, which I grew to accept as my home.

When Catherine was two years old, Jeb and I welcomed a son named Joseph W. Preston, Joseph for Jeb's father and the middle initial standing for Wolf. Old Red was tickled to have a namesake. Two years later we welcomed yet another son, Matthew Redmond Preston, and we couldn't resist letting Old Red have another namesake. He was a beloved grandfather to all the children, even Donny and Bethany's son Joshua and new daughter Sarah. He taught all of them hunting and fishing skills, and he was a great storyteller about what it was like to be an Indian child in the old days. For me, the best part about his likeability was I knew acceptance of a person of a different color and culture came one heart at a time.

There was never any further information about my parents, although Old Red had checked into it a number of times when he was in the military. He told me it was his guess they were still alive, but my Northern Cheyenne band had returned to Wyoming permanently and no longer journeyed as far south as before. It gave me some comfort to think they were still living, but I still wished they could have met their grandchildren.

One day, the local sheriff came by with a large envelope of items for Jeb. They were Benjamin's personal effects and were found on his dead body after a gunfight in Dodge City. After Jeb disowned his brother and threw him out, Benjamin landed on his feet in Abilene, working for the cattle stockyards when Abilene became a cow town with the growth of the railroad. He grew up and did all right for himself, but he got in with the wrong crowd in Abilene, and his troubles followed him to Dodge City. Just as Jeb and Old Red helped me through Tovee's death, I told Jeb he should grieve and try to remember the good things about Benjamin and forgive the bad. Once again, the sacred path of tears became the path of healing and forgiveness.

Jeb and I were naïve to think the Battle of Arikaree Fork on September 17-19, 1868 was the end of the war. In spite of more than seven hundred Indian deaths of Cheyenne, Arapaho, and Sioux in the grassy fields near the Arikaree River, the surviving Indians regrouped and joined with others to continue their killing raids. Things did get gradually better, but not for a few years.

In November of 1868, Black Kettle's camp of Southern Cheyenne, the same tribal band attacked at the Sand Creek Massacre four years earlier, joined other tribal bands at the Washita River in the Oklahoma territory. His band was on its way to new reservation land given in the Medicine Lodge Treaty of 1867. Black Kettle's small encampment was several miles west of the other camps, and a total of about six thousand Indians were wintering along the Washita.

On the 20th of November, Black Kettle and Little Robe of the Cheyenne, along with the chief of the Arapaho, met with General William Hazen at Fort Cobb in the Oklahoma territory. They requested permission to move their people south to the reservation land near Fort Cobb.

The request was denied by Hazen, who did not have the authority to grant it. He knew General Sheridan was pursuing hostile Indians and had declared all Cheyenne and Arapaho hostile, and the Indian chiefs were told to make peace directly with Sheridan. They were sent away. At the same time, a war party of more than a hundred warriors, including Dog Soldiers and other young men of various camps along the Washita, came back to the camps after conducting raids on white settlements.

Black Kettle and the other peaceful chiefs returned to their villages on the 26th of November. Although Black Kettle was warned of approaching soldiers who were after the raiding party, he delayed moving his camp until it was too late. Custer and the Seventh cavalry reached Black Kettle's camp on the edge of the encampments first and attacked, although Black Kettle and his band had not been part of the raid and had sought peace. Among the dead were Black Kettle, his wife, and more than a hundred Indians. Many women and children were taken captive.

The Indian Peace Commission criticized the battle as an assault on peaceful bands on the way to new reservation land. Colonel Edward Wynkoop, the agent for the Cheyenne and Arapaho, published his letter of resignation, calling Custer's fight a massacre of peaceful bands.

Shortly after Custer's attack, Sheridan's larger force also advanced to the Washita River, and the remaining Indian tribes separated and fled. The Cheyenne and Arapaho retreated southward while the Kiowa and Comanche headed for the Wichita Mountains. Sheridan decided to follow the latter group, which surrendered at Fort Cobb near the reservation land, but the Cheyenne and Arapaho remained at large.

The year of 1868 ended in Kansas with the Indian wars briefly improving. A permanent patrol of troops was placed on the Saline and Solomon Rivers, and no raids occurred until the following spring. Sheridan's campaign ended in the spring of 1869, and the war was almost over as far as the southern tribes were concerned with the Comanche, Kiowa, and Apache on their reservations.

There was still dissension with the Cheyenne, however. The Dog Soldier bands under the war chief, Tall Bull, refused to make peace, whereas the majority of the Southern Cheyenne favored accepting relocation to the reservation land in the area known as Indian territory. With the tribe divided, Tall Bull and more than two hundred warriors along with their families joined the Sioux and Northern Cheyenne on the Republican River.

There was temporarily a renewed outbreak of Indian raids in May of 1869. On the 21st of May, the Sioux and Tall Bull's Dog Soldiers made a raid in Republic county, killing thirteen people and taking two women and a child captive. On the 29th of May, the same Indians attacked the Kansas Pacific railroad and the next day, the Saline valley was victim of another raid with another group of thirteen people killed and two more women captured.

Custer left Fort Hays in pursuit, but he failed to catch the Indians. In what would be called the Battle of Summit Springs on July 11, 1869, Colonel Eugene Carr pursued Tall Bull's Cheyenne Dog Soldiers in retaliation for the raids. Tall Bull was killed in combat in the Colorado territory, and the remnants of Tall Bull's band later said they wanted peace. As a result of the battle, no hostile Indians remained on the plains of Kansas or in the Colorado territory.

Although the Indian wars ended in the southern Plains and Jeb and I and the people of Salina began to feel safer, the war was not over but took a detour to the Black Hills in the Dakota territory. The Sioux War for the Black Hills, involving the Sioux, Northern Cheyenne, and Arapaho under Sitting Bull and Crazy Horse, would erupt in 1876 to 1877. American troops would be defeated at the Battle of the Little Bighorn in 1876, but they would eventually go on to win the war.

As time passed and peace prevailed, the prejudices against the Indians began to ease in Kansas. Jeb began to encourage me to publicly share my journals, which I began to do in small ways in my own community. He thought it was important for me to embrace what was good and beautiful about my heritage, but also to be honest about anything negative.

Although it was difficult for me, I believed along with Jeb my words might be a path of healing. With trepidation, I recounted the troubled times in which I lived, and the hope for peace which claimed my heart, even when I was young. My longing for peace was what enabled me to live without the boundaries of skin color for most of my life and to my surprise, my community embraced my story and continued to warmly accept me.

This has been my life story. Although I am a Cheyenne by birth, I am a white woman by adoption. I want to be known not for the color of my skin, but for the inner workings of my soul and my lifelong desire for peace. In our hearts, we are all the same color of blood red and all members of the human family. Our blood looks the same when spilled upon the ground for the causes which divide us. But in our souls, we are the transparent and colorless breaths of God, who gives love and peace and forgiveness.

When I began my journal, I recounted the words of the poet, William Wordsworth, who said, "Fill your paper with the breathings of your heart." These words, then, are my breaths, not good or even bad. I am simply Mokee, a child of God, and an American.

Forgive me, Spirit of my spirit, for this,
that I have found it easier to read the mystery told in tears
and understood Thee better in sorrow
than in joy.

George William Russell

Bibliography

BOOKS

Blackmar, Frank W., editor (1912). *Kansas: A Cyclopedia of State History, Vols. I-II*. Chicago, IL: Standard Publishing Co. Sections: Abilene, Abilene Trail, Battle of Arikaree, Fort Hays, Fort Wallace, Junction City, Salina, Saline County, Saline River, Smoky Hill River, Smoky Hill Trail. (skyways.lib.ks.us/genweb/archives/1912)

Brown, Dee (2001). "War Comes to the Cheyenne," *Bury My Heart at Wounded Knee*. New York, NY: Macmillan, pp.86-88

Connelley, William E., "The Treaty Held at Medicine Lodge," *Kansas Historical Collections, Vol. XVII*. Kansas State Historical Society, pp.601-606

Greene, Jerome A. (2004). *Washita, The Southern Cheyenne and the US Army*. Campaigns and Commanders Series, Vol. 3. Norman, OK: University of Oklahoma Press, p.12, 27

Grinnell, George Bird (1956). *The Fighting Cheyenne*. Norman, OK: University of Oklahoma Press, pp.111-121

Hoig, Stan (1980). *The Peace Chiefs of the Cheyenne*. Norman, OK: University of Oklahoma Press, p.61, 63

Hurt, R. Douglas (1977). *The Construction and Development of Fort Wallace, Kansas, 1865-1882. Vol. 43, No. 1*. Lawrence, KS: University of Kansas, pp.44-45. (kancoll.org)

Hyde, George E. (1968). *Life of George Bent Written from His Letters*. Ed. by Savoie Lottinville. Norman, OK: University of Oklahoma Press, p.118

Maxwell, James A., editor (1978). *America's Fascinating Indian Heritage*. Pleasantville, NY: Reader's Digest Association, Inc., pp.154-203

Sides, Hampton (2006). *Blood and Thunder: An Epic of the American West*. New York, NY: Doubleday, p.379

ONLINE RESOURCES

accessgenealogy.com/native/tribes/Cheyenne/cheyennecustoms.htm
accessgenealogy.com/native/tribes/Cheyenne/southnorthhist.htm
brainyquote.com/
en.wikipedia.org Sections: Abilene, American Old West – Kansas, Battle of Beecher Island, Battle of Washita River, Cheyenne, Chisholm Trail, Dog Soldiers, Fort Hays, Kansas, Kansas Pacific Railway, Medicine Lodge Treaty, Republican River, Salina, Kansas, Sand Creek Massacre, Smoky Hill River map, Smoky Hill River, Washita River, and Winchester Rifle
fortunecity.com/victorian/song/1147/names.htm
kansasmemory.org
kansastowns.us/junchist.html
kshs.org/kansapedia/kansas-frontier-forts/11809
kshs.org/places/forts/graphics/fortmap.gif
legendsofamerica.com/ks-smokyhillstrail.html
manataka.org "Cheyenne Dog Soldiers," by Richard S. Grimes (2011)
vlib.us/old west/forts.html

CPSIA information can be obtained at www.ICGtesting.com
Printed in the USA
LVOW071926101211

258758LV00002B/106/P